CAUGHT BETWEEN THE CINDERS

Dev/Line/copy and proofreading editor: Callista Morgen

Cover Design: Emily - @quirky.circe

Fanart: Fay Bec

ISBN (paperback) 979-8-9896465-2-4

Book 3 in the Dark Curse Series: Prequel to Hidden Beneath the Embers.

AUTHOR NOTES

Caught Between the Cinders is book 3 in The Dark Curse Series. A prequel *meant to be read in publication order*. If you are picking this up and have not read book 1 and 2, please start there to avoid massive spoilers to the series.

This story **follows the parents of our FMC, Davyna.** It takes place **125 years before Hidden Beneath the Embers.** Please keep in mind that there are many time jumps in this book. This is due to covering the 100-year Enemies to lovers relationship of the King of Valyner; Ezekiel, And the Queen of the Cursed; Nyna.

Another thing to recap from Hidden would be the time shifts between realms: **1 day in the Valyner = 1 month in the Mortal Realm.**

You will see on each chapter header (if there is a time jump) how much time has passed for both realms.

This book includes triggers like: Death of loved ones, thoughts of suicide, physical and emotional abuse, mental health struggles, torture, blood, gore, death, violence, Pregnancy, explicit language, and sexually explicit scenes.

Last warning: you are about to FALL IN LOVE with these characters. There is no turning back now.

GLOSSARY

1. Courts in Valyner

Ember Court: They are known to be the strongest with their fire abilities. The stronger the bloodline, the more powerful the flames they can summon. They cannot burn.

Fallen Court: They are known for their shadows, feathered wings, and some have the ability to read minds. They can drink blood but don't have to live off of it. It also makes them stronger.

Crystal Court: They are known as the witches of the Fae. They can cast spells, hexes, and more.

Crescent Court: They are known as the werewolves of the Fae. They can shift at will and are stronger in wolf form. They can also communicate through their minds when they shift.

Salt Court: They are known as the siren Fae. They have the ability to summon water as their power. In the water, their eyes become slits and their skin shimmers with scales. Some Fae, depending on the bloodline, can even breathe underwater.

Sky Court: This Court was made specifically for Akari by her brother, Ezekiel. She was a seer. But this Court is neutral, studying the Fae and gods. They are in charge of the rituals that take place in Valyner. Anyone can give up their Court ability to become a Sky Court member and will be left with the Core abilities of the Fae. Very little Fae in this Court possess the seer ability, and it either comes with older age or based on the bloodline.

2. **Creatures-** Valyner has various creatures. Some that we meet in *Hidden Beneath the Embers*

-

<u>Sentores/Mal-afera-</u> Also known as the dark beasts. They are wolf-like creatures with black glass skin. Very territorial and aggressive. *Mentioned in Hidden Beneath the Embers and Seeking Beyond the Flames.*

<u>The Dark Souls/Mal-kuya-</u> Fae that have died, and their essence is captured in the Dark Forest. If Fae enter the forest, the Dark Souls will try to kill them to have them join their army of the dead.

<u>True sirens /Waar Sairini-</u> Only found in the sea. Their bite is lethal unless treated quickly. They are less likely to attack Salt Court members.

<u>The Cursed-</u> Fae who were cursed to lose their Fae magic and forced to embrace their Court ability. They were exiled to the Mortal Realm by King Ezekiel when some Fae sided with humans in the Great War against his father by supplying dark obsidian to the humans. With the curse placed on them, they went mad over time, becoming more unhinged and attacking the humans they once tried to protect. Some learned control, but not all. Vampires and sirens could not procreate, but witches and werewolves could with other Cursed members.

<u>(Cursed) Witches-</u> Died faster because of the magic in their veins pulled from their life force.

<u>(Cursed) Wolves-</u> Were in pain every time they shifted, and they would shift more frequently the longer the curse was active.

<u>(Cursed) Vampires-</u> Needed blood to survive and couldn't be in the sun.

(Cursed) Sirens- Needed to be near the sea to stay alive, but could be on land for some time.

There were no seers or Embers involved in this curse.

3. **Dark obsidian-** A material only found in Valyner that can kill the Fae. It is an element that was merged into the Realm from one of their creators, Obsidian.

4. **Hell-** This place in Valyner was created by King Ezekiel with Nyna's magic during his rule to protect the Fae of his Court with what was coming. It was a tunnel system under where the Ember and Fallen Lands meet. The spell was tied to Osiris's life force as a fail-safe when Ezekiel died. After Osiris passed, the spell keeping everyone hidden within transferred to Kadeyan.

5. **Lords and Ladies of Valyner**
Ember- Ezekiel
Fallen- Osiris
Crystal- Persephone
Crescent- Keres
Salt- Alaric
Sky- Akari

6. **Lunavas-** A ritual to honor the gods who created the Fae. It is a yearly tradition where their magic cycles into the lands, and a portion of it goes to the Untouched Fae or Ruler over Valyner. The magic also shoots up into the sky as an offering to the gods. Over the years, it has become more depleting for the Fae as it strips some of their power.

7. **Realms**

Mortal Realm- There is only one Mortal Realm, and it has

always been there. Places in this realm include: Armaros, Qeles, and the Cursed Lands.

Fae realms- The fae realms were created by the six gods. They came together with their opposites to create the fae.

Valyner- Created by the Goddess of Light; Tanith, and the God of Darkness; Obsidian. Valyner has six Courts, with a small territory in-between each known as No-Man's-Land.

Gelmyra- (formally known as the Unknown Lands) was created by the Goddess of Day; Amara, and the God of Night; Slate. Gelmyra has six Courts: Glint; Alter; Soyl; Pixi; Frost; and Rayn.

Anawyn- (formally known as the Unknown Lands) was created by the Goddess of Death; Onyx, and the God of Life; Bion. Anawyn has six Courts: Hollow; Scaled; Soul; Sage; Vine; and Phantom.

Solyus- A realm that was created by the gods when they left their maker; Zaryk. Obsidian banished them shortly after and claimed the land as his own with Tanith, his mate. *Mentioned in Seeking Beyond the Flames.*

Oasis- A realm that was created by the gods: Zaryk and Arcadyus after exile. This is where they used the stones to create the six gods using the stones. Those six gods would go on to do the ritual Lunavas and create the three fae realms.

The Abyss- A type of realm/holding place created for Arcadyus by his brother Zaryk when they did a spell that joined the six stones (or known as the Untouched stones by the fae). This place has held him captive long before the fae were created.

8. **The ancient language**- Learned in the early days and used

mainly by the Sky Court and Crystal Court for spells and rituals. However, other Court members did study it. It is not used as much anymore in Valyner. *Mentioned in Hidden Beneath the Embers and Seeking Beyond the Flames.*

9. **Untouched Fae-** These were the original six Fae created during the first ever Lunavas. The humans came together to call upon the gods to make them more powerful in future wars for more territory. The first humans that were turned into Fae in Valyner were: Ezekiel, Elias, Akari, Orla, Persephone, and Osiris.

Pronunciation Guide

Names
Nyna: Neen-nuh
Zaryk: Zar-ick
Osiris: O-s-iris
Kadeyan: Kade-E-an
Akari: Uh-car-e
Marta: Mar-ta
Eryx: Eric-x
Levanna: Leh-vann-a
Davyna/Dy: Duh-veen-a/Die

Places
Valyner: Val-i-ner
Armaros: Arm-a-rose
Qeles: Key-les
Eldros: El-dros
Lunavas: Lu-na-vas

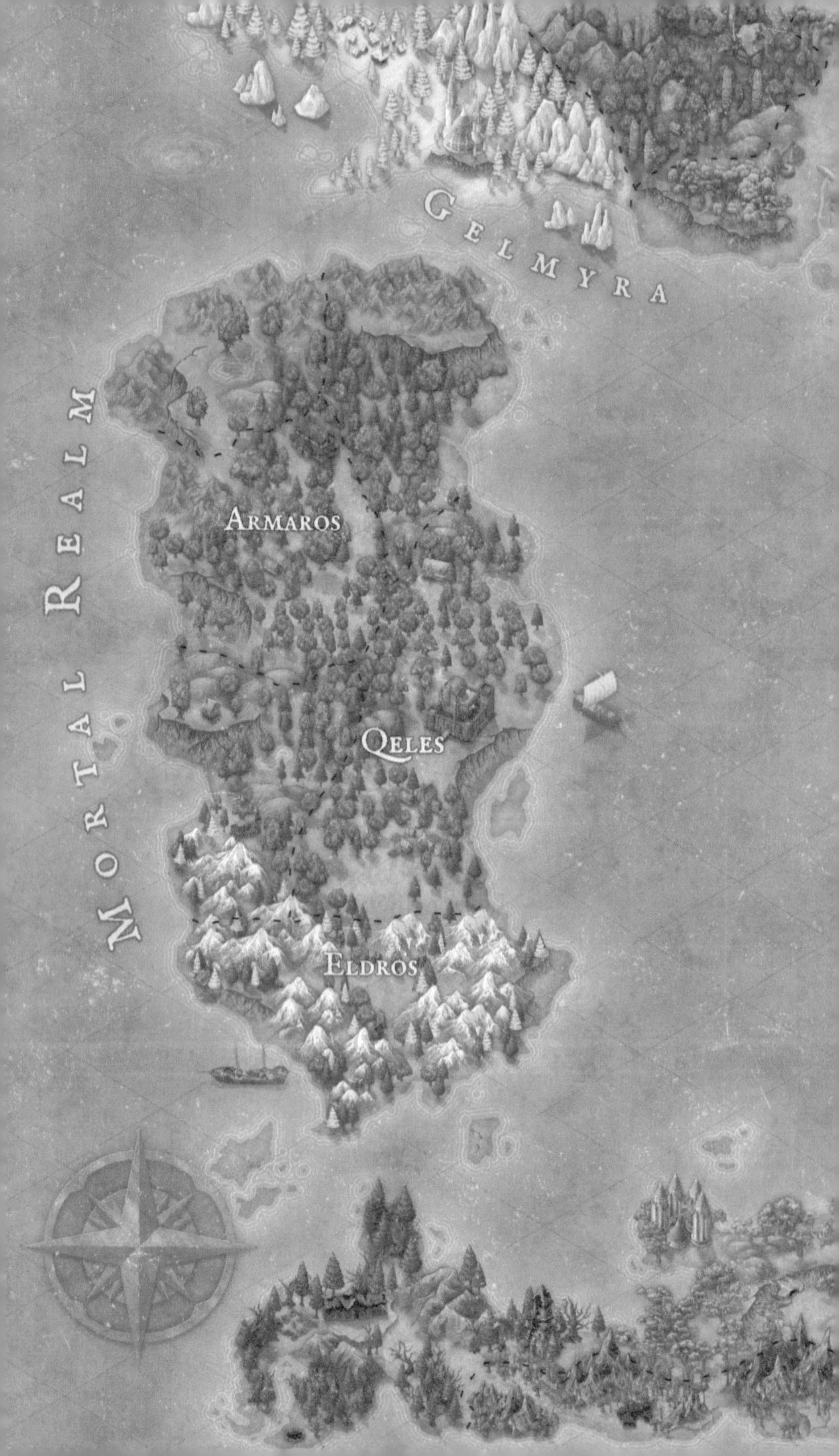

GELMYRA
MORTAL REALM
ARMAROS
QELES
ELDROS

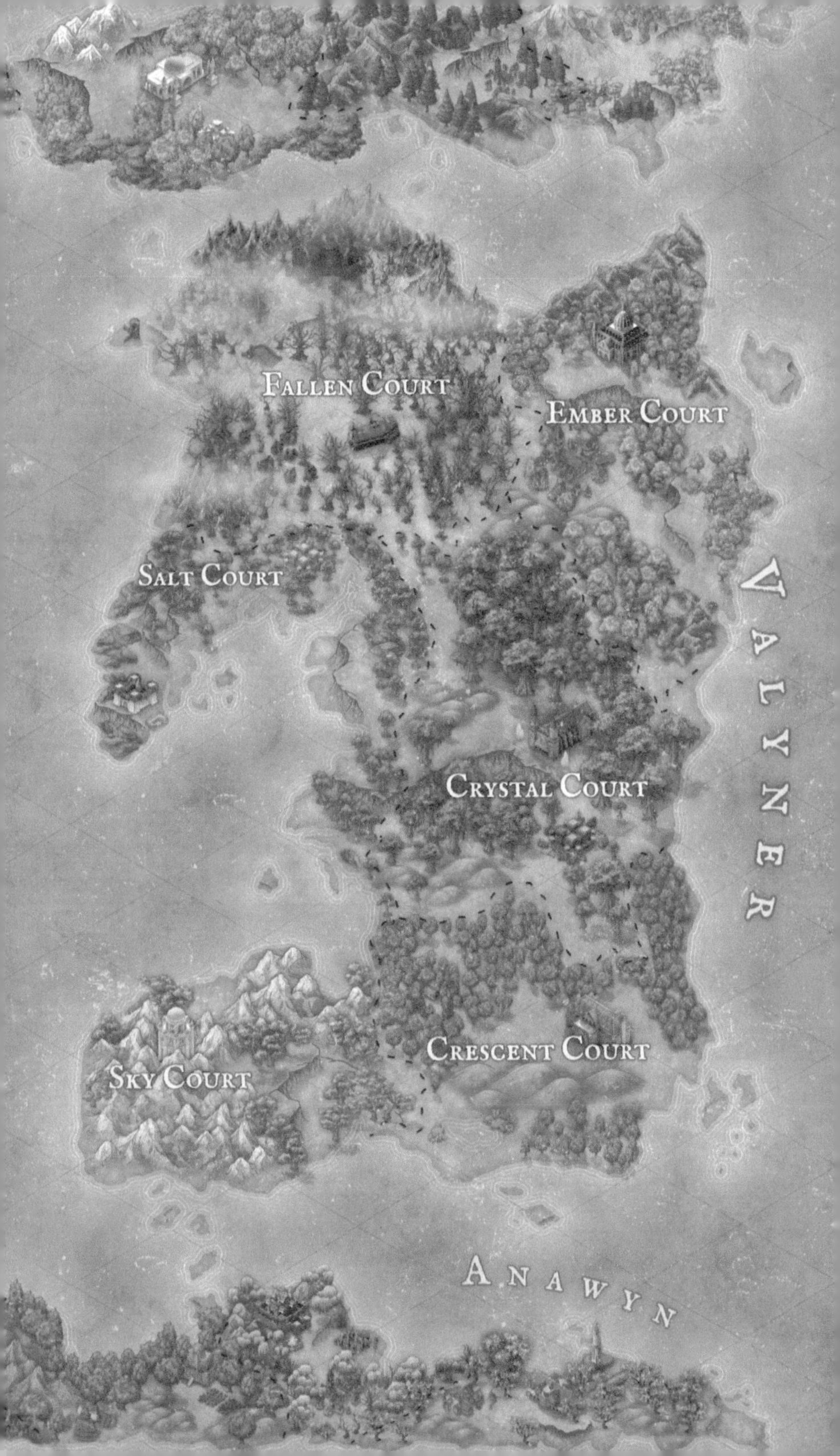

Fallen Court
Ember Court
Salt Court
Crystal Court
Sky Court
Crescent Court
VALYNER
ANAWYN

To the ones who faced their shadows and still fought to give the ones they loved the light—no matter the cost.

To my four children—
You are the reason I chose to heal, so that my demons would not become yours.

PRELUDE

Over 1,400 years ago, the six gods carved three realms from the void and blessed mortal blood with magic. A new race was born—faster, stronger, touched by power not of this world.

These mortals became the fae.

The human king coveted their gift, but the gods chose others—including his three children.

War was inevitable.

Man against magic.

Father against son.

The gods separated the fae realms, isolating them, but left Valyner and the Mortal Realm to war.

Born of ash and flame, King Ezekiel was crowned by Obsidian and Tanith, the gods who shaped Valyner. He ruled without mercy.

After crushing his father and his army, he turned on those who betrayed him—including his own siblings. He cast his brother out of Valyner, along with the other fae who had tried to protect the humans. His sister, siding with their brother, was sealed in her temple, never to see him again.

With nothing left but power, Ezekiel ruled alone on the copper throne the gods had forged.

The Mortal Realm and the Fae Realm parted, though some fae still traveled between them.

The gods saw what he had become and cursed him to live alone —never to pass on his legacy.

But now, something stirs among the Cursed.

A woman born of secrets. Untouched by the curse the king

placed on them. Vengeance in her heart for the loss of a loved one. Power in her veins unlike any other.

Her people need her. She is ready to rise, to fight the war that will free those who call her Queen.

But what if the king she was born to kill is the man she must rely on to uncover who she truly is—and claim the revenge she seeks?

They were never meant to love.

They were forged to fight.

But when the gods' lies spark a new war, only one truth will remain:

ALL PATHS LEAD TO RUIN... EXCEPT ONE.

And it is the only one worth fighting for.

"We are the savage villains in fairytales told to children, but not for my child... In her story, we are the knights in shining armor."

-Klaus Mikaelson

Part one
The Revenge we seek

CHAPTER ONE

NYNA

I was going to kill that son of a bitch.

I kept my head down, trying to tune out the surrounding people, who were sniffling. But more so, I was trying to ignore the rage building wilder than the summer storm brewing above us.

My father cleared his throat, causing me to pull my gaze up to see everyone's eyes locked on me, including his.

"Nyna. Will you join me?" His eyes narrowed slightly.

I couldn't tell if it was out of concern or disappointment, but before I could analyze those hard blue eyes, they quickly scanned over to his side.

Fuck. It was time.

My father continued his speech as I made my way through the community of witches in Armaros, receiving a gentle hand on my shoulder as I passed. Some whispered spells of peace and strength over me, and it took everything in me not to stop and ask them to save their power.

I could use mine with no consequences...because of what I was.

I was always the odd witch out. My power, my aura, differed from those around me. Add to that a temper, like my werewolf father, and it was a recipe for something people didn't like.

Containing more than one power wasn't normal to our kind here in the Mortal Realm or any realm that I knew of. So, I had to pretend to be only one type at my father's request: a wolf.

I say request, but it was more of an order, which only drove me mad over the years. Which is what led me to leave my father's house, despite the tears my mother shed. I couldn't take being under his roof, always telling me to hide what I was.

I just wanted to be me.

But the truth was...I shouldn't have been here. Not after what happened twenty years ago...when I died.

The memory of that night settled into my mind, sending shivers down my spine. Their faces still haunted me—the vampire and siren I thought were friends, but who really just wanted to make me suffer. Before they turned me into one of them.

They couldn't have guessed what would come of my death, the transformation that I still questioned to this day. I should have come back as a vampire or a siren, losing the two abilities I already shouldn't have had. Yet I evolved into something more. Something that scared me.

I went back home, seeking answers, hoping my mother could figure it out, or maybe my father. They didn't speak for a long while, until my father sternly expressed that I never speak of this to anyone else. The warning tainted his words and kept me silenced.

And I could see why he wanted me to keep it hidden. Especially from the King of the fae, since I had defied his curse, never becoming weak or unhinged, as so many did here within our communities.

Yet, for the surrounding witches using their power right now ... It was just one more spell closer to death.

I knew the reason they were doing it, though. So many had to do this on their own. For their husbands or wives, their children taken too soon. Their hands had held the torch, with heat crawling down their skin as tears blinded them. Until they dropped the flames onto the ones that were no more.

And today, it was my turn to burn my mother over the bed of crystals she laid on.

The tradition of Valyner still reigned strong for the Cursed Crystals here, but if our power hadn't been affected under this curse, we could have used magic instead of fire to turn her ashes into new crystals that would have held her aura forever.

I offered to, but my father forbade it. It was "a risk he would not take with my power."

I had lost count of how many funerals had taken place these past few weeks because of that monster. That *King*. Sending his fae here to kill and burn through our streets until there was nothing left of our people.

I wanted him dead.

"This is a great loss for the witches…and my family. Evyra was a woman of power and grace. And the oldest witch to live under the curse passed down by the fae King." My father continued, but I tuned him out.

It wasn't a lie. My mother had defied the dark curse placed on us. Most Cursed witches here in the Mortal Realm were lucky if they lived until they were thirty, maybe thirty-five.

She had been seventy. And her magic hadn't killed her.

Someone had slit her throat.

And I would not stop until I figured out who.

Blood pumped through my veins, causing my skin to itch.

I needed to shift. Or fucking drain someone dry. But I'd save that for one of the fae who dared to cross me.

"She will forever be missed," my father said, his voice somber, but even with his entire speech, something about it didn't say, *"I loved her."* And that only angered me more.

He was always distant from her. From me. That was until it came time to talk about my power. He was a father who was there but wasn't. There had been years I tried, tried everything to be close to him, but that childhood want was gone. And to this day, he had yet to show that it affected him.

Leaning over, I grabbed the torch from his hand and moved over to her body lying on the smooth crystals.

I paused for a second, my lip quivering. Her black hair was draped over her shoulder, doing nothing to conceal the deep cut in her neck, darkening with her decaying flesh. Her skin, once a beautiful olive tone, was now just pale.

A chill ran down my spine, piercing my flesh like kisses made of shattered glass.

I glanced at her face, eyes forever closed shut, and I wanted them to open. I wanted to see the life in her golden pools one last time.

This woman had been my rock. A force to be reckoned with. And I knew something had haunted her, yet she was there. Ever present, her rage from whatever happened long ago extinguished when I was near. She cared. She was a mother...

A mother that I would have dreamed of being if I could have children. But it wouldn't happen. Not in this world, or under this curse. Plus, I probably couldn't now. The only type of *motherhood* for me was turning someone. And I wouldn't do it. I wouldn't inflict this life on any other being.

A tear slid down my face, and anger seeped through the cracks of my grief. She didn't deserve this.

None of them did.

Throwing the torch down, I stepped off the platform, making my way through the crowd, refusing to look back.

"I'll undo this, Mom...I promise," I whispered to her departed spirit.

Making my way past the town, I climbed a hill and sat down, overlooking the stream below. I didn't know how much time passed, but I felt like I was lost in a trance. Until someone sat down next to me.

"I know that look, Nyna," my father said with a hushed tone. "You need to be careful. I know your emotions are heightened right now, but—"

"Heightened?" I laughed, looking over at him, his blue eyes void of any emotion. "You can't stop me from helping them. Not anymore."

My mind was made up. I was sick of living in the shadows when the very power in my veins might just be what would end the suffering of the Cursed. And free me so I could finally be...me. I was done hiding.

"If you expose yourself to the Cursed, they will demand too much from you. And I fear you will open a side to your power that will affect not only your future but the people close to you."

"Do you know what Mom told me the day she died? Before I sent her to that camp to give the vampires the spelled blood I made." I couldn't forget it. Her voice had been so hollow. Her eyes filled with tears, refusing to let them fall. "She told me she lived a half-life, with half of her heart. And she feared I would do the same if I didn't find who I truly was."

I stood up and shook my head, willing the tears to leave my eyes.

"She knew I loved being with each one of the Cursed. That it felt like home. And after losing so many people, friends..." A sharp breath suppressed the sob in my throat. "I'm done waiting to be picked off by the fae. So I'm going to use this power, all of my power, to help stop this curse."

"You can't..." he said flatly, and it broke something in me.

It was his doubt in me. His indifference to everything I'd just said.

I leaned down, gritting my teeth. "Watch me."

Walking away, I took a deep breath, my mind focusing on one thing now.

I was choosing this path. I was choosing to help. And I would not stop until they were free. Even if it killed me.

So, I hoped the fae and their wicked *King* were ready.

Because I was done holding back.

CHAPTER TWO

EZEKIEL

Two weeks later in Valyner
Or one year and two months in the Mortal Realm

If I had to listen to one more person complain about something in this realm, I was going to burn them inch by inch until they begged me to rip their heart out through their throat.

I rolled my eyes, gripping the copper throne until my nails dug painfully into the metal. The male standing before me was rambling about the details of his last trip to the Mortal Realm.

I let out a long sigh, contemplating whether this was worth killing him over. I mean, I had done it for less in the past.

The fae were mostly in line under my rule, but there were always a few who wanted to push certain issues. Like me sending them to the Mortal Realm. Few agreed with my method of hunting parties, but it was beneficial on two fronts.

One: The Cursed fae would stop breathing. And two: My subjects would remember I could make them join the dead just as fast.

Not that I was going to explain this to any of them. If they couldn't figure it out for themselves, then maybe they didn't deserve to be on this earth anymore.

The fire ignited in my palm, and I heard a chuckle escape Osiris. Glancing over at him, his amber eyes were on my hand for a moment before dragging his gaze over the male, whose heart was skipping beats.

Osiris took a step forward, his broad shoulders rolling back, his gaze cold as dark mist circled him. It shot out, pulling the man a few steps closer, causing more fear to bleed out around us. I glanced over at my general of war, my only Emissary in this realm, and leader of the Fallen Court.

His black hair was tied back like always, half up as strands framed his strong features. It looked like he embodied darkness. It was rare to find someone so loyal. A true warrior. But here he was. By my side for the last 1,400 years.

"Your Grace...I mean no offense," the male pleaded, his blue eyes so wide it looked like they were bulging out of his head. "I was just trying to say...something...or someone is very different there."

My fire went out, and I narrowed my gaze at the male.

What the fuck did that mean?

He was trembling, his eyes still locked on my hand, waiting for the flames to come back and devour him.

"What do you mean, someone is different?" I questioned, my voice dropping an octave.

"A woman. I mean...one of the Cursed. She... She isn't like the others."

I tilted my head, my eyes connecting with Osiris. "Has anyone else from the Fallen army reported on this? Have Kadeyan or Silas heard anything?"

"No, my King. None of my soldiers or my sons have spoken of this," Osiris explained, looking back at the male. "What did you see?"

The male let out a shaky breath, taking a step in before pausing again. Like he knew that wasn't a good idea.

And it wasn't.

"She turned into a wolf before the moon was in the sky. Me and some other fae tracked her, but... Everyone was lost during our pursuit. One by being drained of blood. Another being torn apart. And one that was done by spellcasting. All by her hand alone."

"Did it not cross your mind that she was leading you into a trap with more of the Cursed?"

He shook his head slowly, his skin going slightly pale. "There were only six heartbeats. Mine, my three men, my mate, and hers."

"Then why are you still alive?" I demanded.

"I ran, Your Grace... My mate was injured and the power I felt coming from her...it was unlike anything I'd ever felt."

"That isn't possible." I stood, moving towards him. "No fae or Cursed has ever possessed more than one power."

He dropped his head, not meeting my gaze. "I promise, Your Grace. I only speak of what I saw."

"And you couldn't kill it?" I asked.

"I-I wanted to help my mate. S-she was bleeding too much, and..." He paused.

"And what?"

"I didn't want to die," he whispered.

I stepped in, raising his chin to look into my eyes. They were glassed over, his heartbeat erratic and filling my ears.

"I am sorry, my King," he groveled, shaking his head. "She was... p-powerful...I heard others in the village call her t-their Cursed Queen. Please... I don't want to die...or be parted from my mate. I'll do anything. P-please." He dropped to his knees, his fingers interlacing together as if he were praying to me.

"Shhh," I hushed him, placing my hand on the top of his head. "You shouldn't fear the death waiting for you... Fear the one I'll give her."

Fire ignited in my hand, traveling over his head, down his body, until he was completely encased. Screams fell from his lips, the only kind that came with true pain. True fear. They echoed off the walls and back to me, causing the heat in my body to intensify. And I took a slow, deep breath, basking in the inferno's crackling.

"Do I have to do everything myself?" I turned, looking at Osiris.

"Kadeyan and I can take care of it. If you'd like."

"No... I'll do it. Plus, it will get me out of dinner tonight with *her*."

I began walking out of the throne room, my guards standing at attention on each side. I pointed to one. "Find the mate. And bring her to me so I can kill her slowly."

Rolling my shoulders back, I cracked my neck before Osiris appeared next to me, his black vapor fading up into the air.

"Persephone will not let it go that easily. She is waiting for you to set the date for her coronation and the public bonding ceremony."

"Don't remind me." I looked over at him, taking in the subtle smirk. "You and Kadeyan are in charge until I return. Make sure the Lords and Ladies are present for some new laws I'll be implementing."

"As your emissary, Your Grace, I must ask. What laws?"

I stopped, meeting his gaze. "Laws that should have been implemented long ago about mating bonds. They end with my rule until I get what I want."

I fell into the gap, not wanting to discuss any more of this with him. He knew of my curse. And he knew of my anger and who it was directed at. I needed loyal, dedicated subjects who would fight when the day came. Because if this all worked, they would try to kill me for it.

Yet, I didn't want what they took away from me. Not anymore.

Family was nothing.

But power was everything.

I moved through the woods, listening to the breeze pass by, rustling the leaves. It had been a thousand and some odd years since I'd been back here.

I refused to go because I didn't want to see him. I didn't want to feel his anger ever again for what I had done to him. And yet, I could feel him. Feel his power calling me like a siren.

My brother.

I swallowed hard, ignoring how my muscles tensed, and kept moving. Keeping to the shadows, I willed my power to stay deep within to not alert anyone of it. After some time walking, I stalled, sensing something.

I stood still, waiting, my heartbeat racing before I pulled for the throne power to cloak me.

It was him. It had to be Elias.

Shame filtered up, but I quickly pushed it back down, remembering his betrayal.

Looking back out at the clearing, the shadows lurked at the tree line, just waiting to consume the remaining moonlight. Air refused to fill my lungs as I took in the woman standing there. Her golden eyes beamed into the night, her long black-brown hair blowing in the breeze.

She was beautiful. Then I finally felt it. Her power. It was like mine. Strong, with multiple lines streaming through her. And a throne didn't give it to her. She just had it.

How?

She shifted into a wolf, her bones snapping. Yet, she didn't cry out like others I've seen with this curse. She gritted her teeth, enduring each crack as she transformed before my eyes. I had watched the Cursed wolves shift before. It took time as the moon shifted to the highest point in the sky.

You could always count on the beautiful melody of their cries that followed each limb contorting into their wolf form. But not from her...no, it was never that fast. She made it look easy.

She ended up taking off, and I followed from a distance, studying her. I could feel her power come off in waves, and it only added to my anger.

This had to be her. The one they were calling their Cursed Queen.

I needed to kill her. There was no room for another ruler.

Especially one for people who were prisoners of my judgment.

She was my subject. And she would pay for whatever she did to possess this power.

Other wolves joined her through the night. They ripped animals apart, one by one, never fully satisfied. And it made me smile. That they were forced to become the beasts they truly were.

As the wolves shifted back, I stayed far enough away, waiting for her to be alone. When they departed, I moved closer, contemplating how I was going to do it.

I wanted to see how she fought. How she got angry before I burned the beautiful little creature to ashes. But not before she told me what she had done to possess that amount of power.

A power that would make me untouchable to the gods.

She shifted back, and I stopped behind a tree. My heart slammed against my ribs, the adrenaline only adding to the thrill growing within. As I peeked around the large trunk, I saw someone else.

Ice froze the blood in my veins, and I was completely paralyzed.

"Thank you for coming tonight, Nyna. I know you've been busy since you started helping the Cursed last year. The wolves in this area really benefited from your guidance tonight," Elias said, grabbing her hand. Fire rushed up, flickering behind my eyes.

My brother knew her... Was he working with this usurper?

Another betrayal. I shouldn't be surprised.

"Any time, Elias, really. It's the least I can do. But you seem perfectly in control when you shift. You could lead them too."

He squeezed her hand tighter. "I'm not a leader. And my control comes from having people like you in my life."

Bullshit. I made sure his curse wouldn't drive him mad. A kindness I should have never given. But why hide it?

He continued. "You have been doing a lot for each one of the Cursed in the lands."

"Not enough..." Nyna shook her head and walked off. "I am going to figure out a way to undo what he did."

Was she talking about me?

I held back a laugh as she began walking again. As I went to follow her, I stopped, glancing back at my brother. He was looking around, his eyes locked in my direction.

He called out to her, causing her to stall. "Be careful going home. Something is out there."

Fuck...he still had it. That nose like a godsdamn bloodhound, always sensing when I was nearby.

"Let them come for me. I have nothing to lose."

She began walking again, her scent traveling through the air and invading my nostrils. It was warm and sweet. Like roses in full bloom in the middle of summer.

Elias headed back to where he was going, and before I could even think, I trailed behind him.

I didn't want to. I wanted to go deal with the girl, but there was something about seeing him again.

A small wooden cabin was placed deep in the woods, secluded from the town and main roads. I could hear the stream behind the house, but it was hidden by all the trees.

Elias grabbed some firewood, made his way to the front door, and stalled.

"Show yourself, Ezekiel," he whispered, dropping the wood, allowing it to echo off the porch.

I jumped into the gap and landed right behind him, but before I could get a word out, he turned.

His fist slammed into my jaw, stunning me for a moment before I turned back to stop his other fist from hitting its mark.

Gripping his hand, I turned it until I heard it crack and tossed him to the ground. I moved fast, ripping him up by his shirt and slamming him against the cabin. He coughed, his blue eyes burning with hatred.

"Miss me, brother?" I taunted, throwing a punch that made his jaw pop on impact.

He growled, the sound vibrating through his chest. Pushing me, he lifted his foot and kicked me right in the stomach, sending me back. I fell to the ground and watched him come at me, his anger completely unhinged.

As he dropped, I fell into the gap, reappearing behind him and slamming my boot onto his back. Fire ignited in my hand as he looked over his shoulder.

"Go on and fucking do it!" he yelled.

The fire grew hotter in my hand, sending tingles up each nerve until it blazed through my body.

"DO IT! Kill me like you killed Elizabeth."

The reason he turned against me. For the human he fell in love with.

My hand shook, my fire flickering in and out. My lip lifted into a snarl, and our eyes locked on one another. I searched his, wondering if he remembered all those years we kept each other alive. The three of us against our father. His abuse. His cruel words...

Did he even care anymore?

Did I?

But the longer I looked into his eyes, I saw no love. It was gone.

He pushed my leg away and turned over, sitting on the grass, his breath heavy. "Why are you here, Ezekiel?"

"Do I need an excuse to see my bastard brother?"

"Fuck you," he seethed, pushing himself off the ground and looking me over. "I haven't seen you since the beginning of this hell you inflicted on us all. And I'd much prefer you kept it that way."

Elias began walking to the cabin, and I cleared my throat.

"Stay away from her, Elias. One betrayal led to this punishment on you and all the fae who followed you. The next will be your death."

"Good. Then we will all be free of you," he countered.

"Watch your tongue, brother. I am still your King."

He turned, walking right up to me, our noses just barely touching. "No. You stopped being my King the day you killed innocent lives."

"The humans were not innocent. Our father was leading them in the war against us. And you supplied them with the only thing that could kill us!" My voice roared, echoing out into the forest surrounding us.

Elias stepped back, turning away from me briefly before turning back, his expression colder than I'd ever seen before.

"We were HUMAN once! Or have you forgotten that?" he questioned, his heartbeat drumming in my ears.

I looked away.

"Do not come back here. If you want to raise hell over the lands because you are convinced everyone is plotting against you, go ahead. But leave me alone."

"Everyone is. Do you think I don't know what your little creature over here wants?"

"Leave Nyna out of this. She just wants to help the Cursed. The people *you* left to go mad."

I laughed, glancing back at him. "Well, that's never going to happen." I took a step in, lifting my hand and pointing at his chest. "Mark my words, brother. I will rain fire down on her. And you can either help me stop her and be freed from your curse or you'll go down with her."

He swallowed hard, not moving an inch. After a tense moment passed, he nodded and took a step in.

"Then give us your best shot."

Before I could respond, he turned around, walked into his cabin, and slammed the door shut.

CHAPTER THREE

NYNA

Three years later in the Mortal Realm
Or thirty-six days in Valyner

Rain hammered down, soaking my long hair and the muddy forest floor. The early sun's rich morning colors were subdued by the storm's shadows. But the night was over.

The vampires were finally in the caves across Qeles. I was bitten a half dozen times, having to snap some of their necks to stop them from pursuing the humans in the nearby town, which put them in a deep sleep long enough to get them away from the mortals.

I'd have to glamour some mortals today, and get more blood for the vampires, spelling it to curb their hunger.

My body was beyond the point of exhaustion.

I'd been working with more of the Cursed for over three years now, and the rumors had spread like wildfire of my power.

How I could walk in the sun as a vampire and not burn, or get lost in bloodlust. How I could shift at will, even during the day. There was pain, but I could force the shift to happen faster.

My magic as a witch did not drain the life from me, putting me in an early grave. My powers extended to manipulating water near any water source, without the need to transform or return to the ocean.

Many were stunned at first, but over the months, I met more and more of the beings in our realm. Some were humans who had been changed. Some were so old that they remembered Valyner when they had lucid moments. But regardless of their age and how long they had been suffering, they all had the same thing in common.

They hated King Ezekiel. And they wanted things to change.

My power had been tested over the years, and with that, a restless energy fought to be freed from deep within.

I did my best to control it.

To prove my father was wrong.

And yet, sometimes it frightened me. Like I wasn't ready for what might come next.

I shook off the chill running down my spine and looked up through the trees. The raindrops fell onto my face, and I took a deep breath.

Did my mother see me? Did it bring a smile to her face that I was being myself now?

Heat ran down my spine, and I looked over my shoulder, feeling something.

Something that had been constant over the last few years. I didn't dare ask my father, because I already knew where he stood with what I was doing. But I had scanned text from Cursed that talked about Valyner, powers of the Cursed, and more before they succumbed to their fate of bloodlust or death itself. And nothing.

This feeling was completely unknown, and yet it told me everything I needed to know at the same time.

Someone had been watching.

Waiting.

The question was who? Was it a Valyner soldier? A Lord or Lady? Someone from the King's Court who did his dirty work? Or could it be the vile serpent himself? I held my breath, listening, but there was only the droplets of rain and the hushed breathing of humans in a nearby town.

Maybe I was just paranoid.

Furrowing my brows, I went to turn, and a hand reached out, wrapping around my throat. The air instantly left my lungs as my body was lifted into the air.

Panic surged through me as I fell back, my body slamming down into the mud and sticks below.

I coughed, looking up into silver eyes. And my heart stopped for a moment.

He was frozen in place, kneeling over me. His hard gaze locked on mine, and I noticed that the sound of the world was gone. The rain fell silently, our breathing nonexistent. All things were mute, and it was just me and my attacker, lost in each other's eyes.

Heat bloomed within, turning into a fierce and uncontrollable flame. And I wanted it to stop.

Snap out of it, Nyna.

Grabbing his arm, I partially shifted, feeling each one of my bones break. I stifled my cry, my claws tearing through his red leather until they reached his flesh. He let out a hiss, looking down, and I took in his pointed ear peeking through his chestnut-brown hair.

A fae.

I ripped through his flesh, cutting him deep until he let out a growl of pain.

Iron instantly filled my senses, blood rushed through my veins into my face, and the ache in my jaw grew.

He dropped his hold on my neck and I brought both my feet up, kicking him in the chest. The fae stumbled back a few steps, *laughing.*

"Is that all the *Queen of the Cursed* has for me? You've got to do better than that, Nyna." Fire ignited in his other hand, strands of hair falling over his forehead and hiding those hypnotic silver pools that were swirling.

"How do you know my name?" I breathed out, pushing myself up. My eyes locked back on the fire in his palm, growing wilder.

I had never seen an Ember or fought one out here. Only witnessed the aftermath of what they could leave behind. Bodies completely blackened, the flesh and bones crumbling into soot.

He threw the fire out at me, and I dropped to the ground, rolling away.

Black shadows like the Fallen fae held me in place, forcing me to feel the heat sear against my flesh. It coerced the hairs on my neck to stand, and I gritted my teeth together.

Holy shit.

Dropping me from his hold, I pushed myself up, slipping in the wet soil before standing my ground.

How was he using other power? Were we alike?

Another line of fire rolled out towards me and I threw up my hands, placing a barrier between us. Mud coated my fingers, dripping before me as I tried to steady my breathing.

He tilted his head, taking in the shield for a moment. "So, it is true. You are more than one thing. How?"

"Oh, I'm full of surprises." I taunted.

A vile smile pulled his lips up before he ripped my spell down, undoing its magic, thread by thread.

What the fuck?

Another pillar of fire darted out toward me and I got up, running to where a large puddle of water lay.

Shoving my hands into it, I pulled it into my body and sent it out, creating an enormous cloud of steam in the fire's wake.

My heartbeat grew, filling my ears like a war drum as my eyes met the male before me.

"Do you really not know who I am?" he asked before giving me a mischievous grin.

No fae had more than one power, which meant...

My eyes widened, the words on my tongue vanishing as I took in every feature of his face.

I wasn't expecting him to look...like he did. And yet, he was so much more.

I'd built him up in my head over these years—someone so monstrous, so vile. And yet, he looked so normal.

Silvery scars graced his cheek and forehead, while other small ones danced across his hands and knuckles. He was a lot taller than me. My head looked as if it could rest perfectly on his chest. Broad shoulders that spoke of strength. And a face that looked as if it belonged in a painting... Or carved out of stone to last forever.

But I knew better than to be deceived by looks.

The anger returned, and with it, what I set out to do for the Cursed and my mother.

"You're King Ezekiel..." I seethed, slowly pushing myself up and holding my ground before him.

"Aw, aren't we brave? That's sweet," the King of the fae teased before sending out another wave of fire.

I focused on my power, stilling it to wait for my command. I pulled everything within to the surface, feeling it burn in my veins.

Along with something else...something deeper, rattling, and wanting to be unleashed.

Closing my eyes, I felt the heat of the fire grow hotter as it came rushing at me. My skin protested the heat, but that thing deeper within welcomed it—told me to let it hit me.

Trepidation wracked through me, and I tried to send out a spell to push it back, but my power denied me. My eyes widened, and my throat closed up.

No.

I was going to die... I was going to fucking die all because my power denied me the ability to kill the son of a bitch who cursed us? Before the war even started against him?

The gods and stars above could fuck off with this fate they had for me.

Fire slammed into my chest, pushing me back a good ten feet.

I gasped and took in the cyclone of fire encasing me. I waited for every nerve to scream out in pain, for my throat to turn raw from screaming. Yet, I wasn't even making a sound. I wasn't feeling anything. It wasn't burning me.

My jaw dropped.

What was happening?

Meeting his gaze through the dying flames, I took in his satisfaction. Well, that was until he realized I wasn't dying.

The flames themselves only ignited my power, but it was more than that...they were fueling something within. Challenging my magic to grow, to unleash something untamed. Something wondrous...yet dangerous.

He stepped in and his brows furrowed, his anger growing unhinged. And I pushed my hands out, using a spell to throw the flames back at him.

They slammed into his body, forcing him to steady his footing against the force.

The fighting ceased, the sound of our breathing mixing with the rain falling from above. Raindrops trailed down his face, making his chestnut hair stick to his cheeks.

"What are you?" he asked after a minute passed.

"I'm the Cursed who is going to kill you," I growled, narrowing my gaze at him.

He chuckled, looking me up and down. "I'd like to see you try, Ruin."

"Ruin?" I questioned, arching a brow.

"Yes, it's fitting, no? Because it's exactly what I am going to do to this land." He gestured to the forest beyond. "To your precious creatures calling you *Queen*..." He took a few steps in, groaning. "And then...to you."

Closing the distance between us, the heat within grew with each step. I brought my hand up, unsure of what I was doing. Placing it on his chest, he froze, and our eyes connected.

His scent of ashes surrounded me, and I focused on who he was. What he had done.

"You think death scares me? I've already been through it. And it made me stronger."

Lifting my leg, I grabbed the small blade I always kept on me.

Dark obsidian.

I buried the blade into his stomach, taking in his sweet gasp as I pushed it up through his flesh to his chest. He pushed me back, and I sent out another spell, tossing him through the air.

Ezekiel opened a portal between our realm and his and fell into it. I focused on the power, studying it as it closed before me.

It spoke to something within, like a distant feeling I once had... and then it was gone.

Stepping back, I tried to steady my breathing once more, my eyes going wide.

I just stabbed the King of the fae... And not even a blow that would kill him.

Cursing under my breath, I let out a long exhale.

I just started a war I wasn't ready for.

CHAPTER FOUR

EZEKIEL

Six months later in Valyner
Or fifteen years in the Mortal Realm

"How are you feeling today, Your Grace?" Osiris spoke, pulling my gaze away from the map of Valyner laid out before me on the table.

I took a deep breath, my rage still nagging just below the surface.

That woman, that *thing,* had me in bed for over a month healing from the dark obsidian she plunged into my stomach.

How did she have it? Who gave it to her?

I had used it a few times in the past, but never felt its toxic signature of magic within me. It was written that this mineral of power was from our god Obsidian and it was the only weapon—aside from our power—that could kill the fae. Even me. And it made me hate the bastard even more for making it. He was always playing a sick game. And I wanted to make the rules now.

If I had more power...

I could.

I could even kill him. He would deserve it. He was the author of this fate forced upon me. But not the author of who broke me first.

That title belonged to one man. One human who I killed.

"You are weak, Ezekiel. You will always be weak."

Silencing my father's voice, I concentrated on the present.

"I'm fine," I finally responded. "Tell me about the attack last night."

"It was done by the wolves again. They were searching for something in the Ember Lands. My soldiers eliminated them all."

"And do we know what they were searching for?"

"No. Their memories were spelled to protect that information," Osiris said, looking over the map.

"Which means the wolves weren't behind it." I breathed out. This was the fourth time in a month. "Those fucking witches."

"Would you like me to get Persephone here to ask her?"

I ground my teeth together. "No, I plan to see her in a couple of weeks. I will ask myself. But I'd like to ask around more first." Because I didn't really trust her if I was being honest, but I needed the Lady of the Crystal Court. And I needed to find the source of this inconvenience without alerting the culprit.

Pulling the Mortal Realm map over the one that was already spread out on the table, I ran my finger over the land where I last saw her. I still couldn't figure out why I'd hesitated when she touched me. Or what I'd felt deep in my bones. I had spent months trying to figure out what happened. And it was driving me madder than ever before.

It was unsettling.

Unnerving.

But most of all...thrilling.

"Have our men returned from the last hunting party? Have they got her yet?"

Osiris pulled out a chair across the table and sat down, leaning back. "They should be back tonight if all goes well."

It had been six months since I had her in my grasp, about fifteen years in mortal time. I could have ended this. Ended this one problem. But now I had ten times more since returning home. Courts were disobeying laws, conspiring to do something that we still hadn't unveiled.

I needed this one thing.

I needed her dead.

Sparks fell from my skin, landing on the map, and quickly ate away at the parchment.

My fire didn't work on her...why?

Fuck.

I didn't need this right now. This distraction.

I pushed the maps across the table and stood, making Osiris follow my lead.

"I'm going to have to visit her. Inform my soldiers to follow. Now."

I fell into the gap, knowing Osiris was diving into the minds of the soldiers I trusted. He didn't need to ask where I was going. Or who I was going to speak with.

He knew all too well.

Landing in the Sky Court Temple, I squinted my eyes from the blinding sun pouring in from the large window. As my eyes adjusted, I took in the peaks of the mountains painting the land-scape outside, the lush colors intensified as though the sun only shined this bright over this Court.

The black and white circular room was cut down the center. Both sides contained a small couch, with bookshelves wrapping around the room from the door to the large bay window.

Swirls of ashen sunlight beamed from the ceiling on the light side, while on the other side, a silver moonlight slithered in the darkness, casting a subtle glow. Neither crossing over into the other.

But it was that each side was drenched in darkness or light. Both holding the essence of our power and the divide between us.

You were good with your power. Or you were evil.

I knew where I fell. And I'd made peace with that long ago.

The presence of my soldiers appeared in the temple, and I trusted they would hold their posts.

The door swung open, and I felt her anger, her thoughts raging into a ball of chaos.

"I thought I told you to stop visiting over a hundred years ago."

"Come on, big sister." I turned. "You know you missed me."

"What do you want, Ezekiel?" Akari asked, moving over to the desk by the large window that overlooked the mountains beyond. Moving some books over to the side before taking a seat, she then dragged the silver crown off her head, followed by her black veil.

Her silver eyes beamed just as brightly as mine, but her demeanor was hard, waiting for an explanation.

"I need you to look into my future... Tell me I will be rid of these problems and get what I want," I demanded.

"It doesn't work like that, and you know it," she huffed.

"Do it. That is an order," I growled.

"You lock me in this temple, exile our brother, and now you want me to look into your future? Are you serious?"

"You know why I locked you here! You sided with him!" I yelled.

"Gods, Ezekiel. Do you hear yourself when you talk? He is our BROTHER!" Akari stood from the desk, walking up to me. "And you haven't done a damn thing to help him."

Slowly, I brought my gaze to her, the memories of the past filtering in.

Growing up in our small village. How close Akari and I were despite our father punishing us for standing up for each other. Practicing with swords when our father was away because girls weren't allowed to wield weapons, but she was a natural. She put me on my ass more times than I could count.

Or raising Elias... We were the reason he kept breathing. How he made it to adulthood. Not on my father's coin or bread. We gave him everything because if my father had his way, he would have left my newborn brother to drown in the stream by our home.

He was not worthy.

We all weren't in his eyes.

Wrath caused my blood to boil, and my skin glowed.

"You know what's the saddest thing about you," Akari stated, taking another step in, dark brown hair just like our mother's falling over her shoulders and framing her face. "You hated him. Hated him more than me and Elias combined. But somehow through the years, you have become him... You have become our father."

"Watch your tongue. Or I will rip it from your mouth," I shouted, a growl tainting each word.

The door swung open, and I turned to see a male acolyte enter, his eyes wide as he looked at Akari. I felt his worry for her, his devotion to her...

"Is everything okay, Akari?" he asked, taking a hesitant step in.

"Calvin, please..." She gestured for him to leave, but that wasn't happening.

I smirked, walking up to him and grabbing him by his throat. Akari yelled, her small hands pulling as hard as she could on my arm.

"Ezekiel, stop!"

"Why? I'm just like our father...right?" I locked my gaze on her for a moment, watching the realization of what I meant to do.

Fire ignited in my arm, traveling down until it covered each finger around the male's neck.

Screams rang out from the both of them, and I kept my hold on him, my vision blurring with tears as I watched the flames grow.

I was not my father.

I was a king.

I was his better.

I was... I was...

I tightened my hold, crushing his windpipe before dropping his burning corpse to the ground.

Alone.

Just. Like. Him.

Turning to my sister, I pushed her back and buried down the emotions that sat on the surface. Ones that would do nothing but show weakness.

Taking hold of both her arms, I shook her, forcing her eyes to meet mine. "Now tell me what you see!" I yelled.

She continued to cry out, her pain and loss slamming into me like massive waves crashing over jagged rocks.

After a long moment passed, she pulled back, her anger growing as she looked at me. I held my ground, waiting.

Akari stepped in, placing her hand over my wound, and a chill ran through my body, turning it to ice. Glancing down, I saw the white light illuminate her hand before gazing into her frosted white eyes.

My heart beat faster, my muscles turning to stone as she pushed deeper. Her pain fueled her power, and it washed over the entire room, completely paralyzing me.

"You will fail. Become what you fear. Fate and ruin are your path...until you fall. She will free them. She will reign forevermore." Akari chanted, stunning me further.

She repeated it over and over, my heart slowing with each passing word.

What did this all mean?

I snapped out of it and shook her again, my eyes hardening as I waited for the silver to return to her gaze. And once they did, tears streamed out.

"What the fuck does that mean?" I demanded.

She leaned in, another tear trailing down her cheek. Her lips quivered before they thinned out, her teeth grinding.

"WHAT DOES IT MEAN?"

She whispered, "Figure it out for yourself, *Your Grace*," she whispered before recoiling and collapsing to the ground.

Turning from her, I tried to make sense of it, but I couldn't focus. Not as my heartbeat drummed in my ears like a call to war.

I glanced over my shoulder, seeing her gaze fixed on the body. Sobs broke past her lips, echoing up to the enchanted ceiling that swirled with sun and moonlight.

"We are stronger when we are alone, Akari." My lip rose into a snarl.

"Love is deadly..."

Akari met my gaze. "Get. Out. Of. My. Temple."

I went to speak, but held back the words on my tongue. My eyes burned once again, and I pushed my body to walk. The gap opened around me, pulling me into the void. Rage fueled by regret? Past pain? I couldn't pinpoint what it was...but it was overwhelming.

Her vision had to be about Nyna... It had to be about her. And for the first time in over 1,400 years, I feared. A violent cry fell from my lips, quickly being swallowed by the darkness that was my only company.

I wouldn't let her take this from me.

I wouldn't let this be the end.

"Ezekiel?" Persephone asked, placing her hand over mine. "What's wrong?"

I forced a smile, glancing over at her. She was dressed in a black gown, cut out on the sides, revealing her sun-kissed skin. I slowly met her dark purple-blue gaze, noticing for the first time the way they glinted in the dim light of my parlor.

"Nothing. It was a busy few weeks."

She nodded, lacing her fingers through mine. "The Crystal Court will not give any pushback on your new orders. You have all of us behind you."

"Are you sure about that? Wolves attacked the Embers multiple times this month, and last week they got closer than they ever have. And we couldn't figure out who sent them. Which means..."

"What?" she said, her shock quickly turning to anger. Her eyes turned a lighter shade of purple. "I will handle it. And they will be executed in the town square for all to see."

I smiled, nodding my head.

She was a fierce creature. I'd give her that. And maybe this would solve the problem. I wasn't so naive as to believe it would.

Yet, perhaps the sight of their Lady killing their own might remind them of our supposed alliance.

Or I could just burn them all.

"My Court is yours. And I will make sure everyone follows," she said.

"Yes. Three Courts on my side. But what of the other three? I cannot gain more power without alerting the gods. Which means there will be a war. We need power to win," I countered, pulling my hand back and standing. I walked over to the glass doors, looking out at the terrace behind my castle.

"They will fall in line," she affirmed.

I laughed. "Right. Keres loves doing that." I rolled my eyes.

"He is a bitter little wolf with a temper, trying to be alpha. But he knows he will never be one."

"No...he will not," I added, thinking of the true alpha of the wolves...

My brother.

"I will speak to him if you'd like me to. He might not like falling in line, but he loves his ego being stroked. Which would be better coming from me than you." She rolled her eyes, smirking.

I nodded, and a few seconds later, I felt her hands wrap around my arm.

"The binding spell I have created will combine our power. It will give you what you need to break your curse and be truly untouched...by anyone. But we will need our untouched stones to do it," Persephone said.

She knew this wasn't an arrangement I came to lightly, and was not fueled by any form of lust or love to bind myself to her. It was a necessity.

But since I had made it known, I'd felt her excitement. Her joy. She truly wanted me, which put me on edge.

For what?

My sister's words filtered back into my mind. And the fear of falling was all-consuming. But something else inside me screamed against this plan. Screamed to never bond with her.

We weren't mates. I was pretty sure my curse kept me from ever having that, too. And it didn't bother me. True mates made you lose touch with reality. I could see it in each fae. It blinded them. It changed them, stealing their minds to think only of their mate. Abandoning the life they had planned for this...what? Fate?

That wasn't *love*. It was just as toxic as dark obsidian.

I looked up at Persephone, the words on the tip of my tongue to tell her to set the date for this week. I needed this. Needed this power more than ever before.

But I couldn't.

I dropped my head again, my eyes closing, and all I could see was *her*.

I needed to get rid of her first. And then I would be able to think straight.

"As soon as I handle these issues, we will set the date. But the realm needs to be ready. This means I need more Crystals and Acolytes scanning the text we have on the gods. I will not be unprepared if they strike."

"Of course, my King." She rose to her toes, kissing me on my cheek, and my stomach turned.

As she moved in front of me, placing a hand on my chest and smiling slightly, I glanced down at her hand, her long black nails lightly grazing my shirt. But I felt nothing.

"I must go, attend to the soldiers going on the next hunt."

She nodded her head and leaned in, her lips brushing mine. I closed my eyes and allowed it, but in the darkness, all I saw were golden eyes staring back at me. Filled with power and hatred.

I could feel Nyna's touch again on my chest, causing my heart to skip a beat.

What the fuck?

I pulled away, forcing another smile, and pulled her hand back, giving it a quick peck before leaving the room. Each breath grew more ragged as I made my way to my study off of the throne room, imagining our last meeting.

How she'd fought back. How those pools had glowed brighter

when she realized who I was. There had been no fear. No resistance to her attack. She'd given it to me...

Closing the door behind me, I placed a privacy barrier over the room and tried to steady my breathing. I didn't like this feeling. I didn't know what it was, nor did I want to find out.

My sister's haunting words chanted in my mind, and I slowly lowered into my chair at the head of the charred wood table. I rested back, interlacing my fingers and bringing them to my chin.

You will fail.

Was it because of her?

Become what you fear.

Weak?

Fate and ruin are your path...until you fall.

Was she going to kill me?

She will free them. She will reign forevermore.

I leaned forward, looking over the map of the Mortal Realm.

It was all about her...

She was my downfall.

Standing, I grabbed the map and pulled it to the edge, seeing her dagger resting below it. Slowly, I picked it up. I looked over the toxic metal, still stained with my blood. And the faintest scent of her still lingered on the leather.

I needed to learn more about her, to study every single thing that made her smile, made her tick. I needed to know my prey as well as I knew myself.

Smiling, I whispered a locator spell and placed the dagger down. It spun, growing in speed. As it finished, the blade slowed, pointing to Armaros.

"I'm coming for you, Ruin."

CHAPTER FIVE

NYNA

Two years later in the Mortal Realm
Or twenty-four days in Valyner

My breathing was heavy, the blood thick on my skin as I looked around at the fae lying out before me, their bodies blending into the ground from the night sky above. The attacks from the King had been coming consistently for the last seventeen years since I met him in the woods and stabbed him. And with it, more Cursed began banding together in their lands to the south.

And somehow, I fell into an unexpected role among them.

A leader. A ruler.

"Nyna," Vennyx called out to me, his black hair falling into his eyes as he looked over the dead. He walked past it all, placing his hand on my cheek. "You okay?"

"Yeah. The bastards got some good hits in. But I'll be alright." I smiled.

He moved back, pulling his dagger from his hip, and slit the wrist of the fae on the ground. Slowly, blood trickled out, collecting in his hand.

My veins itched as the iron seeped into every sense, but I stood still. Breathing in and out.

Vennyx moved back over, offering his hand up, and I slowly leaned in. Parting my lips, I drank down the sweet crimson, feeling the soothing effects on my muscles and bruises that I would still have tomorrow, just not as bad.

I met his gaze, the veins under his eyes slithering like snakes as his own bloodlust grew.

I pulled back and wiped my mouth. "Can you tell everyone to get their horses and head back tonight? We need to come up with a better plan. We've lost too many of our people."

"You're being too hard on yourself, Nyna." Pulling me in, he kissed my forehead, and I welcomed the comfort.

I might have welcomed it a little more than I should have during these few months with him. We were friends, but I needed to escape thinking about all this, even if it was only for a few minutes.

I had made some progress with the magical essence of the portal the fae used, which they referred to as the 'gap'. We could access it. But the problem was, it took a lot of magic. And we didn't know what would happen to us if we passed through it.

Some of the Cursed had gotten too close to fae using it and described agonizing pain. I assumed that's what we would face on the other side. And then how were we going to fight?

No, we needed to understand the curse that had been placed on us. And how to undo it. And I needed the King's blood.

"Nyna..." The voice from behind me pulled me out of my thoughts.

Turning, I took in my father.

His light blonde hair pulled in the breeze, and his blue eyes scanned over the fae on the ground. Glancing over at Vennyx, I gestured for him to wait there and walked over to my father.

"What are you doing here?"

"I needed to see you," he said before meeting my gaze. "You need to be careful. You are using too much power."

"And?" I retorted, moving past him to lean against one of the large pines.

"Nyna... Your mother wouldn't have wanted you to put yourself at risk. She wouldn't—"

"Don't." I stopped him. He didn't get to mention my mother—his wife—when he had been so indifferent towards her.

Towards me.

He turned away from me, his shoulders falling. "I can't lose you..."

I stalled, unsure what to make of that. For a split second, it made me aware of every crack from childhood he silently gave me that dragged into my teenage years, and into adulthood. And those four words should have filled them in. But they didn't. The damage was done, and I didn't believe him.

Pushing myself up, I walked over and looked in his eyes, my anger evident. "I'd rather die fighting than hide. Can you say the same?"

"You need to be careful with your power..." he warned, and I rolled my eyes.

Here we go again.

"Why do you always make this about my power? I know how to use it," I bit out, my hands balling up by my sides.

"You haven't even begun to understand what you..." He trailed off, closing his mouth quickly.

"What the hell does that mean?" I said, raising my voice.

He avoided my stare, shaking his head before closing his eyes.

"I know who I am. And you trying to keep me locked up didn't work before, so stop thinking you can do it now." I moved away from him and spotted Kali.

I called out to her, and she mounted her horse and began riding over.

"What do you need, Your Grace?" she teased, her long black hair flowing in the wind, blood still trailing down her chin.

I shook my head, and she grinned, knowing I hated when she

called me that. Some Cursed members would say it out of respect, but it was something I corrected right away.

I was one of them. Not royalty.

Kali was a new vampire, turned recently, and I had been helping her through her transition. She was doing well, and all the attacks were giving her practice and allowing her to drink her fill.

"Can you escort my father to wherever he came from?" She nodded, and I walked away.

"Nyna..." my father called out, and I resisted turning to look at him. "I hope that one day you understand that hiding something you love, or need, is the only choice."

I turned to look over my shoulder, but my father had already walked back to his horse.

Vennyx moved over to me, his hand falling to my lower back. "Do you want to get out of here, maybe get a drink before we head back?"

I let out a long exhale and walked to where our horses were with the other Cursed, who brought them in from the woods. Gods, I needed a release. Getting onto the back of my black mare, I looked back at him, caught the intense look in his eyes, and grinned.

"I need a bath first."

The night blanketed us, the cool summer air causing my nipples to pebble up as I arched out of the pond.

My fingers threaded through Vennyx's wet black strands, his fingers circling over my clit with perfect pressure. I moaned, leaning back more until my skin pressed into the rough outer rock of the pond.

His hand stopped, and my eyes shot open just in time to feel his touch return to my body. Lifting me out of the water, he rested me on the edge of a large flat stone, moving between my legs.

His tongue slowly circled over and over, and I was pulled back into the feeling I was chasing.

Oblivion.

I wanted to say I'd found it before. Felt completely absent from my body, but even when I hit those peaks, I was still aware of the problems I faced. The responsibility on my shoulders growing by the day.

Yet, I kept trying, trying to find it because I needed just one moment of feeling completely free from the chains I placed on myself.

Would I change anything about the path I chose, or what I'd done?

No.

I wanted to help the cursed. I wanted them to live because they deserved more than this life. The witches deserved to grow old and appreciate their power. The vampires and sirens deserved to be without the bloodlust that drove them crazy. And the wolves, they didn't deserve to turn, breaking every bone in their bodies until they became animals with no remorse.

And somehow, I didn't suffer the same. I needed to help where I could.

So, maybe it was guilt. I felt it so much in the beginning after I transformed...maybe that still drove me.

Vennyx pulled me down, and my back scraped against the rock, pulling my thoughts back. He slowly pushed the head of his cock into me and I moaned, wrapping my hands around his neck.

He slid in and out of me; the water creating a louder slap between us and echoing out through the trees.

I focused on the way he felt inside me, each inch sending vibrations through my body.

"Come for me."

His lips touched my neck, and my eyes closed, focusing on the feelings, begging them to take me away.

A power washed over me, and I felt every nerve light up within. It was breathtaking, waking up every line of power in my body.

Vennyx held me close to him and began walking out of the

water to lay me on the large stone. He began thrusting again, and I welcomed the heat growing in my limbs, traveling to my core.

I wanted it to consume me.

My climax continued to build, and I chased after it, moaning louder and louder.

Vennyx stalled, a gasp falling from his lips before droplets fell onto my chest and face. I opened my eyes, biting back the curse on my lips.

Did he have to come before me right now?

Although...that wasn't the case.

Blood flowed out from his chest, and his eyes were glossing over. My body stiffened, my breath nonexistent, as his body was pushed to the side, exposing who was behind him.

My anger overwhelmed me, washing away every other emotion.

"Sorry, maybe I should have let you come first...before I killed you."

Ezekiel's hand wrapped around my throat, pulling me in.

He stalled, turning to stone. Lifting my foot, I kicked him in the stomach, hoping it hit his old wound.

I stood up, looking him over, waiting for his next move, not caring I was completely bare before him.

He began laughing, holding his stomach, before looking back at me. "You don't have your dagger anymore, Nyna. You can't win."

I smiled, placing my hand out wide towards where my clothes sat with my dark obsidian sword. It floated through the air; the hilt falling into my palm.

"You sure about that?" I questioned.

His eyes hardened. "Where did you get that?" he demanded, his silver irises melting and his skin glowing.

I wasn't going to tell him. I'd die before I gave him that information.

"Did you give the order to kill my mother?"

"Who in the voids is your mother?" he questioned before laughing. "Aw, is that why you hate me? You think I did it?"

I rushed in, twisting and slashing the blade through the air. He vanished into the portal and reappeared behind me, his fire rushing out.

It slammed into my back, but like before, did nothing to me.

"How are you doing that?" he yelled.

And honestly, I wanted to know too.

I chuckled, turning to face him. "What is it, *King*? Do you have performance issues?"

His eyes scanned my body, growing wilder by the second. I moved in, swinging the sword in a circle before bringing it up.

A sword of fire appeared in his hand, blocking my blow, and he began moving me back. With each hit, he gave more of his wrath. And I got to see how unhinged he was. How dark he would go.

Good.

I wanted to see it. Study it so that I could find a weakness.

And it was clear. It was his anger. He became too agitated and sloppy with his strikes.

Spinning, I brought my blade up, slicing into his face. He stumbled back, his eyes going wide as he let his fire sword rest against the ground.

I lifted my other hand, my breathing heavy, as I began chanting.

"Lo venos, le trebua, vas lotasa, es valtu." His blood filtered through the air, the droplets creating their own spiral as they made contact with my palm. His blood sank into the layers of my skin, and as it did, my breathing paused.

Stumbling back, I gasped at the feeling of his blood in me and looked down. The blood was swirling, creating lines that resembled a gem...

What the hell?

He moved in, gripping my throat again, forcing me to look at him. "What did you do?"

But I couldn't speak. Not as I felt his essence within me. And then it clicked. This power. It was what was stronger in his presence.

When he stalked me for that year. When I stood close to him before sinking a blade into his stomach. It was like something deep within awoke when I was near him. And part of me wanted it to come out, while the other side begged for it to stop.

His magic ripped my sword from my hand, and he brought it up to my neck, moving back until I was pinned to the tree.

"What are you?"

He leaned in, causing the metal to bite into my skin.

And something inside me heated, my nerves firing off like embers popping off firewood.

He didn't move, didn't breathe. His eyes just studied mine, and I couldn't help but study his. The flex of silver swirled, like melted iron that screamed of war. Of pain. Of longing... And at that moment, it made me feel more exposed than I already was.

"I have killed many in my lifetimes. And yet here you stand. Still breathing..." His other hand came up, wrapping my hair around his finger.

"Then get on with it."

He paused, his face going cold, eyes hardening. "With pleasure... Ruin." He pulled the blade back and spun it so that the tip was pointing at my heart.

Just as it was about to hit me, power erupted from behind him, pulling him into the portal.

I let out a ragged breath, dropping to my knees.

What was that?

Was that me? I didn't feel my power come to life, nor did I really think of anything to stop the King...

I couldn't even begin to understand the remnant of power still lingering in the air. Strong and mysterious. I listened, but heard no other heartbeats. Sensed no other presence but my own. It was like magic just appeared to protect me...

It had to be my own...right?

Looking around, I waited for him to reappear.

But the King was gone.

My breathing hitched and deepened as the shock took over.

My body shook uncontrollably, and I picked up my sword and ran over to where my clothes were. Dressing quickly, I got on my horse. I glanced back at Vennyx's body and sorrow slammed into my chest.

He was dead...

Tears lined my eyes, but I didn't have time to do this here. I needed to go.

I grabbed the reins of his horse to follow us and began riding through the night, not stopping for anything.

And my eyes kept looking down at the mark on my palm, with his blood fully formed into what I thought.

The shape of a gemstone.

I needed to figure out how to undo all this before he came back, because I didn't know what had just happened.

But it could never happen again.

CHAPTER SIX

EZEKIEL

Three months later in Valyner
Or eight years in the Mortal Realm

The witches were all in attendance in the town square, listening to Persephone speak. The large crystal in the center created various hues from the sun's rays that beamed onto the ground.

But it was the sobs coming from the three witches with dark obsidian chains around their wrists that were truly breathtaking.

Persephone had found the traitors who had come onto my land, looking for the closest guards to interrogate. They had wanted information about my movements and my plans for gaining more power.

"In the name of our King. And as the Lady of the Crystal Court, you are sentenced to death," Persephone said after finishing her speech. "Verena. Marta. Come forward."

Marta's iridescent hair beamed, the pink and blue hues shimmering with each step. She stood in front of one male.

Verena moved in next, standing before the female. I glanced

back at her mate, Jax, and their daughter, Levanna. She looked like she would rather be anywhere else than here.

Persephone walked up to me, placing her hand on my arm. "Would you like to do the honors?" she asked.

"No, by all means..." I smiled.

She winked and moved back over to the prisoners, her hips swaying from side to side, her black hair pinned up. Standing before the last female, she turned and nodded to Marta and Verena.

Verena went first, placing her hands on the female's face, and the screams grew. Blood quickly poured from each opening on her head, and within a few breaths, the female's body fell to the ground.

Marta went next, the male before her breathing heavily. She didn't even touch him; instead, she sent her words through the air, her magic thick and coated in death. And if you paid attention then you saw it: the light purple mist that shimmered before stabbing into him like a blade.

The male cried out, trying to fight the power inside him. His death wasn't as fast as the first. It took time, working its way through him, and I was impressed. Pushing my power out, I studied the spell and was even more shocked when I found no way around it. Once it had made its mark, death was certain.

Persephone began as the male continued to suffer and pulled a dark obsidian blade from a sheath on her thigh. She spoke a spell over it and moved in, sinking it into the last witch's chest.

Pulling back, she looked over at the male still alive, still crying out in pain, and threw the dagger at his head, bringing the town square to utter silence.

"This is the fate you will all face if you try to rise against me," I called out as I began walking forward, looking over each one of their faces. "Mark my words. I will burn this Court to the ground if need be." Fire spiraled down my arms, falling to the ground and slithering like snakes.

They devoured the dead, and I turned back to the fae.

"You are dismissed."

Slowly, they all left, and I made my way down to the edge of the

Dark Forest. Persephone showed up a few minutes later and kneeled at the edge where light and darkness met. She whispered her spell, and before my eyes, creatures formed in the shadows.

"Why move their essence here?"

"Traitors don't deserve freedom. They deserve to suffer. Dark souls deserve an unending darkness," she said, standing and wiping the soil from her hands. "It's their punishment for eternity—to be stuck here, decaying and never leaving the shroud of night over this forest. And to serve the living witches to fuel our spells."

That made me smirk. But I was pretty sure it was more for her than the Court itself, which I understood.

"Ezekiel...what has been going on? You seem distracted."

Well, that was an understatement. I still was having issues within the Courts. More secret attacks and my mind wasn't even here to deal with that.

It was on her.

The one who would take everything from me.

"You have been going to the Mortal Realm a lot. And I fear your absence is what's giving fae courage to rise against you. Their King needs to be here."

It was true. If I wasn't there fighting with Nyna, I was watching her. Who she spoke with. But my body also felt pulled there. The power burning like venom in my veins if I denied it.

"I need to finish something there first."

"Maybe I can help...if you told me what it is," she breathed.

And every alarm inside my body went off. I didn't want her anywhere near Nyna. I didn't want her to know she even existed because then she would want to...

Wait...

Was that what I needed?

"I need to go."

"Ezekiel!" Persephone called out, running to catch up with me. She grabbed my hand, turning me to face her. "I need to ask you this. At least once..." She swallowed hard. "Do you want me as your Queen? Do you want me?"

My stomach turned. I think we both knew the real answer to that.

Smiling, I pulled her in and kissed her, doing my best to give her the passion she craved. Not because I wanted to, but because I needed to put this off a little longer. Because if I was right, I wouldn't need her spell.

After a minute passed, I pulled back and looked into her shimmering eyes. Slowly, a smile rose on her face, painting a picture of pure bliss.

"I will be back soon."

Landing in the Mortal Realm, I placed the dark obsidian chains in my jacket pocket and started walking, the power in my veins guiding me through the town.

I cloaked my ears as I moved past the humans, ignoring their conversations and attempts to sell whatever they had.

Using the gap again at the edge of town, I landed on a familiar dirt path. It was the one that led to my brother's cabin.

Was she with him?

I focused on my hearing and heard heavy breathing, and the blood in my veins passed the point of boiling. I moved through the woods, following the sound, when I heard a sword cutting through the air.

The rage inside me died down for a moment, and I was thankful for...what?

My brother could fuck whoever he wanted...

Just not her.

I stalked closer, seeing her through the trees, her hair tied back, strands sticking to her face as she moved through the dance of death. The tight fight leathers molded to every curve perfectly. She moved like a warrior and struck like one too.

It was...beautiful.

My heartbeat doubled over, and I shook off the hesitation and moved in.

Stopping a few feet behind her, I pulled the chains from my pocket, and she paused.

"Just the person I wanted to see," she said sarcastically, turning, her breathing heavy. She spun the sword in a circle. "I need something from you."

"What a coincidence. So do I." I brought my hand up, showcasing the chains.

It was a chance. I didn't know if they would work on her. But they should, since she was under the curse. So, there was only one way to find out.

She rushed in, and I jumped into the gap, reappearing next to her. I grabbed her arm, but she dropped, kicking my foot out, and causing me to lose my balance.

Fucking little brat.

I recovered, spinning her around and bringing the shackle down towards her arm. Both her feet came up, kicking me right in the face, and I laughed, the sting of her blow causing me to let her go.

"Come on, Ruin. I just need all the power in your body. And then I'll leave your corpse alone," I argued, and she sat up, taking her fighting stance.

"And I just need your blood to undo the curse on us."

I chuckled. "Do you think it is that easy to undo dark magic?"

"It's worth a shot," she protested before pulling a dagger from her back and throwing it at me.

Grabbing it in mid-air, I let out a harsh breath as I glanced down and saw it was another dark obsidian blade, sitting inches from my heart.

I was going to kill whoever was giving her these in the worst way possible.

As I threw the dagger back, she tried to move out of the way, but it buried itself in her thigh, causing her to cry out. Dropping to the ground, she tried to breathe through the pain.

I moved in, kicking her sword away, and for a moment, I felt something...

Regret? Shame?

"Now, let's get this over with, shall we?"

I grabbed her arm, and heat flooded through me, sweet and intoxicating. The shackles hovered next to her skin, and anger rose.

Why couldn't I do it?

WHY COULDN'T I DO THIS!?

Nyna spun her body, screaming out from the wound in her leg, and took both my feet out. My back slammed into the ground and, before I knew it, she was using her vampire speed to straddle me. The shackles were on both my wrists, and my arms were above my head.

Gods damn it.

My power faded, and the feeling itself was strange, making me feel...human.

Pulling the dagger free from her leg, she held it to my neck. Her eyes filled with tears, her anger growing with each violent breath she took.

"Why do you want my power?" she asked.

"Because everything I want is mine."

She pushed the blade deeper, my flesh burning from the toxic metal.

She stood like that for a long moment, her emotions just as chaotic as mine.

Did she feel this too? This unbending and unwavering call.

Bringing my hands up, I wrapped the chains behind her neck and brought her face closer to me. Her full pink lips hovered so close to mine that I forgot about everything.

My kingdom. The fate my sister told me. My power.

"Undo the curse, Ezekiel. Or I will kill you."

"You sure about that, Nyna...because here I am, waiting for you."

Pulling the blade back, her fangs sunk into my flesh of my neck, snapping me back to reality. I shoved her back, clutching the wound, forcing more blood to pour out.

I sat up, stunned. The veins below her eyes grew dark, flowing with her own crimson, and she rushed back in at inhuman speed. And pain erupted in my neck again.

She was behind me, holding my head still as she drank deep, and my vision quickly blurred.

Fuck, she was really going to do it.

Throwing my head back, it slammed into hers, and I wrapped my chains around her neck, pulling as hard as I could.

Her power seemed to dull but I couldn't tell. I just hoped it was working. That she would become just like me...

Powerless.

But as she gasped for air, I felt the world spinning even more.

Our eyes met, and something passed between us. Something I wish I could figure out because I wanted to know what it was.

Why could this *thing* be affecting my mind? My body...my—no —I had no soul anymore...she couldn't affect something I didn't possess.

And a faint whisper within said I knew why.

But then everything went black, and it didn't matter.

I didn't know how long I was out, but I remembered hearing a man's voice... before the chains fell from my wrists.

My power bloomed once again, causing me to suck in a sharp breath. I looked around, searching for someone, anyone, but I was alone.

Who removed the dark obsidian?

After a minute passed, my eyes scanned the woods beyond, and I realized I couldn't feel her.

I couldn't feel her anywhere...and for the first time in ages, that made me truly afraid.

Part two
The deals we make

CHAPTER SEVEN

EZEKIEL

One year later in Valyner
Or thirty years in the Mortal Realm

I couldn't take this anymore. Seeing golden eyes every time I closed mine. The smell of roses was forever ruined for me. I had them removed from the Ember Court entirely. I couldn't focus...couldn't live like this.

Fuck.

Was she thinking of me? Waiting for me?

My mind drifted back to being in each other's presence. The first time she touched me. The second time, taking in her bare skin as she fucked someone else. I wish I could say killing that vampire was just to scare her...

It wasn't.

Or the way she straddled me during our last encounter. How her lips were so close to mine. How utterly powerless I was, and yet, it didn't feel so wrong.

I wasn't sure what--or should I say, who--intervened that day, but maybe if we both had died, this horrible chapter would've ended. Or maybe only more suffering would've found us.

Why did I believe it was the latter? Why did that make me hate her even more?

But I refused to give her another thought, just as I had refused myself the freedom of returning to that horrid place. I needed to let it...let *her* go and move forward with what I needed to do here.

Just like she let go...when she sank her teeth into my neck.

Fuck me.

My dick hardened, and I denied myself from going any further with that thought... Not that I had been strong enough these past few months.

She was a problem.

A beautiful, ruinous problem.

My hand moved to my slacks, grabbing my cock and stroking without permission.

A knock on my door stopped my movement, and I groaned. "What is it?"

"Your Grace, I have word from my father."

I got up, adjusted my slacks, and swung open the door. Kadeyan stood there, his hands behind his back.

I began walking, and he matched my pace as I headed towards my study. The grey stone around us looked brighter today, shimmering almost. And I couldn't explain it.

Everything seemed brighter lately.

"What news do you have?"

"He has located some bases there, but it seems they are cloaked. He can't enter. None of the fae can."

I laughed, shaking my head.

Yeah, I was doing a great job of letting her go...

"Not surprised," I mumbled.

Did she use my blood to amplify a barrier?

I looked over at him, his amber eyes locked forward and his long hair pulled back just like his father's.

"Can I ask something, Your Grace?" He slowed as we approached the door, turning to face me.

"Of course." I stalled, looking him over, and felt a sense of peace wash over me.

I always did like having Osiris' boys around. They were loyal, and most of all, made in the image of what this realm needed: more fear.

"Do you believe in mating bonds?" he asked.

I pulled back a bit, considering his question.

"Why? Have you found someone?" I was genuinely curious, especially since I knew he wasn't one for showing much love outside his small circle of friends and family. Probably because of how he was raised—with two of the cruelest men in the realm.

"No...not me..." he explained. "Do you believe they weaken who we are?"

Pausing, I rolled my shoulders back. That question held such weight now, but I gave him the answer I had believed since I became King of Valyner.

"I do. I think it affects us on a level that is damaging to who we need to be. You can love if you can. But your soul is yours alone. No one should ever have that much of you...." I stopped, clearing my throat. "Why do you ask?"

"Silas... He is spending a lot of time with a Crystal and there is just something I feel from them both."

I laughed, shaking my head. "Silas is a hopeless romantic. He always has been, but mating bonds are not that common. And when they do happen, they seem to alter the person's loyalty against all else..." I trailed off, my heart tightening in my chest.

"Is that why you don't want fae to be mated anymore?" Kadeyan asked before swallowing hard. He stood taller, knowing he had overstepped.

That information was between me and the Lord and Ladies of Valyner.

"Who told you that?" I stepped in.

"No one. I read Keres' thoughts when I was in the Crescent Court this past week to...intervene for his wife and daughter."

That fucker needed to be put down like the dog he was.

"She is here. Katarina. She is asking for a meeting," he added.

I let out a long breath and nodded.

He opened the door, and sitting in one of my chairs was Keres' *mate*. Her red hair was pinned up, exposing the bruises on her neck, and her black eyes she wore as if they were plated armor for war.

My blood boiled, and I walked in, nodding to Kadeyan before closing the door.

"When did he do this?"

"Last night, my King."

I nodded and moved over to the chair across from her. "Did you come to tell on him, or was there another reason for your visit?"

"I want to help..." Her voice shook.

I arched a brow, looking her over. "What do you mean?"

"By stopping you from making one of the biggest mistakes of your life."

"Careful, wolf," I warned, but she continued.

"Persephone had a son with Keres. A little over 400 years ago now."

I placed a privacy barrier over the room, and she looked around. Her eyes widened with fear that she was even speaking of this, but again she carried on.

"I found out it was hers after he brought the child into our home. That's when he started beating me. To keep me quiet and pretend that the boy was mine. That Alastair was mine..." She stared off, her eyes hollow. "He is just like his father...and his mother." She looked back at me, her eyes colder. "I am a prisoner in that house until he goes on hunts to the Mortal Realm. And this past week before he returned, I found notes from Persephone."

"What did they say?" I leaned in, and her head dropped. She picked at the skin on her palm and I noticed the scrapes already there. "And be careful to speak the truth with me."

"Do you take me as a liar?" she asked, her green eyes cast with a sheen of tears, slowly meeting mine.

"No...I do not."

"Persephone may care about you. But I think her true passion lies in power. And she wants more. She wants to be unstoppable. And I believe she will do anything to get it."

"What was said in those letters?"

She straightened. "Something about the untouched stones. She was asking him to find the Crescent one."

I stood up and moved closer. "Well then, it's simple. I'll kill them both."

"You can do whatever you want. As is your right. But my suggestion would be to play the game and find out more. Use it against them."

Her response shocked me, but I could see the benefit. Killing two leaders, one being an untouched fae, could stir up political problems...

I grinned. Yes, I liked her plan much more.

"And what do you want for telling me this?" I asked.

"Protection. For my daughter, Alta, and me when the time comes. I will go back there—"

I placed my hand up, stopping her from speaking. "You don't have to go back to that house."

"No, but I do. Because you can't trust either of them. And you need someone on the inside. Just get me out before it's too late."

I looked at the mate—or, I should say, *forced mate*—of Keres. They weren't truly bonded by fate. She was just convenient. There. Able to bear him children and to strengthen his standing in the Court. But I guessed she was taking every herb she could to avoid another pregnancy by that man. I didn't blame her.

"Why are you doing all this? Why not just take your daughter and leave?"

Katarina smiled—it was weak—but there. She stood and met my gaze. "He would hunt us down. And he would kill me to take her back. She is his blood..." She paused, burying down her fear of that happening. "This is for my daughter. I want to show her we don't run; we fight."

I was taken aback, shocked by the love I felt pouring out of her. That parental protection was more vicious than any power or creature alive. It stunned me, ripping at the wound in my soul I buried long ago.

I would never experience that love.

Who could ever love the vile and cruel King for who he was?

No one.

"Then you have my word. We will set up some patrols on your estate. Osiris will be your point of contact to get information for me. And if he is unavailable, then I ask you to give it to Kadeyan, but it must be in writing. I want to keep him out of this as much as possible."

She nodded and moved a few feet away before her orange mist swallowed her whole.

I ran my fingers through my hair, the itch in my veins growing because here we were again. Someone was always undermining my rule.

My power.

My wrath.

And it was the woman I'd chosen to sit beside me on the throne. Honoring her and her Court. My ally, who wanted to make me untouchable by all forms of magic.

I should've seen this coming.

There was no trusting anyone.

Except maybe one. And it made me want to speak to him. The one who understood my deep pain, the damage...

I fell into the gap and felt the rush of darkness pass over me. But now the real question was, would he be there?

I landed in the woods, just outside the cabin that my brother had occupied some years ago. It was cool, the leaves on the trees shifting from their bright green hues into autumn.

The cabin itself was under construction on one side, the foundation laid in the dense soil.

Sun rays beamed overhead, and the sound of wood splitting drew my attention to behind the property.

I could feel his emotions—subtle, unbothered. Yet with each step I took, it shifted. The axe came down harder as I came around the cabin, his shoulders rising and falling with his heavy breathing.

"What do you want now?" he asked, not turning as he grabbed another piece of wood and placed it on the stub before him. The axe flew, slamming down with a force that made even my bones quake.

Slowly he turned, and I stopped, looking him over. His reddish-brown hair stuck to his face, sweat coating his brow. I went to open my mouth but closed it, avoiding his gaze.

Taking a few steps in, I watched him grip the axe in his hand. "I have a problem..."

"You always have problems, Ezekiel. And you eliminate them each time." Elias turned, grabbing another piece of wood.

"Persephone is up to something with Keres. I need to know... Do you still have it?"

He stopped, turning over his shoulder to look at me.

"Do you still have the Crescent stone?"

He chuckled, the smile on his face not surprised. "You want that from me, too? My last connection to my Court?"

"No...I want you to keep it safe."

"From who?" He dropped the axe, moving in towards me. "From who Ezekiel? Keres?" His eyes flashed a yellow haze, and I felt a stab in my chest.

I took his Court from him...and gave it to that dog. A dog who was sitting at the feet of my *betrothed*.

"Why are you here?" he asked, looking me over.

"I saw our sister a little over a year ago in our time."

"It's not my time anymore," he mumbled.

"She told me something." I moved over the tree trunks laid out across the lawn and sat down.

"I assume it went as well as our last meeting," he retorted, and I gritted my teeth.

"I have enemies everywhere. In my realm, my home, in this land...and I just... I need it to stop. I need everyone for..."

"You are still hell-bent on lifting the curse on you by the gods?" he huffed. "You eviscerated more lives than anyone combined. As far as anyone is concerned, it was a blessing for you to never carry on a line of your own."

Standing, I moved over to him. I wanted to bring my fires to the surface, to cover him from head to toe...but I couldn't.

"I didn't care about that! I didn't need a child or a mate! You were to be my heir... Did you know that?" I growled. "My little brother. The one who fought to make me see life could be different."

"I was clearly wrong in my pursuit of your redemption," he said flatly, and it was worse than being stabbed with dark obsidian.

My gaze hardened, and the walls within built themselves back up, shutting out the pain. "You were. Because there is no redeeming a monster like me," I whispered and walked away.

"Ezekiel..." Elias called out, and I felt his sorrow surface. "Instilling fear will never get you anywhere. Look how it ended for our father."

I winced at the mention of him.

"I am not our father." My voice rose as I turned slightly.

"No...you are not. Because I knew the man you were before this. One who bled for his family. Willing to do whatever it took to free us. And that man is not gone, just lost."

"He is gone. Love and mercy did not secure our lives or our futures. Power did."

"Can you truly be this blind?" He moved in, his boots crunching down on the dying grass. "You did those things for the love of our family. And in your actions that drove you to seek more power, you destroyed it all. And you alone can choose to make it right."

He placed his hand on my shoulder, and tears flooded my eyes. "Power will not keep you from hurting, brother. Your pursuit of power will continue to steal a life worth living. And I don't think you are so far gone to realize that yet..."

After a few moments, his touch fell away, and I turned back, watching him pick up another piece of wood and bring the axe down.

Making things right would force me to face that I was the one who ruined it all...

Ruined our family.

And I couldn't.

There was no way out of the firestorm I created... I was caught between the cinders of my mistakes. My choices. And I needed to continue living with them.

Because admitting that would reveal that I was alone, not because of some curse...but because I was the problem.

And that would swallow me whole.

CHAPTER EIGHT

NYNA

Six years later in the Mortal Realm
Or two months and twelve days in Valyner

Screaming rang out in the distance, and I jumped up, looking around. I was in a hut, the walls shaking from the force of the wind that was howling outside.

I slowly got up, recognized one voice, and felt for the sword I had been sleeping with. The same sword the king tried to kill me with by the pond.

But it wasn't there.

"Father!" he yelled, and I dragged back the wooden door.

I could see Ezekiel. He looked about the same age as when I'd last seen him, but somehow felt younger. More human. His eyes were a duller grey, but just as hard.

My gaze traveled over to where his was locked, and I spotted a woman on the ground, her lip split and bleeding. Her eyes matched his perfectly, her hair just a few shades darker.

A sister maybe?

Next to the woman was a young man with a stab wound in his

stomach. His eyes were wide, showcasing his blue eyes. And that reddish-brown hair...

He looked so familiar.

Oh my gods... Elias?

I stepped out, seeing a man standing over them.

"They are an abomination to my house. You all are!" *the man yelled, and looking at him, I was stunned, unable to move.*

He looked so much like Ezekiel. Same color eyes, and chestnut hair the same length, just hitting the top of his shoulders.

Ezekiel moved in, gripping his sword and lifting it. "If you touch them again, I will drive this through your heart!"

His father laughed. "You? The weakest of them all? You all have disgraced me for long enough."

"Then end it here. With me. Leave Akari and Elias alone," *Ezekiel countered.*

Their father laughed harder, his tone sending chills through my bones. He moved in, swinging his sword with such fury. Such rage. But Ezekiel held his own, meeting his father's attack with brutal ferocity.

After a few minutes of their fight, his steps faltered as his father pushed him back. His father used his failure to advance, plunging his sword right into his shoulder. Ezekiel gasped, and so did I.

Akari and Elias swallowed their screams, and without hesitating, I ran over, looking down at him. The fear in his eyes was all-consuming, crippling.

Their father stepped back, leaving the sword in his son's flesh. "The gods will grant me true power and warriors tomorrow night. And I will be rid of you all."

He walked off, and Akari got up.

"Ezekiel!" *she cried, running to him.*

Ezekiel pulled the blade free with a cry. Akaria tore the hem of her dress and pressed the fabric into his wound, forcing him to grit his teeth and stifle a scream. They both made their way over to Elias, and she did the same for him.

"I don't want to die...I don't want to die," *Elias repeated, tears falling from his eyes and staining his cheeks.*

"I won't allow it, brother," *Ezekiel whispered, grabbing his brother's hand, looking to Akari and back to Elias.* "We are going to that gathering. And by the gods' mercy, we will be chosen. All of us. And we will never see him again."

I jumped up, sweat trickling down my neck as my hand went to the sword at my hip.

It was there...

It was just a dream...another dream of the King.

I had seen him as a child, cowering from a man yelling at him, with bruises on his face. And a woman crying, trying to protect him.

Him screaming near a river to spare the child when he himself was so young, saying he would raise the newborn. He fought for approval for so long, and then it shifted.

It made me think of my father. How I tried. And I gave up as well...

There were also dreams where I saw him as he was now. Sitting in a throne room, cursing the gods above, his anger growing wilder.

And some that seemed so far off, I couldn't believe I was having them. Seeing him smile, genuinely laughing. They were always blurry, being swallowed by a void. Those felt like nightmares compared to all the others. And it had nothing to do with the darkness.

It had to do with seeing him like that.

He was different in the past. Still vicious, but with purpose. And somehow over the years, that light went out. And he was nothing but a monster that mimicked his father.

It was...sad. And against my better judgment of who I knew him to be, I felt sorrow for the life he had to live.

I had pulled his blood out of me. What, thirty-six years ago now? I had used it to enforce barriers in each city for the Cursed to use as sanctuaries from the fae. And I feared they would not be a long-term solution.

Many of the Cursed were growing impatient with my ability to understand the curse placed on us, but the blood wasn't enough. There was something in it that was completely untouchable, dark.

He was right. It wasn't as simple as having his blood. So what did I need?

The faint markings on my palm remained the outline of a gemstone, and over the years I wondered if it was something that could help. Yet again, I had no answers. No leads.

Until now...

Fuck.

I got up and walked out of my small cabin and looked around, the night still upon us.

Spotting Kali talking to one witch, I moved over.

"Hey, where is Elias?" I asked, scanning.

It looked like most of the wolves were already gone.

Shit.

"He left about an hour ago to go back home. Why?"

Kali had been slowly becoming more agitated with feeding. And all the spells I placed on her weren't holding back the inevitable... I feared how long she would have until the bloodlust would take her. Until my friend's blue eyes were hollow.

I cursed under my breath and walked over to the horses. Untying the reins from the post, I pulled myself up quickly.

"Nyna? What is it?" Kali asked, running over to me.

"The sun will be up soon. Make sure all the vampires are in the caves. Break their necks if need be."

She nodded, and I took off.

I rode fast, watching the sun rise through the trees as I made my way through Qeles. Voices from the humans filtered through the city streets, and I overheard some talking about *the monsters*. They were scared, angry, and determined to protect their families from us.

They knew we were here, among them, and with more Cursed

falling away from their humanity...it was just a matter of time before they planned to fight us too.

Armaros came into view, and I cut through the woods until I was off the beaten path. And my mind replayed the dream.

Why didn't he tell me?

Why wouldn't he have told me about his brother?

Making it to his cabin, I glanced at his window and saw him yelling and waving his hands, but I couldn't hear anything.

I tied my horse's reins to the tree and walked towards the door, and if I hadn't already spotted him, I would have been convinced he wasn't even home.

It was utterly quiet.

I knocked and waited, but after a few moments, I pushed open the door, seeing him, his face red, his chest rising and falling.

I moved in, looked around, and saw nothing before turning to face him. "What the fuck is going on?"

A hand wrapped around the back of my neck, and I instantly grabbed the dagger at my hip.

"Come now, Nyna. We both know you don't have what it takes to kill me."

I could say the same, asshole.

Throwing my head back, it hit his throat, causing him to cough and stumble back. Ezekiel choked out a laugh, and I turned, looking him over before glancing at Elias.

"It's true. You are his brother."

Elias' brow furrowed. "How did you—?"

"Why didn't you tell me? Oh my gods... that's why you never struggled with your power. You're an untouched fae." I took a sharp breath, my mind racing.

I wasn't one, yet I had control. And so did my father. I shook my head, letting the thought go for now because there were more pressing questions that needed to be answered.

"Why didn't you tell me you were one of the untouched fae? Why didn't you give me something on him to help our people!?" I yelled.

Ezekiel straightened, looking at his brother. "Yes, Elias, please explain."

Elias' face hardened on his brother, his blue eyes darkening. "You know why, you fucking prick."

"Shame?" he taunted.

"Where is the stone?" I asked, which grabbed both of their attention.

Elias looked sick, worried even, but Ezekiel didn't.

It was just pure wrath.

Shadows poured out, slamming me against the wall, shaking the books behind me, and causing some to fall to the ground.

"Ezekiel!" Elias yelled.

But it was too late. He was moving in, meeting my gaze. "I should have killed you the moment I set eyes on you," he seethed.

The power between us grew, and while it sent chills through me, it also shook something within. Something that hid behind a closed door. And from the shift in his eyes, I think he felt it, too.

Yet, just as fast as that awakening came, it was devoured by my fury. And those eyes were nothing but a reminder of why I was fighting.

"And I should have drained you dry." My fangs ripped through my jaw, sending heat through my veins.

"Ezekiel! You will not kill her," Elias demanded.

"Oh, I won't?" he laughed.

Pushing my hand through his toxic embrace of vapor, I went to strike him but he grabbed my wrist. He slowly glanced at the fading scar of the stone his blood left behind on my palm.

His shadows fell and he pulled me closer.

"What is this?" he asked.

"Bite me," I seethed, and it brought a smile to his hard features. And as much as I didn't want to admit it, it made my stomach flutter.

Elias moved in, pushing his brother back and causing him to drop his hold on me. He stood between us, a growl rumbling in his chest.

"You will have to go through me."

This stopped the King, his lip pulling up in disgust.

"You would choose this traitor over your own blood?" he asked.

Elias took a step forward. "You chose power over family. So tell me, why can't I choose a friend over you?"

This shut him up, making him take a few steps back. "Tell her to explain. Now."

"I'm right here, asshole," I objected.

Elias turned, looking at my palm. "What did this?"

I narrowed my gaze at Ezekiel, and his eyes were already fixated on me. "*Your blood* did this."

Elias turned, looking at his brother. "You used the Ember stone to curse us, didn't you?"

"Careful, brother."

"What is the Ember stone?" I asked, but neither man looked at me, lost in their silent conversation. "If you don't tell me, I'll ask Akari."

Ezekiel pointed at me. "I am going to make you wish you were never born if you say another word!"

It was my time to laugh.

"How do you know about our sister?" Elias asked. "Where is this coming from?"

I closed my mouth, swallowing hard.

"Oh yes, please, at your own convenience, usurper," the King seethed.

"I'm not a Queen!" I shouted. "Just someone willing to go up against you. And have people who support me in that cause. That must be hard to understand, having people who are loyal to you."

"You little bitch," he fumed.

"Gods above, will you two stop? It's like watching two children fight over a toy," Elias yelled. Turning to me, he took a deep breath. "How do you know about our family? About the stone?"

"I had a dream. Many dreams...of him."

Ezekiel looked stunned, and it was a weird expression on a man so cold. Then he grinned, and that alone terrified me to my core.

Because he was breathtaking.

"Was I any good? Because I assure you I'm much better in reality."

I gave him my middle finger and a dirty look, which made him silently chuckle. Glancing back at Elias, I saw my friend, the worry in his eyes, and took a deep breath.

"I think it was from his blood being inside me. And the blood made the mark of a gemstone. I figured I'd just throw it out there, and now I know what I need to free our people. With no help from you."

Ezekiel interjected, "You are no untouched fae."

"No. But I've been strong enough to take you on, so what do I have to lose?" I walked to the door and stopped. "Be careful, King. Not every fae who comes here is fighting us. Some would rather see you burn than follow you into an unknown war."

Walking out, I was stopped by Ezekiel as he appeared before me, his light grey mist holding a scent of smoke and ash.

"What do you know about that?" he asked.

I went to walk around him, but he grabbed my arm, spinning me back to face him. I stumbled into his chest and placed my hands on him. We both froze, the heat between us growing past the point of soothing. It was ravenous, like a hungry blaze determined to devour everything in its path.

And it scared me.

His hand slipped around my waist, and I held my breath as he pulled me closer.

"What are you doing to me?" he whispered.

I slowly met his gaze, his silver eyes shimmering as if they were their own light source, putting the moon and the sun to shame.

"Get your hands off of me," I whispered back, my voice shaking. But it wasn't because I was afraid of him...I was afraid of whatever I was feeling.

He listened, slowly letting me go. And I turned, walking away with one thought...

What the fuck was that?

CHAPTER NINE

EZEKIEL

"**B**ring in the next one," I demanded, my hands already tingling from the last pillar of fire I released on the corpse before me.

Osiris nodded and moved out of the room. Screams of prisoners filtered in from down the hall, and instead of feeling joy from it...

I felt nothing.

She was right. I returned home last night and started torturing the fae who went out on hunts.

My people were helping the Cursed. Giving them dark obsidian, explaining my plans to gain more power.

Which meant my plans were falling apart.

This realm was going to fall apart. Just like my sister said.

I continued on for hours, interrogating prisoner after prisoner, all ending with their death. Blood coated my face and my clothes. The white shirt I was wearing was stained a deep crimson, as if that was the thread used to create it.

I slumped against the wall, my power and body succumbing to exhaustion. Ashes lay before me, and I barely heard Osiris come in and take a seat.

"May I speak frankly..." he asked, and I glanced over at him, knowing the shield I kept up was completely down, That I was showing him the brokenness I guarded with my life.

"It's okay to care."

"Not for me, it isn't…" I whispered.

"When I met Celeste…it was the first time I cared for something more than myself. She was my heart. And losing her right after Kadeyan's birth…it killed me."

"It was my fault. I demanded she fight with us in the great war…" I gazed out of the ashes again, but he continued.

"She wanted to fight for you…and so did I." He breathed out. "I found comfort after the war with another—you remember, Isolde…"

I nodded slightly, and he continued.

"But again, she died after Silas was born. It hardened me. It made me fear letting anyone close again."

"Why are you telling me this?" I asked him, slowly turning and seeing his amber gaze locked on the grey stone wall in front of us.

"Because I think you need to hear it. Love doesn't make us weak. It would never make *you* weak. It would only strengthen you, even if you lost it. You would be stronger for having let love in and carrying it with you."

"Who could love me after what I've done?" I waited until his eyes met mine.

"You might be surprised. And I know of three people already." He smirked. "You are like a brother to me, Ezekiel. And regardless of what you do, I will stand beside you, because I know you need it. But you also have your brother and sister."

Resting my head against the wall behind me, I chuckled. "Elias would rather protect the Cursed."

"You say that, but if he had shared information with the girl who wants to undo the curse, he could have given her direction in her pursuit. And yet, the Cursed attacks have not escalated. They have remained the same. He cares for you."

"And Akari?" I asked.

"She is pissed at you for sure." He laughed. "You probably

shouldn't have killed her friend. But it's been what, two years now? Go speak with her. Hear her out on this vision that has you on edge."

"What of Persephone and Keres?" I looked over at him, and he shrugged.

"She can't do anything without the throne's power. And she will not get it. Not while either of us breathes."

Faelynn opened the door, her black eyes landing on me and Osiris.

"What is it, Faelynn?" Osiris asked, standing and moving over to her.

"The Sky Temple. Crystals have—"

I vanished into the gap, pushing my power to get to her as fast as I could. I landed in the temple and felt her power coming from the lowest levels and used the gap again to appear there. The black stone walls promised shadows, if not for the orbs of white light floating overhead, showing the circular atrium.

My eyes darted to the two Crystals who held my sister down, while another was trying to undo the enchantments on her stone in the center of the room.

Anger flooded every nerve, and I moved in.

Accessing the Crystal power in my veins, I crushed their spells. One turned, and I brought my hand up, sending out my fires to consume them. The other two looked over at me, their eyes wide.

Osiris appeared behind me and sent out his shadows. The vapor slithered into their bodies, causing them to scream out. I resisted the urge to kill them, to rip out their throats with my bare hands, and rushed over to my sister.

Dropping to my knees, I pulled her into my lap, and her breathing grew wilder.

"Who sent you?" Osiris asked, looking at the both of them. He touched both of their heads, and I could tell by his anger growing that their minds were spelled. I sent out my power, cracking the magic within and giving him a place to enter.

"Fuck, their memories were wiped." He stepped back after a moment, his shadows crushing their insides.

They gasped and tried to scream, but nothing came out of their mouths but blood.

"Ezekiel...my office, now. It's spelled," Akari whispered, her chest rising and falling.

I glanced up, looking up through the hollow center of the temple, sensing other fae descending the stairs to various levels, on their way to study.

We needed to move before they saw their Lady like this.

"Osiris!" I yelled, grabbing his attention.

He moved over and we all fell into the gap, appearing in my sister's office at the top of the temple. I walked her over to a small couch on the light side of the room where warmth radiated, like the sun itself. Placing her down gently, I turned, listening to her uneven breathing. My eyes were locked on the shadowed side of the room where darkness lived, beckoning my wrath to come forth.

Osiris stood off to the side, waiting.

"I will kill Persephone for this," I growled.

"Ezekiel," she called out as I tried to leave. "You can't stop her."

"Don't doubt my anger, sister," I shouted.

"Valyner will fall. It is not for you to save," she said, sitting up and wincing. Osiris moved in, helping her stand. She locked her eyes on me, and that look alone stopped me from moving an inch. "You will fail. Become what you fear. It's already begun."

"I do not need your visions to tell me that when I see it."

"Listen to me!" she yelled, wincing once more before coughing. "You need her..."

"Persephone?" Osiris asked, stunned by her statement. As was I.

"No...the one they call the Cursed Queen. She holds the key to the future of this realm. She holds the key to you."

What the fuck did that mean?

Akari's eyes shifted into a white fog for a moment before blinking it away. She slowly walked over to me, wincing from the pain no doubt still coursing through her.

I moved in, supporting her weakened body as she wrapped her hand around the back of my neck.

"You have torn the hearts of too many. And now you will know what it feels like to love something more than the air you breathe," she proclaimed, her heart pounding like a drum in my ears.

I pulled away, my eyes wide.

"Tell me what you saw," I demanded.

"No," she countered. "Because then you will do everything to avoid it. And I will not allow you to keep on this path. I will not allow you to affect my future."

Osiris moved in, standing by my side. "What is your order?"

But I was still lost in my sister's eyes, her emotions swirling around me, begging me to listen, to heed her warning.

I moved in, looking down at her. "If I do this...if I make this deal...what will happen?"

"Freedom."

I looked away, my anger faltering before I met her gaze again. "And I need her? The Cursed Queen?"

"Brother. If you ever loved me, Elias, even Osiris...then you will do this. This affects all of us now."

The thought of being near Nyna again...scared me. It scared me more than death itself. She was turning my life upside down. Everything I fought to become.

I backed up, moving to the door. "Osiris. I want guards posted in the temple. Their job is to protect her with their lives." I pointed at my sister. "Embers and Fallens only."

I met her silver eyes one last time and felt my throat tighten as though the hands of life wanted to steal the air from my lungs. "You have my word, sister."

Osiris followed me, and all I could see as we went down the spiral staircase was red. A burning fire that kept growing in power. Making it outside, I let it free, the fire consuming me from the inside out.

"Ezekiel!" Osiris yelled, forcing me to turn and look at him through the blaze.

I took a few deep breaths and with it, the flames died out. "Get those soldiers here and then go to our meeting spot. Have Kadeyan and Silas stand post at my castle. We leave tonight."

I began walking off, but he called out, "Where are you going?"

"I'm going to see my betrothed."

Throwing open the crystal doors that held various shades of purple to her castle, I made my way past her guards. Not one of them tried to stop me. They knew better. I went upstairs; the sun creating an array of colors in the air as its rays reflected off the crystal pillar and onto the walls.

Getting to her office, I paused at the dark amethyst doors as voices filtered out.

"It's a problem for me and Jax. She cannot be with someone like him."

Verena.

What the hell was she doing here?

I pushed open the door, taking in Persephone, Marta, and Verena.

"We will discuss it later. If you both would please give me a moment with the King." Persephone gestured for them to leave, and I watched as they left. Verena didn't look at me once, but Marta... Her eyes were locked on me, the powder blue growing brighter.

Her rage towards me was evident. So many looked at me that way because I killed their friends or family, passed more restrictions in their Courts, and whatever else I deemed necessary. I couldn't care less about why she was pissed. She could get in line.

"Hello, my love." She moved over to me, and I gripped her by her throat, moving her back until she slammed into the wall.

"Did you send Crystals to the Sky Temple? Did you give the orders to attack my sister?"

"N-no," she choked out.

She looked so convincing. Shocked by my reaction, even fearful.

I let her go and stepped back, watching her hands go to her throat, coughing.

"Ezekiel, why would I attack someone who will soon be my sister?"

"You tell me?"

Witch bitch.

"I would never..." She moved in slowly. "I know you. And what you do to traitors," she said, her voice calm and understanding.

Yet, there was no ignoring what my body was screaming. That this was all an act, a strung-out play that I had unknowingly been playing, where she slowly became the lead. And I was done acting.

"Why do you want to be bonded to me?"

"Because I see who you are. Who you *really* are. And I choose to love that man. Support my King."

She was such a good liar. How did I not see it before?

Well, two can play this game.

I forced an apologetic smile and gestured for her to come closer. I picked up her hand and gave it a light squeeze before kissing the top. Bile rose into my throat, and I swallowed it down.

"Forgive me."

"There is nothing to forgive. You are a King. As your right to question us all." She ran her fingers through my hair before lifting my head to meet her eyes. "It is us from here on out."

"Indeed, it is..." I moved back and cleared my throat. "I will be gone for some time. I need to attend to some things. But when I return, we will set the date for your coronation."

Her eyes lit up, and I saw it. The faintest desire of love...and it wasn't for me. It was for what it would give her.

Power.

I pulled her in, running my hands down her body, before lifting and placing her on the desk. I shouldn't have said it, but I needed to see her face. Gently, I wrapped my hand around her throat. I resisted laughing at how easy it was to make this witch moan.

I studied her, her soft expression. "As long as you stop meeting with Keres."

She froze, and it felt like the first time I ever released my power.

Good.

Empowering.

"I'm not sure what you mean..."

I leaned in, my lips brushing her ear. "Yes, you do," I whispered. "And if you want me. All of me." I rolled my hips into her and ignored how my body turned to ice. "You will stop fucking the dog. And making him do tricks for you." I pulled back, her gaze hard for a moment before it returned to confusion. "You want to be a queen? Earn it."

I released her and walked away, feeling her anger shatter through the walls she hid behind so well.

I smiled, letting the gap take me away.

Didn't she know I was the best at bringing that out in people?

CHAPTER TEN

EZEKIEL

*L*anding in my bedroom, I grabbed a few things, stuffing them in my leather bag before heading to the throne room.

With the bag slung over my shoulder, my heartbeat quickened as I passed the fae workers, my soldiers.

This was insanity.

This girl would not want to work together. And now I had to convince her it was needed. For my realm...

For my reign.

Fuck.

My hands shook as I pulled open the doors to the throne room and took in my soldiers standing at attention.

"Get out. All of you."

I watched them leave, but reached out, stopping Ash. She looked up at me, her fiery-colored eyes meeting mine. "I need you to round up your most trusted soldiers and be ready when I call on you."

"Of course, Your Grace," she said before I let her go.

Shutting the doors behind me, I took a breath, but it did little to settle the panic growing in my veins. I stared at the throne, my fires growing wilder inside.

Part of me despised it right now, what it had done to me over the last 1,400 odd years, but it wasn't the throne's fault. A chair made of copper wasn't the problem...

I was.

Tears fell from my eyes, stunning me as I brushed them away.

Emotions slammed into me from every angle, and the pain was too great...too much.

Power will not keep you from hurting, brother. Your pursuit of power will continue to steal a life worth living.

This affects all of us now.

My eyes narrowed, my breathing rapid.

I convinced them to go to that first Lunavas. I made us what we are...and now it was my duty to save them again.

To save Osiris and his boys.

I would not lose them.

Dropping into the gap, I landed in the tunnels below the Fallen and Ember Lands. I walked down the long hall, the water dripping to the same beat as my boots slamming against the ground.

"Osiris," I called out, but stalled as I looked over the large room. He wasn't here.

I waited a few minutes, the silence itching at every nerve. I made my way downstairs to the bottom level, un-spelled the room holding my stone, and placed it in my leather jacket before going back. But again, he wasn't there.

Something was wrong...

"Ezekiel, Come!" His voice invaded my mind, shocking me.

I traced his magic back and used the gap to pull me there.

My eyes focused on him in the dead woods of the Fallen castle, and grief captivated him. Everything slowed, my heart aching to take its next breath.

Then I heard it...a broken cry that brought me back to reality.

Looking down, I saw Levanna—Verena's daughter—crying over Silas. The side of her face was stained with his blood.

I stumbled back, gripping the tree next to me.

No.

No.

NO!

Blood poured from his ears, nose, eyes, and mouth. And my stomach turned, forcing me to look away. My vision tunneled, my stare becoming vacant until the fire in my blood pulled me back. My eyes landed on Kadeyan, his hollow stare locked on his brother. The brokenness was clear for all to see.

The pain of loss drowned me, my sister's words pushing me further into the depths of the chaos I never thought I would face.

This affects all of us now.

It was starting...

"Levanna found him on Crystal Land..." Osiris choked out. "She... used her power to call Kade and me..." Tears fell to his cheeks.

His knees slightly buckled, and I moved in. Grabbing his shoulder, I pulled him towards me and held him tightly.

Seeing dead bodies was nothing new to any of us. But this was different. This plunged the steel deep into my chest...and I hated it.

I hated this feeling.

A feeling that I thought I could control. A feeling that I had buried so long ago that I felt untouchable. But I wasn't. None of us were.

And it made me feel...human.

"They will pay. Mark my words, Osiris. They will pay with their lives."

Eight months later in Valyner
Twenty years in the Mortal Realm

Months passed in the blink of an eye. And my problems in the realm multiplied.

Courts were at each other's throats. Fae were meeting together, from the reports I had received. And I hunted down every lead, only to be left with nothing.

Silas' funeral had been the day after we found him, all of us numb, broken by his loss. But no one more than the mate...

She went home and tried to kill her parents, and a warrant was out for her head. If they hadn't named their daughter, I could have gotten it thrown out, but the order came down from them, given to Persephone. The Courts had their own laws that were approved by me long ago...and this was one I couldn't undo at the moment. But at least I could offer her my protection. I wouldn't let them touch her. Nor would Osiris or Kadeyan.

Her pain reminded me of my fear of the past. When I thought I was going to lose my sister. Or my brother under my father's hands. It shook something inside me every time I was near her.

And there was no running from that pain. Not anymore.

I tried to get to Verena and Jax...but Persephone swore up and down they were not involved, and that they were being held for investigation.

It was bullshit. The laws of our Courts were bullshit. But if I intervened...what would happen next?

Would they kill Kadeyan? Osiris? My sister?

Would they go find Elias?

I was becoming her puppet, and it brought on a wrath I didn't even know I could possess.

The last time I saw Persephone was a week ago, when she pressed the issue again that we should bond soon to unite our two Courts. That was the last thing on my mind. She claimed I had been absent, and I was. With her.

I was doing everything in my power to scare the realm into listening, which meant I had killed my way through them, passing new laws, and avoiding her like a fucking plague because I didn't want to be anywhere near her.

And I couldn't stop thinking that she had a hand in Silas' death, knowing it would keep me here, pushing me closer to her coronation.

I was the King, and yet...I had no control right now.

I looked over the room Osiris had given me in the Fallen castle, the war table in the center with Valyner carved into it. It was a place to get away, with only a few knowing it existed.

"Kadeyan. Listen to me!" Osiris yelled, and I turned my head towards the hall. "You will let this go. The Fallen Court needs a leader right now. Promise me you will do this."

Hesitation and anger flooded in, and I stood, moving towards the door.

"I promise," he finally said.

"They will pay. I promise you, Kade...they will," Osiris stated.

I opened the door, and Kadeyan avoided my gaze, but I saw his eyes lined with tears.

"Your father will return soon. I promise," I said. "But until then... Raise hell."

His eyes met mine, and his amber eyes shifted into a deep crimson before he nodded.

He walked away, and I took a deep breath, looking at Osiris.

"Are you ready?" I asked.

"Let's go get what we need...so we can kill them and be done with this."

CHAPTER ELEVEN

NYNA

Cool ocean water caressed my feet, and I welcomed the embrace. The air was thick with salt, the sky taking on shades of pink and purple.

"Thank you, Orla," I said, turning to face the former Lady of the Salt Court in Valyner. She had given up her position to her son many years ago, allowing him to lead and advising from a distance behind closed doors. She was happy that way. And it gave her time to help others...like us.

"It is the least I can do for my people."

Orla had been here since last night, swimming with the sirens and directing them to different prey further out in the ocean, and creating water chains that held them back from boats. She didn't turn into a beast like them, but it was almost like they viewed her as a leader in the water, following her commands.

"It is something else...to see them become like the true sirens in our realm," she stated. "Do you struggle like them?"

"No... I try to help them the best I can. But I can't do what you do."

She looked me over and smiled, tucking her long silver-blue hair behind her pointed ear. "I think you are capable of more than you know."

We both stood, and she grabbed my hand. "I spoke with Akari. She wishes she could meet you in person, but often sees you in her visions," she said. "Her message for you, though, was cryptic. Most seers are, but she says to be ready for change. One that will turn your life upside down. And let your eyes be open to who the real enemy is."

I nodded, and she released my hand.

Well, that wasn't so cryptic. She was speaking of her brother. Wasn't she?

"Well, I hope to see you again soon...but in Valyner as a guest of my Court. I'd like you to meet my son, Alaric, the Lord of the Salt Court, and my grandson, Eryx."

I nodded and met her sea-blue eyes. "It will be an honor...when the day comes."

She fell into the gap, and I watched as the blue salty mist of her power vanished into the air before letting out a long exhale.

The water brushed up on shore, the sound lulling me into a trance. I needed to go, and yet I savored it. The smell, the breeze, the sound. I found a moment of peace, and I wanted it for just a little longer.

"What are you doing?" my father called out from the sand-banks, causing me to turn and come back to reality.

I walked over to him, looking around. "I was meeting a friend. That's all."

He looked me over and began walking with me. "It's been almost fifty years, Nyna." He stopped, but I continued on. "Are you ever going to forgive me?"

I stopped and turned around. "As soon as you tell me what you meant about my power."

"I can't. Not yet."

"Well then, Dad, until then, I am going to keep living my life. And burying friends. You should do the same."

"I am sorry to hear about Kali. You two were close."

I stopped, closing my eyes... She disappeared four years ago, and my heart hadn't been the same since. That was until I found a skeleton a few days ago. One that had a leather bracelet around the wrist with a silver locket on top. The same bracelet I gave her when she turned.

We buried her that night.

She wasn't the first friend who came and went. And it hurt, the realization that she wouldn't be the last.

"You have been fighting this war since your mother passed away. It's been what...ninety years? I think you need to come to terms with—"

"At least I fought for her."

"This was never my fight," he said calmly.

"How can you say that as one of the Cursed? This is your fight!"

"There are things you haven't even begun to understand about the word *fight*. Or war. Exile. Shame. Curses." He raised his voice, his face turning a shade of red.

"Then tell me!" I yelled.

He closed his mouth, his anger fading away, and I wanted it to come back. I wanted him to fight me, to fight anything. Show emotion and want to...be my father.

"Was this not the life you wanted? Did you not want us?" Tears flooded my eyes, and I couldn't help but let them fall. "Look at me..."

He did as I asked, his blue eyes filled to the brim. He moved in, pulling me to his chest, and held me as I let out sobs that had been held back for far too many years.

After what felt like a few minutes, my father cleared his throat.

"I wanted you, Nyna...I did. You were the hope I waited for. That I begged the stars above to give me and have protected every day since you were born." He squeezed me tighter, his heartbeat filling my ears.

Pulling back, I wiped the tears away.

Someone standing off to the side caught my gaze, making me furrow my brows.

"Elias?"

He approached, smirking, but it was uneasy. "I need to speak with you."

"Okay... Um, Elias, I don't know if you remember Zaryk from Valyner, but this is my father."

My father offered his hand, nodding. But Elias looked confused.

"It's good to see you again, my Lord. I will let you guys go." My father gave me a quick hug and walked away, disappearing beyond the sandbanks and into the woods beyond.

Glancing back at Elias, I noticed his eyes were still lost in thought.

"What is it?"

"Nyna..." he started and shook his head. "I have never met your father before."

"Well, I'm sure the pack in Valyner is much larger—"

He cut me off. "No...I knew all the wolves in Valyner, and I'm telling you—I have never seen him before."

Shaking my head, I looked to where my father just stood. "He always said he was from the Crescent Court in Valyner. He was cursed in the beginning for fighting for the humans. What are you saying?"

He swallowed. "I'm saying that he isn't from my realm."

My stomach dropped, and I thought back to all the times he spoke of my power. How I needed to be careful. And to only show one of them.

Oh my gods.

He knew all along why I was different, didn't he? So why couldn't he tell me yet?

I wanted to run after him, to ask him why he would lie about this all my life. Why he let me live thinking I was the only one who was different?

"I'm sorry, I didn't mean to..." Elias started, but stopped. "I need you to come with me."

"Where?" I asked, still feeling lost in my own thoughts.

"Do you trust me?" he asked. His eyes were begging, his body tense, yet eager to move. He was nervous, and that got my attention.

Elias was noble. Respectful. And aside from him withholding his secrets about his family, I did trust him.

I nodded, and he led me through the town, the night becoming a roaring celebration among the humans. For a moment, I fell into their joy, their free spirits.

Music played on violins, and couples got up, dancing. Laughs filtered out from the pub, and I glanced through the window, taking in their smiles.

The humans were something to behold. Cherish. Their lives were troubled with mundane things, and it made me wonder what it would be like to experience the seventy to eighty years as one.

We walked to the edge of the town square and entered another pub with the name "Brooks" on the door. It was quaint in here, holding a warmth in the small space. The man behind the counter was pouring drinks, and a woman walked over to him, kissing his cheek before cradling her belly.

It made me smile.

Elias took my hand, moved over to the bar and leaned in, grabbing their attention. "My friends went upstairs?"

The bartender's eyes shifted to a rich brown hue, and I leaned in. I'd never seen this with glamouring from the vampires...which meant it was true what I heard over the years about some of the core fae powers.

And then it hit me. That means a fae was here.

"Yes, my lord. You will not be disturbed."

The glamour fell, and he went on filling drinks for the men lost in their stories of some battle the king's great-grandfather had won.

We made our way up the spiral stairs, and my heartbeat grew with each step. My power felt more on edge than I had in over twenty years.

And I knew what that meant.

"Elias," I called out to him as his hand wrapped around the doorknob. "What is behind that door?"

"A bargain...if you will accept it."

He opened it before I could ask any more questions, and standing before me were two fae.

One that I had never seen before, with almost black hair tied in a bun and amber eyes. And the other...I knew all too well.

"What the fuck is he doing here?"

I walked in, and Elias closed the door behind me. Just as I was about to throw my fist at the king, large wings appeared, blocking me from getting any closer. The feathers were as dark as onyx, lying tightly together and cutting off my view of the King entirely.

"Sorry, little one. Can't have you doing that."

"Who the hell are you?" I asked, stepping back and meeting his powerful gaze. He was Fallen. I knew because of the wings. It made them harder to catch in raids; that, and their shadows.

"My name is Osiris. Lord of the Fallen Court. And General to the King," he answered, looking over at Elias. "It's been a long time, Lord Crescent."

Glancing over, I took in Elias' expression. And for the first time since I've known him, I saw sorrow fill his eyes.

Was it because Osiris was using his title? Sorrow for the life he lost? The freedom of his true power? All our power... And that only added to my anger because the son of a bitch in this room was the reason for it all.

"Why are you here, Ezekiel?" I called out, and Osiris looked over his shoulder, his wings slowly retreating into him and exposing the King.

"I want to make a deal with you, Ruin," Ezekiel stated, but each word came out with so much disdain, like he would much rather do anything else in this world than work with me.

And the feeling was mutual.

"A deal?" I arched a brow, watching him as he took a few steps forward.

"Yes. You help me by using your power for a spell I need. And I'll help you with something you want."

"Well, I don't trust you, so you can see the problem in your delusional proposition," I retorted.

"No one is more unhappy with this than me. But my sister insists you are going to help me with the problem I face."

I laughed. Laughed until my stomach hurt. Elias just stared at me, concerned, while Osiris smirked. But Ezekiel—it only made his forced features of peace fall, showcasing his cold-hearted annoyance. And satisfaction came over me. I'd gotten under his skin and forced the real him out, and it felt pretty damn good.

"And what do I get?" I chuckled, meeting his silver eyes.

"I will free you and my brother from the curse," he countered. "You will join us in Valyner. Fully pardoned for your crimes."

The amusement fell from my features, and anger boiled up from within.

My crimes?

Was he fucking serious?

My eyes hardened, my fists tightened at my sides.

I walked right up to him, hearing the Fallen soldier next to me pull his sword from the sheath.

"Nyna..." Elias warned, but I ignored him.

I studied Ezekiel's face, his eyes, and couldn't help but think back to all the dreams I'd had of him. Where I'd seen him in a different light. Someone who was capable of empathy. Love. And then, something flickered across his gaze... Fear? Yet, I didn't want to believe that.

"Give your fae vampire the order. Because I will never work with you."

I waited, my heart racing. Ezekiel's eyes burned with an intensity that I knew all too well. A minute passed, and I stepped back, keeping my gaze on him.

Turning, I whipped open the door, hearing it slam into the wall as I was already rushing to the stairs. I didn't look back. I couldn't.

After what just happened with my father...and now this. My mind was lost in a haze.

What was inside me?

Why would Akari tell me to be ready for change, warn me who the real enemy was, and then send her brother to me?

He was the problem.

He was the enemy.

He had to be.

No, I needed him to be...because if not, then I had to face the truth.

That maybe this was the change.

That *he* could change.

I finally slowed in the town square, surrounded by humans dancing, and tried to catch my breath.

Hands slid around my waist, and I jumped, ready to tell the person I wasn't in the mood for a dance. But they spun me around and pulled me in.

My body stiffened as I caught sight of Ezekiel. My gaze flicked to the humans surrounding us, and my hand hovered near the hilt of my blade.

"Lay your sword before me and make the deal, Nyna, Or I will kill every human here," Ezekiel said calmly.

"I will not work with you..." I seethed, and the surrounding lanterns shattered, the flames pouring to the ground.

The humans screamed, scrambling to get away from the growing fire.

"I will do it. And then I will go find every Cursed tonight and slaughter them before you."

My eyes scanned over to the humans running, and I stepped back from Ezekiel. Some flames slithered up the coats of the humans, and their screams pierced the night sky.

"Please, take your time..." he called out, raising his hands and causing the fire to grow.

It traveled up the buildings, the wood blackening just as fast as the flames hit it.

"Ezekiel!" Elias yelled from behind me.

"Leave the curse on me. Save everyone else!" I yelled out at Ezekiel, the words burning as they made their way up my throat.

"Such a martyr." He laughed, taking a few steps towards me. "Lay the sword before me."

I gritted my teeth, watching the flames travel down the streets behind him, going straight for the woods... We had a base out there, and he must have known that.

I pulled my sword free and threw it to the ground. He dropped his hands, the fire around us extinguishing just as fast as it took off.

"Do we have a deal?" I asked bitterly.

He walked up to me, smiling.

"We have a deal, Ruin. You alone in this world might just be the best part of all of this... Cursed to be alone, just like me."

"And yet, I can survive it. Can you?" I walked away, not looking back.

I had just made a deal with the wicked King himself, and something stirred inside me.

A warning I couldn't ignore.

There was no coming back from this. Not with my soul intact. Yet, somewhere deep within, a haunting melody rose, sweet and terrifying all at once. One that sang of belonging, that recognized the connections between us and tried to bind us together.

And that alone made me fear what nightmare lay before me.

PART 3
THE LINES WE CROSS

CHAPTER TWELVE

NYNA

One week later in the Mortal Realm
Or six hours in Valyner

"Again..." Ezekiel demanded, as I sat down on the forest floor.

"Give me a minute."

My breathing was heavy, my body even more so with the exhaustion of the last week.

We had come to the woods outside Elias' new home, which was just past the river from his old cabin. It was a nice two-story brick structure, with a large porch.

Not that I'd been able to enjoy the confines of the home much because every day for the last week, I'd been out here with *him,* testing my power. I decided to stay at Elias' while I worked with his insufferable brother, and with each passing minute I regretted that choice.

His friend Osiris left the morning after I made the deal with his King, and his parting words still had me on edge.

"Give him a chance to prove you wrong."

A chance... Yeah, well, it was hard when the asshole barely talked and just shouted out demands. It was clear he wasn't happy with the results.

And let's not forget, this was all happening because he'd forced my hand in this godsdamn deal.

Asshole.

"You're holding back," he bit out, and I looked up.

"I'm doing everything you asked of me. It's not my fault you can't figure out whatever you are trying to find." I stood up, my body protesting the movement. "And what are you looking for, Ezekiel? What does my power have to do with anything?"

"That isn't information I'm willing to give you," he huffed, turning away.

"Of course not." I rolled my eyes and walked over to where the cups of water sat and drank down mine before picking up his and drinking half of it.

He could go get more. He wasn't doing shit, anyway.

"Can you stop with your snarky emotions...they are distracting me."

I turned, watching him pace.

"Can you read my mind?" I asked, anger rising at the thought that he was in my head.

He stopped, smirking. "No. But I don't need to when your emotions say it all."

My heart doubled over, the sound filling my ears. Ezekiel's lips only turned up more, which meant he heard it too.

Fuck...he shouldn't be allowed to smile, grin...or do anything that repaints the image I need to have of him.

There was something about being this close over the last seven days, though. His presence was something my power was affected by, but when he left before all this, it went away.

Now it was constant.

He took a step closer, and I snapped out of my thoughts, watching him intently. My hand wanted to go to my hip, to grab my sword. And then I remembered he took it.

He moved in, and my breathing became shallower with each

step, each inch he closed between us. Ezekiel stopped just before me, his chest still like he wasn't breathing at all.

His hand came up to my chin, softly pulling it up to meet his gaze.

"Let's try it another way, then," he whispered, before wrapping his hand around the back of my neck.

He closed his eyes, focusing, and I didn't know whether to pull back and hit him.

Or lean in...

The world faded from my eyes, and I was pulled into a dark abyss, with strings of color. I saw black, blue, orange, purple, and a soft, almost translucent white molding together and radiating their light outwards. They danced, creating effortless arcs of power and beauty. It brought a smile to my face.

It was my magic.

What made me...me.

The smile fell. My mind filled with my father's voice.

"I fear you will open a side to your power that will affect not only your future but the people close to you."

"You haven't even begun to understand what you..."

What I was capable of? What I truly was?

I'd asked him to explain what he meant, and he'd said, *"I can't. Not yet."*

Glancing back at the strings of light, I didn't feel joy anymore. I just felt lost. Lost in the secrets that he knew... He knew what this all meant.

Pulling back, I turned away, tears filling my eyes.

Ezekiel didn't speak.

"There you go. Now you see my power," I fumed. "Did you get what you need?"

He moved away, and I listened to his boots crunch down on the debris on the forest floor. He cursed under his breath. "What does she have, Akari?" he whispered, and it made me turn.

"Excuse me?"

He let out a long exhale, pinching the bridge of his nose.

"Ezekiel, what do you need from my power?"

His features hardened before dropping his hand. "Your power was supposed to save my family. Save my realm..." He stopped, almost like he didn't want to finish the last part. What else was there? "But from what I can see, you have nothing that can truly do that."

"Isn't the all-powerful King of the fae enough to do all that on his own? What is this really about?" I asked, but it only angered him more.

"I'm running out of time, and I need you to try harder!" he yelled, his tone screaming the urgency.

I was sick and tired of this. Of him. Of secrets and half-truths when I needed the whole story... Yet, I never got that from my own father, so why was I surprised that another man in my life was doing the same?

"And I need to go make sure the Cursed are safe." I started walking away, but he grabbed my arm, stopping me from taking another step. "Let. Me. Go."

"Then don't walk away from me." His eyes slowly met mine, and the pain inside them shook me to my core. He was...scared. "I can't lose them. They're all I have...if they will even have me after what I've done."

"Ezekiel, please...let me go," I asked again, my heart racing.

He leaned closer, and I held my breath.

"I need you to try...please."

And against all the insults swirling in my mind, the desire to push him away, I said, "I will."

He let me go, and I took a breath and moved away from him, but stopped and looked back. His eyes were hollow, lost in thought.

"What did Akari tell you?"

I expected him to get enraged at my question, but he just slowly met my gaze, his expression unchanging. "That you hold the key to the future of Valyner..." He paused for a moment, swallowing hard. "That you hold the key to me."

I was stunned, no words forming to even respond to that.

I couldn't tell him she sent me a message, but it aligned. Change was coming. For him. For me...

So who was the enemy, if not him?

"I'm going to go check on the Cursed," I finally said and walked away to Elias' house, where my horse was next to the stable he was building.

"I'm ordering all hunting parties to stop. Osiris is overseeing my orders in Valyner. And I have placed trusted soldiers throughout each city to watch. Their orders are to kill on sight if any fae tries to harm the Cursed."

I paused but didn't look back.

"I gave you my word, Nyna...but if you need to see it for yourself, go... We will try again in the morning."

Why did I believe him?

Moving again, I got to my horse, seeing Elias come out of the house. His gaze met mine before looking over to the tree line. I glanced back and saw Ezekiel watching me, his entire demeanor different from what I knew.

Getting on my horse, I rode as fast as I could, trying to clear my mind from the cyclone of thoughts until one remained.

I needed to see my father.

———

Night had fallen over us, blanketing the lands in an onyx cloak. And it settled deep into my bones, resonating with me more than I wanted it to.

I was in the dark.

Years back, I had asked some of the Cursed to monitor my father. I found two witches who told me my father was at a bar in Eldros. He would usually visit after it closed to have a drink. I rode fast through the woods, seeing the fae as I entered the town, dressed like humans, but their power gave them away.

Ezekiel was telling the truth.

The witches also told me over the years that my father bounced around, disappearing for days before reappearing. Which didn't bother me...but it was different now.

He had secrets, and I needed to know what they meant.

I pushed open the door to the empty pub and spotted my father.

He was sitting on one of the bar stools, his long blonde hair hanging over his shoulders, his eyes cast down at the glass before him.

Closing the door behind me, I moved over to the bar. I grabbed the bottle of bourbon that was out and popped off the top. Taking down a good amount with only a slight burn, I savored how it felt before having to talk to *him*.

Placing the bottle back down, I looked over at my father, waiting.

After a minute passed, he finally met my gaze.

"Where are you from?" I asked.

He smiled, but it was broken. "Valyner..."

"Bullshit! Elias was the Lord of the Crescents. You were never there," I shouted. "Where are you from? Is it from another fae realm?"

"If I say yes, will you let it go?" he countered.

"Are you serious?" I stood up and walked a few feet away from him before turning. "Did you know I was different?"

"Yes."

"Is that because you are too?" I waited, my skin crawling with rage and anticipation.

"Yes."

"Gods, Dad..." I ran my fingers through my hair, turning slightly before dropping my hands and meeting his gaze. "Why would you lie? Why would you hide that from me?"

"Because hiding was the only choice."

"What else are you hiding?" I asked, stepping closer.

He rose from the bar and walked up to me, stopping by my side. "Do not speak to me that way. I am still your father."

I stood on my tiptoes, getting as close to his face as I could. "A real father would help his daughter."

"I have lied to protect your future. I have steered you away from becoming like me! Because if you do..." He stopped, gritting his teeth. "You don't need my help anymore. You are exactly where you need to be."

A shimmer of power emanated from him, his aura radiating more authority than I had ever felt before.

It was chilling.

Panic rushed through me like the winds of a devastating storm, taking out villages in its wake. I swallowed hard, avoiding his gaze, trying to make sense of what I was feeling.

And then I remembered. I had felt that type of power before. In the very beginning of my war with the King. Near the pond...when we fought in the woods.

It was my father's.

I turned, watching him head towards the door.

I wanted to demand answers, but who was I kidding? This was just another question he would refuse to answer.

"If you walk out, I am done! I will no longer be your daughter. Or *you*, my father."

Turning his head over his shoulder, he smirked. "That's just the thing, Nyna. You are going to need me soon. You are going to need the truth. I just refuse to give it to you when you aren't ready to hear it. But the day will come...and I will be the only one who can show you what you truly are."

He walked out, and I just stood there, unable to move. Unable to feel anything anymore. I was just numb...

What I truly was?

I don't know how many hours passed, but at some point, I got back on my horse and rode back to Armaros, everything a blur around me.

Dropping from my horse, I walked to the front of Elias' house, seeing Ezekiel standing in the window.

Like he was waiting for me. Like he knew I would come back.

And I didn't know why I did. I could have stayed anywhere else tonight, and not in the room down the hall from the King.

But I came back.

Tears filled my eyes as I walked towards the door, my legs shaking. And before I knew it, Ezekiel was there, holding me up. And the distant sounds became louder and louder.

I was crying.

I was crying in his arms.

"Nyna... what happened?" he asked, his voice tainted with a growl like he would kill anything and anyone who made me cry like this.

And slowly, the tears stopped falling, and my cries turned into soft sobs, fading away with the young girl who wanted her father. Who needed more than the scraps he was willing to give.

I looked into Ezekiel's silver pools and felt the heat build deep in my core. He brushed my hair back from my face, and that soft touch alone cleared my mind. Allowing my rage to come back. And I focused on what I wanted—no—needed.

"You were right...there is something more to my power. And I need your help to get it out."

CHAPTER THIRTEEN

EZEKIEL

I paced back and forth in my brother's spare room, my heart racing. I didn't sleep at all last night. My body physically couldn't decide if I wanted to go hunt down who made her cry like that and rip them to pieces, or sit by her door if she needed anything.

And because of that, I was beyond confused.

I hadn't shown affection like that since...I couldn't even remember. Every emotion felt foreign in her presence. It was maddening, but it also felt good. Like the blood in my veins was warm again. It was an odd feeling since I was fire and ash down to the last fiber of my being. But for centuries, I had been so cold. And now, the warmth had found its way into the frigid shell I wore.

I should have questioned it, pushed it away. But I didn't want to.

The door down the hall creaked open, and I stopped, looking at my brother as he stepped out of his room. He furrowed his brow, studying me, and I cleared my throat.

"I'm just waiting for Nyna to start her training today." I said.

"She's been outside for an hour at least, swinging a sword."

Did she go out the window?

Elias studied me. "Are you okay?"

"What does that mean?" I walked past him and down the stairs, sending out my fires to light the fireplace in the main living area.

"I saw you last night with her... Do you want to talk about it?"

"No." I began walking again, but his hand grabbed my arm, pulling me back. "Elias. You are my brother, but if you say another word, I will—"

"You'll do what? Kill me?" he added.

My lips thinned out, my eyes hardening on him.

"This past week, I've seen it. How you both act when you are close. And you look at her like she is your—"

"Enough!" I yelled, pushing him back. "I'm cursed to be alone, and I prefer it that way."

"No, you don't," he stated before continuing. "And we are all cursed by something. Whether that be dark magic, our failures, our fears...regrets."

I shook my head, avoiding his gaze, but he moved in, wrapping his hand around the back of my neck and forcing me to look at him.

"I see my brother again. So please... Don't run from whatever you are avoiding." He let me go, and we stood in silence, the only sound coming from the crackling wood burning beside us.

"No one could love who I've become. I made peace with that long ago."

He walked to the door and opened it. "I've loved you my entire life, Ezekiel. Even when I hated you, I loved you. So does our sister. There is a lot to love if you let people in."

He left, making his way across the lawn to where the horses grazed, and mounted his. I watched him ride away, my breathing growing heavier.

I needed this to go away. Needed to stay focused. I couldn't let warmth back in. Because love hurt. It shattered you. It brought you to your knees, screaming at the gods why they would allow you to feel *that* alone.

Love only guaranteed death, leaving nothing but ice within.

Yet, when I look at her, I felt warm...and I missed feeling warm.

Walking outside and around the house, I stopped, leaning

against the side. I got lost in how she moved through each swing with her sword. And without thinking of anything else, I smiled.

She stopped, turning to face me, and those full pink lips parted. Lips that drew me closer.

Fuck.

Snapping out of it, I picked up her glass of water and began walking over. Handing it to her, she slowly took it, our fingers touching for a moment.

"Thanks," she said, drinking half of it down before placing it on the ground. Stabbing her blade into the grass, she slowly met my gaze, her golden eyes bright and welcoming, but also heavy with a burden I wanted to understand.

"I need you to explain what you said last night. How do you know there is more to your power?" I asked, avoiding the fact that she was in my arms when she said it.

We didn't need to talk about that.

"My father isn't from Valyner."

I arched a brow, waiting for her to explain.

"I felt his true power last night, and it wasn't the first time. He stopped you from killing me once...with my sword by the pond. And another time when we were in the woods."

I thought back to those times, and I never did understand what pulled me into the gap—or whose voice it was that I heard in the woods. I only knew the chains were no longer on my wrists, and that a fae must had removed them because they were the only ones who could.

She continued. "It was something more. Like mine, but more. Which means I have it too. My whole life he has warned me about *using* my power, and now I need to figure out how to use it."

"What is his power?"

"He can shift into a wolf," she said, wiping the sweat from her forehead.

"Then he is a Crescent. I mean, even your power is centered on Valyner. The other fae realms have unique abilities. Ice, light, earth wielding, dream walking, skin walking, and the list goes on. But no one else shifts."

"How do you know that?" Shock was plastered on her face.

"You forget, I was made in the beginning. Making me untouched. I met the other fae before the walls went up, locking them out of the Mortal Realm and Valyner. I also know one who is locked in my realm. Faelynn has no sight, but doesn't need it with her power. She has also studied a lot from all realms and never forgets a thing."

Nyna let out a short exhale, shaking her head.

"There is more to this. I know there is..." she whispered.

And then I felt it--her anger towards her father--and I could relate. The type of rage that was deep, suffocating, mixed with sorrow from how they let you down. Over and over...

"Then let's figure out what you are," I said.

She stood there, quite for a long moment.

"How?" she asked, and I noticed none of that rage was directed at me. She seemed to be nervous being near me, but it wasn't accompanied by her normal emotions.

Hatred.

Disdain.

Disgust.

And part of me was glad I wasn't alone in feeling the same.

"Well..." I smiled, hearing her heart skip a beat, mine following suit. "I find that getting angry is the best way to make your power grow. So go ahead, Ruin. Get mad at me..." I leaned in, her scent making my dick twitch. "Give me your best shot."

She didn't move, but she let out a slow exhale as I moved back, her emotions spiraling.

"I cursed all the fae here. To go mad... To become beasts," I taunted her, watching her golden eyes deepen a shade.

Walking around her, I leaned in again. "I sent my soldiers here to kill them. I sent them to kill you..."

Making my way around, I watched as her breathing picked up.

"I tried to kill you. And what a regret that was. That I didn't finish the job."

And as the words fell from my lips, I realized. That was the farthest thing from the truth.

She threw her fist, hitting me in my jaw, and I stepped back, rubbing the spot.

Good. It was working.

"You never got to have friends for long...or true love. Because of me."

Another hit. And somehow the words I spoke hurt more, piercing something within.

"I ruined you. Ruined the life you could have had."

Her power shot out from her hands, the spell sending me through the air.

Slamming into the ground, the impact buried deeper than just my flesh and bones. It went somewhere so deep that it started to rip down the walls I had constructed around myself.

As I pushed myself back up, a yell poured from me and my fires ignited, engulfing everything that I was until I saw what I hid behind those walls.

The monster I became.

The mistakes.

The pain.

Regret...

I stopped, my heart twisting in my chest and causing pain.

Nyna ran at me, her eyes glossed over with a watery sheen, and I didn't move.

I would deserve whatever she gave me.

I would deserve it all. And then some.

She took me to the ground, her fangs out, and I welcomed it. They pierced into my neck and I thought back to every decision that brought me here.

My obsession with killing my father after I was turned, to prove I was better.

Killing Elias' lover because he loved someone more than me.

Locking Akari in the Sky Temple because she sided with our brother.

Cursing my people for trying to help beings that had no fighting chance against us.

Becoming focused on more power because I still felt powerless.

More fear...because I was still afraid.

I sat up, wrapping my arms around Nyna and holding her close. The darkness that I had lived in for so long was shifting before my eyes, small beams of light filtering in. And while my mind told me to shut it out, to not let it in...my heart refused the command.

I was open. Exposed.

And I didn't want to fight it anymore. Not when she was the one leading me out.

Whether she knew that or not.

⁂

After the other day, Nyna avoided me at every turn. I understood. I'd struck a nerve...and I didn't want to push her. Plus, I was deep in my thoughts. With the past mostly, and then the reality of the future. What was coming for the people I cared about?

Sitting in the window seat of my brother's study, I spun the Ember stone between my fingers, staring out of the window.

Elias went out a few hours ago with Nyna to help some wolves steer clear of the humans. I should have gone to sleep, but I couldn't. I needed to make sure they made it back okay.

Her presence grew closer, and my spine straightened. She shifted back, just beyond the tree line, and her bare silhouette was outlined by the moon above.

Fuck...she was breathtaking.

She grabbed some clothes from a stump and slowly put them on. I turned away, but with each second that passed, my heart slammed harder against my ribs.

I stood still, watching her make her way up the front lawn, slowing her steps when she spotted me. We stood like that for a moment before she continued on. I heard the door open, her boots making their way through the parlor and towards the stairs. And then she stopped. Her emotions traveled into the study in waves, with one thing...

Hesitation.

I closed my eyes, spun the stone again, and contemplated whether I should go see her, but then her steps got closer.

"Hey..." She stepped into the office, pausing near the door.

Slowly, I opened my eyes and gave her a small smile.

Her gaze traveled down to the stone, her eyes widening. "Is that the..."

"It is." I said, looking at it. "The stone the gods gave to each untouched fae of Valyner."

Making her way to the other side of the window seat, she sat down. "What can it do...other than curse people?"

I chuckled, shaking my head. "It can hide things. Memories. Plans. I still have it in here." I pointed to my head. "But no one can access them unless they also have this." I held up the stone.

"The power it's giving off... It..." she said, sensing its magic.

"It was made by the gods..." I let it fall into my palm and held it tight, taking a deep breath before placing my hand out. My fingers slowly fell open, and she looked over it. "Want to take a peek inside my head, Ruin? It will scare you..."

"Why would you do that?" she asked, her emotions shifting into panic.

"Because...I think I trust you. And if we are to work together, then you need to know everything."

I didn't know what I was doing. But it felt right. And for years I'd ran from that feeling.

I didn't want to run right now.

I wanted to let someone in...even if it scared them away.

Slowly, I grabbed her hand and pulled her towards me. She sat between my legs, looking me over before placing her hand out.

Placing the stone in her palm, I took her other hand and placed it on my cheek. Her warmth sent tingles down my spine.

She pulled back slightly, but stopped herself, giving me a slight nod.

I focused on the stone, letting the connection between me and it grow until I was pulled into the ruby walls.

Nyna stood beside me, looking at each cut of the stone holding a different memory.

I didn't move, letting her take it in. She started when I was a child. My father beating Akari, me, our mother...

Her eyes welled up, her hand slowly going to her mouth as she saw the one where my father killed our mother in front of us. The way we screamed.

And I could hear it all over again.

She saw Elias being born. How our father had tried to throw him in the river. And more horrendous memories over the years that I wished had never happened.

She saw some of my kills I'd had to hide from the Lords and Ladies of Valyner because I'd needed them to believe it was someone else to get the Court on my side. And looking at them right now, they scared me. I didn't look like myself. I was just...a monster.

I'd done whatever I needed to show my power, my control.

It was funny, because where was my control now?

She even saw the spell I'd used to curse the fae that lived in these lands, with the proof that she could never undo it. It had to be me. My blood.

She listened to what Akari had told me about her vision. How she'd said I needed Nyna. She saw Katarina talk about Persephone. Seeing what my plan was to gain more power...and the reason I wanted it.

But nothing angered her. She just took it all in, her eyes filled to the brim.

Nyna pulled her hand back, forcing us both out of the stone. Opening my eyes, I watched the tears fall, her shock filling the room.

"I told you it wasn't pretty," I whispered.

She leaned in, her lips so close to mine, and I stood completely still.

"No one should ever have to live with so much pain... So much anger. Not even you," she whispered, and our eyes connected.

And everything that I was, am, and would be, didn't matter. Nothing mattered when those golden pools offered a warmth my fires could never give me, or peace I'd never known. No—I was at the mercy of that breathtaking shade of gold, glowing softly with the moonlight slipping in through the window. And in that moment, I realized it was the only thing I ever wanted to look at again.

I leaned in, closing the small space between us, and captured her lips with my own.

There was nothing sweet about the kiss. It was hard and needy. And I wanted to stop.

She didn't want this... She didn't.

Yet, she started kissing me back, her mouth meeting my intensity, everything in me burning hot. My skin glowed as she straddled me, her one hand that wasn't holding the stone lacing through the strands of my hair and pulling me deeper.

I wrapped my hands around her back, sliding them down and grabbing her ass.

I needed her closer.

Fuck, I needed more.

A soft moan fell from her lips, and I swallowed it down like it was life itself. Because in this moment, in this entire life, I was finally living...

I don't know how long it went on for, but the world around me faded away. Every problem, every worry.

Well, that was until I heard my brother clear his throat.

We both pulled away, our breathing heavy. And embarrassment flushed her cheeks red.

I met my brother's gaze, and the smirk on his face said it all.

Glaring at him, I looked back at Nyna. She was already on her feet, trying to hand the stone back to me.

But as she offered it, she sucked in a sharp breath. Dropping the stone to the ground, she grabbed her hand, and I jumped up, moving over to her.

"What happened?"

"I felt something..."

I waited for her to explain, but I was half tempted to shake it out of her if she made me wait another minute.

"What did you feel?" I demanded, my blood going cold.

She shook her head, her wide eyes meeting mine, and whispered...

"I don't know."

CHAPTER FOURTEEN

NYNA

*One week later in the Mortal Realm
Or six hours in Valyner*

Ezekiel went back to Valyner about a week ago to help Osiris with some issues that were taking place within the Courts, and to ask his sister about the stone.

I spent every day riding and walking through the areas where the Cursed lived, trying to stay focused and help, but I couldn't think straight.

What happened with the Ember stone didn't make sense.

Why did it feel like it was trying to tell me a story that was lost long ago? It was as if fire and fury ran through my veins, and yet, it didn't harm me. But it did frighten me...

And then there was what happened between *us*...

I wanted to tell myself that I hated it. That it felt wrong in every way. Yet, I couldn't.

I had never felt so absent from my body, and yet wholly present.

I walked past one of the soldiers he left behind and gave her a smile. Her light blonde hair faded down to red at the tips, her eyes embodying fire.

Walking up to a small pack, I said hello before asking their leader, Jason, to talk.

"What's up?" he asked as we made our way toward the tree line of the clearing.

"Have you seen my father, Zaryk?" I asked, keeping my voice down.

"No...not at all."

I nodded, looking around.

That son of a bitch...back to hiding.

"Thanks, Jason. If you want to move the pack up closer to Armaros, I've been running with the wolves there. I can help the older wolves avoid the town."

"It's alright, there's more land out here. The mountains keep them focused on the animals."

"Good. I'm glad. Are you guys good on dark obsidian?" I asked.

Ezekiel's men and women might had been here to help protect the Cursed, but I wanted to make sure they were able to protect themselves.

"Yeah. We're good." He glanced down at my empty sheath around my thigh and arched a brow. "Looks like you aren't."

My hand went to it, gripping the dark brown leather. I hadn't even realized I forgot until now. But then it made me think about the past week. I hadn't carried dark obsidian at all.

When did I stop thinking about carrying the weapon that protected us from them? When did being around the King of the fae make me feel...

Nope, not finishing that sentence.

"Here take mine," Jason insisted, grinning as he unsheathed his and handed it to me.

I nodded, and watched him walk away. "If you hear anything on my father, or see him..." I paused, wanting to tell Jason to tell him to come see me, but the thought alone made me pause. "Just get me the message."

He smiled, nodding before meeting back up with the pack.

Looking up at the sky, I noticed it was getting dark. I sheathed the dagger and started my way through the camp back towards town where my horse was.

I was probably going to end up staying in town through the night to make sure the vampires and sirens stayed away from the humans. I heard the fae soldiers had been helping with that, which I appreciated. Yet it still felt like it was my job alone.

Making it into town, the night had already fallen, and the humans were still on the streets and talking with their neighbors. Some were discussing the ball that was to take place tomorrow night for the king and queen and that it was only for lords and ladies. They talked of the food and the dancing that would go on until the moon was at its highest point in the sky. Some women even gushed about the gowns, wanting to wear one of that quality.

I could tell many wished they could be there to see it. And I realized...I had never danced, nor worn such a breathtaking gown.

It sounded nice, but at the same time, maybe I was never meant for that type of life.

I sensed power behind me and for a second, I thought it would be Ezekiel...Maybe even wanted it to be.

It wasn't... I could already tell.

He asked once what I was doing to him. But what was he doing to me?

Turning, I forced a smile for the fae with cloaked ears and short red hair, wearing the Ember Court color leather.

Red.

"Nyna, right?" he asked, and I nodded. "I'm Keres. The King sent me to give you a message. Could we?" He gestured to the edge of the town where the woods hugged the road.

I nodded and moved with him, thinking of where I had heard that name before. Was it in Ezekiel's stone? The man who was helping Persephone?

Maybe it was a common name over there.

The thought of the fae Lady made my heart hurt. That he was going to bond himself to her just for power... And yet, she was using him as well for the same thing.

Maybe they were perfect for one another.

"Where's the King?" I asked, secretly hoping he wasn't with her.

"King Ezekiel was having a meeting with the Lords and Ladies of the realm when I left." He smiled. "The King seems fond of you…"

I laughed. "Yeah. Just about as much as he is with everyone else, I'm guessing."

The memory of his lips on mine made them tingle, and I cleared my throat as we made it to the entrance of the woods.

"So, what was the message?"

The male stood unmoving, looking at me with honey-brown eyes that turned vile. And my stomach dropped.

"There is no message…just orders to kill."

Before my eyes, he shifted, and I stumbled back. His deep red fur and his form—twice the size of any wolf here—took my breath away.

As he pounced into the air, his growl echoed through the woods. I raised my hands, casting a barrier spell. He slammed into it, and I let out a yell.

What the fuck was going on?

Power from behind me appeared, and I turned, seeing five others dressed in red fighting leathers. But as they started using their power, I knew they weren't Embers.

Purple mist flowed out of them, slamming against my barrier, and my panic grew.

Screaming, I sent out a spell, throwing them all back. But it had barely knocked them down before they were getting up again.

Shit.

I used my vampire speed to run as fast as I could, trying to get to the Cursed.

I couldn't take on this many fae at once by myself.

Keres appeared before me again, wrapping his hand around my throat and tossing me backward. I fell into the hands of one witch who began chanting.

I screamed out in pain, feeling her spell work through my body with fervor and determination. Blood dripped from my nose, coating my lips, and I let out another cry.

"Ezekiel!" I yelled, gaining a laugh from the witches moving in front of me.

"Oh, sweetheart. He won't save you. No one can," one of them said. Her light blonde hair blew with the wind she was creating from her own spell. The ball of power grew in size, darkening by the second.

Pulling my dagger from the sheath, she let out a breathy laugh. "And what do we have here?" She inspected the dark obsidian. "You *Cursed*, always trying to kill your superiors."

The blonde brought the blade closer to my face, and I tilted my head back.

I took in the other woman holding me, her blue eyes filled with joy, her black hair dancing in the wind, with Keres over her shoulder.

I was going to die...

Fuck.

I didn't want to die.

Another scream passed my lips, and just as the next wave was about to hit, the woman's hands fell from me, and she vanished, along with Keres.

My body fell, the world through my eyes blurring and tilting until my back connected with the soil.

I sat up slowly, my head pounding, and saw Ezekiel standing behind the witch in front of me. Her sphere of power was gone, and a look of horror was now plastered to her face.

He pushed her body over, her heart still in his hand.

His eyes connected with mine, and they were wild with anger and fear.

Purple tendrils reached out towards him, and I yelled.

"Watch out!"

Turning, he sent his fire out, devouring two of the witches, and my heart pounded as I looked for the other two.

Scrambling to grab my blade, one of the witches appeared, grabbing it and giving me a smirk before fixing her lilac eyes on the King. And I could see it...

The rage. The fury she held towards him.

It all happened so fast, before she fell back into the gap.

Standing, I ignored the pain and felt the dagger fly past me, heading right towards Ezekiel. He turned, and a chill swept through me, freezing everything within. It was going to hit him.

No... No.

I sent my power out, stopping it before it hit his chest, and my entire body quaked.

The witch reappeared, her eyes hard on me, like I stole her right to kill him. Stole the vendetta she came out here with. And I understood that anger... I did.

But the difference between us now was that I needed him to make good on his word for *my* people.

Fury took over and I sent the dagger back towards her. Rushing in, I held her by the back of her neck as the toxic blade sunk into her chest.

Ezekiel held the last witch in his grasp, his face more enraged than I had ever seen it before. "I would ask who sent you, but I don't need to."

Fire poured out of him like water, completely devouring the witch, and the adrenaline faded. Falling to the ground, I took a few deep breaths, my vision spotting with black.

"Nyna..." Ezekiel called out, running to my side and dropping to his knees.

"I'm okay... I'll be okay."

I looked over at the dead fae next to me, the dagger still embedded in her chest.

Another wave of pain passed over me, and he met my gaze.

"Here, drink." He pulled the blade out of the fae and stabbed his palm. Crimson pooled up almost instantly, and the smell of iron made my jaw ache. Yet, I didn't move.

I watched him for a moment, watching his chest rise and fall, his eyes still lost in...panic?

"Gods damn it, Nyna, drink or I will force it down your throat," Ezekiel shouted, placing his hand right in front of my lips.

I slowly opened my mouth, drinking down his blood and savoring it. Wrapping my hands around his arm, I drank deeper, and he didn't pull away. No—he did the opposite. He wrapped his hand around the back of my head, holding me there.

He groaned, and my core tightened from that sound alone.

Letting go of him, he quickly picked me up, holding me close to his chest.

"Did any of them give you a name?" he growled, his eyes locked on the path before us.

"One... Keres."

He stopped, his breath growing more agitated. "I will have Osiris kill him in the morning."

"How did you know I was here?"

He stopped, looking down at me. "I was already on my way back... I sensed your power as I was passing through the gap and came."

My brows furrowed, and I pushed myself out of his arms, stumbling slightly. A little voice within told me there was something else...and I needed to know what it was.

"Let me carry you."

"I don't need you to carry me. I need you to tell me the truth. You're lying," I bit out.

"How would you know?" he asked, stepping in.

I honestly didn't know how. He could have been telling me everything, but this feeling... It wasn't something I could ignore. And I needed the truth. Even if I wasn't sure I truly wanted it.

"I heard you," he finally said. "I heard you say you were going to die."

Shocked, I took a step back.

"You said you couldn't read my mind," I said.

"I can't... Or...I guess I couldn't." He stumbled over his words before running his hands through his chestnut-brown hair.

We stood locked in place, the heat circling us.

I think the real question was...why did I call out to him?

Pushing the thought away, I looked back at him. "What happened with the Lords and Ladies?"

He shook his head, his jaw tense. "Fuck everything else right now." He closed the distance between us, slamming his lips to mine.

The shock faded quickly, and I fell into how his mouth possessed my own. Like it was always his to kiss. I opened for him, his tongue tasting every inch of mine, and I moaned.

Picking me up, he moved us back, slamming me into a tree. Thrusting his hips forward, I felt his cock and gasped before he swallowed it down. And my hips moved to feel it again.

"Tell me to stop...and I will..." He broke the kiss, our breath matching one another.

"Don't you dare." I pulled on his leather jacket until his lips were back on mine.

This made no sense. We made no sense. And yet, I would curse the stars above if they tried to stop this.

His hands traveled down my body, leaving a trail of blazing fire in their wake.

I wanted more... I needed more.

Dropping to his knees, my body slid down the tree, and I hissed from the pain. Until I saw him looking up at me.

"Are you sure? Because I don't think I will ever be able to stop if I taste all of you."

My heart beat against my ribs, probably creating a bruise, but I didn't care. Because those silver eyes pulled me in, hypnotizing me.

"Please..."

He slowly smiled before whispering a spell under his breath. My pants vanished, and I sucked in a breath, the cool air hitting my entrance.

"Fuck," he said in a hushed tone before looking up at me. "You've got the King who bows to no one, on his knees...serving you. What have you done to me?"

My heart stopped in my chest, his words like an arrow piercing its mark.

He moved in, his tongue slowly sliding up my center, and my eyes rolled back. A deep growl fell from his lips as he flicked my clit. I moaned, falling deeper into the chaos that was him.

Digging his hands into my inner thighs, he spread them wider as he looked up at me again.

"Don't stop..." I begged.

He slowly circled over my clit, sucking and biting, and I lost sense of everything around us. I forgot almost the last century fighting him. Hating him.

It felt like a distant memory. One I wasn't sure ever happened.

I rolled my hips into him, basking in the pleasure building in my core because it had never felt like this.

Nothing compared.

"Fuck, I could do this forever." His voice entered my mind, and I should have been shocked, afraid, anything. Yet, it was right, comforting. I savored the grit and lust coating each word, because it was just for me. And it only added to the feeling deep within, growing like wildfire.

The world washed away to nothing. Not my breathing, nor the heart pounding in my chest remained.

I was there...

In oblivion, only feeling him.

My hands went into his hair, and I rode out my climax, pulling him closer until each wave passed, and the world came back into view.

Holy shit!

He laughed, and I looked down at him just as he pulled me onto his lap, replacing my pants with the same spell.

Exhaustion came over me, and he quickly picked me up, walking us back towards the town. I barely registered the world around me—too tired to feel anything but the bone-deep weariness and the strange comfort of his warmth. My thoughts blurred, and satisfaction hummed beneath the haze. I was content to stay here. In this in-between.

And I realized the unknown feeling deep within had a word. That I could name it, and finish that sentence I refused earlier.

Safe.

He was making me feel...safe.

I wasn't sure what to make of that. So instead of letting the thought linger, I let each step he took lull me to sleep, where dreams awaited.

CHAPTER FIFTEEN

EZEKIEL

I sat in the chair by the fireplace, my leg bouncing as I watched her sleep.

I glamoured the innkeeper to kick everyone else out, hearing complaints about needing their rest before the ball tomorrow night.

Ignoring them all, I moved up the stairs, taking her to the nicest room, and placed her on the bed. And I hadn't moved since from this chair.

My knee was bouncing up and down, watching her roll over, the sheets twisting between her legs.

It made me jealous.

Fuck...

The sheets were making me jealous.

What was I becoming?

"My King..." Osiris' voice filtered into my mind before I sensed his presence through the door. *"We have a problem."*

I was counting the minutes...the minutes since I left her. Was she awake yet? I needed to get back soon. Yet here I was, putting the Lords and Ladies in their place after finding out from Osiris that more secret meetings were happening. He discovered some gatherings with Kadeyan, and they killed everyone. And I threatened each one of their family members, their friends, that they would meet the same fate.

How many people did I need to kill for the rest to fall in line? How deep did my threats need to go? Down to the pits where not only were they erased but their entire bloodline? I needed them to be afraid, and yet the bite in my tone was off. My wrath and focus on this realm had faltered.

Maybe they could see that.

Stars above, it didn't take a genius to see my mind was elsewhere.

And I knew it was probably always going to be with her now.

The night replayed in my mind, seeing her in pain, how she protected me...

She protected *me*.

Slowly, the anger within grew past the point of anything I had ever felt before.

They needed to pay. And there was no way I could just sit here and let them get away with any of this.

I was their King. Made of wrath and fire, turning my enemies to embers and cinders if need be. I needed more time to figure out this power. Then I could crush the serpent's head—my *betrothed's* head.

Yet, there was something I needed to do before I left my realm, before I returned to her.

And that was seeing my sister.

Appearing in the Sky Temple, I stood behind my sister, my breathing unhinged. She slowly turned, looking at me, and the silence between us took on a life of its own, our heartbeats almost falling in sync. And then I heard it...a third, smaller one.

My brows furrowed, and I looked around.

She slowly met my gaze, her eyes wide like she had just discovered it before I arrived.

Then I realized. That sound...it was coming from within her.

She was...

"Akari—"

A presence emerged from within the Sky Temple, some levels down from us. One that promised honey, but was filled with poison, waiting for you to take the first bite. The same presence I knew because I was going to tie myself to it.

Persephone was here.

Akari's eyes turned white, panic washing over her and turning her skin ashen. Her hand went to her stomach, grasping at the black fabric of her gown.

"Ezekiel. Cloak the child. No one can know...especially not her," she begged, tears building quickly in her eyes.

I moved in, placing my hand on her stomach, and spoke the spell over her, hiding the second heartbeat within her womb. I stepped back, my eyes narrowing, still stunned.

"Who is the father?"

"Ezekiel, there is no time for that—you need to leave. You need to get out of Valyner. It's only about to get worse here."

"I will not leave you and your child defenseless. You will come with me and stay with Elias." I channeled the spell I made long ago, locking her in this temple, but she reached out, grabbing my hands.

"No. I need to be here. That's how I survive. That's how my daughter will survive," she explained.

"A daughter?" I asked, stunned.

"Yeah...her name will be Maeve. After our mother."

I closed my eyes, seeing her again, but I didn't need to. Just looking at Akari was always a reminder of her. Her sweet voice, her compassion, her fight to protect her children against a man who wanted nothing more than to slaughter us. But then he got rid of her, and eventually, us.

"You need to go back to her. You need to be with your mate."

My breathing stalled, my eyes widening. "No...I'm cursed. I can't... I..."

"You came here wanting to ask me again about your path. I'm telling you—she is the key to you, Ezekiel. And she needs protection. And you need hers."

It's why I couldn't kill her. It's why my power came alive in her presence. Why I felt pulled to her, my thoughts wholly consumed by her.

"You will fight for each other, for…" She paused, holding back the rest of her sentence.

I wanted to rush in, to shake her and demand she tell me, but part of me believed she already had.

"You will fail. Become what you fear. Fate and ruin are your path…until you fall." My voice grew more somber as I recited.

My pursuit of untouchable power was failing. I feared many things…but caring for someone, even just a little, terrified me. Yet, I had never felt as strong as I did earlier in the night, defending her.

Until I fell… Was I going to lose the throne? Was I going to be replaced? Or was it something more?

She will free them. She will reign forevermore.

Was that about Nyna? Did it anger me like before?

It didn't. I would bend the knee to her if it meant I could keep her.

And that alone told me everything I needed to know.

"Ezekiel…there is so much more to all of this… So much more to your story."

The door opened, and she dropped my hands, forcing a smile.

"Oh, Ezekiel. I didn't know you were here," Persephone said, her tone sweet and yet, it was the most vile thing I ever heard. "I have set the coronation for next week. The Courts are thrilled and falling in line now. I was just finishing the last touches on the spell."

"Akari. Leave. Now," I demanded.

She met my gaze, hesitating. I glared at her and she nodded, vanishing and leaving behind her white mist. Turning slowly, I met her dark pools, taking in the glint of joy within.

"You will never be Queen."

"Oh, but I will…" She smiled, taking a few steps in. "We will rule like no other with what I'm capable of now."

"What are you talking about?"

She glanced down at her hand, swirling her purple mist between her fingers like snakes. Her smile grew, glee pouring from her, along with something I couldn't place. A power that exceeded her abilities since the last time I was around her.

"I will burn your entire Court to the ground!" I shouted.

"Go ahead. I don't need them to get what I want." She placed her hand on my chest, and I gripped her wrist hard. She smiled wider, leaning in. "How is your plaything doing? Such a shame that your soldiers didn't listen to your orders."

My heart doubled over.

"Do you take me for a fool?" I asked.

"I would never, Your Grace…I take you for a King…my King… my mate."

I pushed forward, forcing her to walk backward until her back slammed into the wall.

"You are *nothing* to me."

My heart was pounding so fast that it felt as if it was going to give out.

"I'll be all you have after today…I mean, you left her all alone…" She smiled.

I stepped back, sending out my fires, my wrath fueling each flame. Persephone threw out her hands, a blast of power slamming into me and throwing me through the air.

And that confirmed it. Her power had changed.

The glass shattered against my back, and I took in the temple's top as I fell further away from it.

"Ezekiel?"

Nyna's voice filtered through my mind and I opened the gap, letting it take me away.

Anger fumed from every pore on my body. I wanted her dead. I needed her dead.

Because I needed Nyna…safe.

I dropped into the room, looking around, ready to fight, but realized no one was there.

"Are you okay?" she asked me, sitting up in the bed, the sun dancing across her face from the window.

She was my mate.

I had a *mate.*

Making my way over to the side of the bed, I dropped to my knees, the air refusing to fill my lungs.

I should have left, gone back to Valyner and killed Persephone right then. And the person I was before would have never hesitated. But now... This feeling from this person before me made me fear being alone again.

It wasn't only that, though. That power Persephone held...it was more than any Crystal fae. More than the Untouched fae.

"I am now..." I finally said, pulling a small smile to her lips before she dropped it. Almost as if she didn't want me to see it. I got up and moved across the room. "We need to go talk to my brother."

"I thought we were going to work on my power?" She asked, placing her feet on the creaky floorboards.

"It can wait until tomorrow."

"But your people... Your realm and our deal with the Cursed?" she countered.

I turned and looked into her golden eyes, reminding me of the sun burning just as the ocean swallowed it up. And here I was, wanting—no—needing to swim out to it...to her.

I didn't know if I had much time. I didn't know what I was going to do about Persephone's new power, or how she even got it, but I had an idea.

And yet...

I just wanted one more night with Nyna. With no training, plotting, or surviving another day.

I was sick and tired of living my days for the next threat. They were there, but I just wanted to live.

In this moment.

With her.

"It can wait until tomorrow... I have something else in mind for tonight."

CHAPTER SIXTEEN

EZEKIEL

I paced back and forth at the gates of the king and queen's castle in Qeles, taking in the sky's battle between day and night. The light fought to stay alive while slowly becoming consumed by the darkness.

Osiris stood close by, and our soldiers were positioned throughout the woods. I wanted the traitors to come. To expose themselves here.

And yet, there was a part of me that hoped they didn't, because I wanted this night with her to be perfect.

"Do you think she will like it?" I asked, glancing over at Osiris.

"It's a beautiful dress, Your Grace. She would be crazy not to."

My stomach was in knots as I waited for her to exit the inn just down the hill. I stopped, waiting...yearning.

"Ezekiel..." Elias called out from behind me, but I didn't move. He came to my side, and I glanced over slightly. "I have heard talk among the wolves—"

"Not tonight, brother." I bounced on the heels of my feet, the nerves growing wilder.

"I need to tell you something else then," he said, his trepidation slamming into me.

I turned, looking at him, his blue eyes duller, his face a shade lighter.

"I am getting married to a lady in Armaros...and I'm going to be a father in 5 months."

What was in the water? First my sister, now him?

"This affects all of us now."

Akari saw this... She knew...

I closed my eyes, taking a cleansing breath.

"You will be a great father," I said, maybe a little colder than I intended. "Do you love her?"

He hesitated, almost like he wanted to lie, but decided not to.

"No...but maybe I could. I have to try, especially for my child, who will bear my curse. I need to do everything to protect them and give them a life with both their parents."

"Always the noble brother," I teased, smirking at him.

"I learned it from you long ago... How could I be anything else?" he whispered and I turned, meeting his gaze.

"I never—I never told you I was..." I stumbled over my words, causing Elias to place his hand on my shoulder.

"I forgive you...but I think you need to forgive yourself now."

His gaze fell to the path, a smirk gracing his face. I turned my head and the breath was ripped from my lungs as I saw her.

Nyna was dressed in a red gown, with sleeves that fell from her shoulders and rested on her arms. The corset was made of fine jewels sewn close together to create a soft resemblance of flames. As she walked, the tulle of the gown shimmered, even without the sun's brightness.

No, it was her light that made that dress shine. And hers alone.

"Close your mouth," Elias said. "Before you drool on your suit." He chuckled, patting my shoulder before walking off.

She avoided my eyes as she approached me, clearing her throat. "So, this is what you wanted to do tonight?"

"I wouldn't want to be anywhere else." I offered her my arm, and she slowly laced hers through mine.

"You know, I just thought it would be more important solving the problems we both have at hand...and upholding the bargain made so that we can be done with..." She trailed off, her heart racing as I pieced the rest of her sentence together in my mind.

Be done with this deal. With each other.

"Is that what you want?" I whispered.

Her eyes darkened as her chest rose and fell, and I could feel the conflict within.

"No..." she finally said. "But we need to figure this out. My people can't—"

"It can wait until tomorrow." I smirked.

We walked through the gates, making it to the castle, and I couldn't even remember who or what I passed because I was wholly consumed by her presence.

Making our way up through the doors on the lower level, we walked down a corridor and we were ushered into the ballroom.

Chandeliers hung all over, their flames lighting up the ivory room filled with wildflowers throughout.

"This is beautiful," she said as I leaned over and grabbed two champagne flutes.

"This is nothing compared to the balls in Valyner. But there is something that puts them all to shame," I said, turning and handing her the glass.

"What?" she asked.

"You..."

We stood utterly still for a long moment, lost in each other's eyes, before both taking a sip of our drinks. Looking over at Osiris, I opened my mind, asking him if there was anything, and he shook his head.

"Dance with me."

"What?" Her eyes widened. "I don't dance...I never have."

Taking her glass, I placed it on a nearby table with mine and took her hand.

"Then I will lead... I like doing that." I grinned before leading her to the dance floor.

We moved through the music, her feet trying to keep up. Her

emotions were all nerves as she stumbled a few times, avoiding my gaze.

Lifting her slightly, I placed her feet on mine and she finally gave me those golden pools.

Those eyes made everyone around us fade away.

"I want to renegotiate our terms," I said, spinning around and pulling her closer.

"W–what do you mean?" she questioned, her eyes showing a spark of fear. But not over what I said. It was from being this close.

And I felt it too...but I didn't want to fight it.

Not anymore.

"I want you free from the curse too..." We slowed, her gaze locked on me. "I want you in Valyner..."

"As what? A prisoner so you can use my power when we figure out what I'm capable of?"

"Do you believe that? Do you think that's what I want now?" I asked her, the hurt evident in my tone.

"No...but I don't know what you want, Ezekiel."

Bringing my hand to her chin, I pulled her in until our lips brushed. "Then I will put it simply. I wanted to ruin you. Your suffering was to continue until I deemed you worthy of death. Then I would have been rid of the misery you brought me."

She pulled back, studying my face.

"But that's the thing. It wouldn't have been your ruin. It was always going to be mine... And I will gladly let you ruin me for the rest of my days...because I. Want. You."

"Ezekiel..." she whispered.

"Please...don't say anything, not tonight. Just let me feel this. Let me feel alive. Let me feel the light..."

Her eyes softened, her hand coming up to my face.

Glass shattered around us, breaking us from our trance, and we both turned. Cursed beings filtered through the windows, attacking the humans, and the room exploded into chaos.

Osiris began snapping the necks of the ones next to him before making his way towards us.

"What the fuck is going on?" I asked, stunned. I was expecting the fae to plan an attack. But not the Cursed.

"I don't know," she said.

Nyna moved through the crowd, throwing a vampire off a human. I followed her, resisting the urge to use my power because I didn't want to accidently kill any of her people.

"We need to get out of here," I yelled to her, but she ignored me, sending out spells that threw the Cursed back through the windows.

Many began rushing her, and I pushed my way through the horde, trying to get to her. Power erupted, sending me and the others back, and I slammed into the ground. Focusing back on her, she turned, looking at her hands.

They flickered with white light before fading away. Her brows furrowed, and her confusion mixed with mine.

That wasn't normal power...

That was something more.

She looked around, and I pushed myself up, moving back towards her.

Elias rushed in, screaming, "Nyna! Watch out." But as she turned, a vampire stabbed her in the chest with a wooden stake, forcing her to suck in a sharp breath.

No.

No!

"Kali?" she choked out, her eyes wide with shock and betrayal, before stumbling back.

My power shot out, the flames above us in the chandeliers causing the fire to fall like rain. Humans and the Cursed alike began running faster.

I didn't care anymore... I would burn down their entire realm.

Walking up to the vampire, I grabbed her by the back of her neck, the numbness taking over and being replaced with pure, undiluted wrath.

"I'm sorry, Nyna. I can't live like this anymore. She promised us... She promised us we would be free...if you were dead."

Burning her body, I dropped her to the ground. I ran over to Nyna, my heart ripping apart inside my chest. Yet, her eyes were still open.

She was still alive.

Nyna pulled the stake out, and the breath returned to my lungs as her eyes widened. Elias and Osiris looked down at her, their shock mixing with my own.

"Cursed vampires can't live through that," Osiris stated.

We all knew that, and yet, the hole in her chest was already beginning to close.

I picked her up and held her to my chest. "Osiris, glamour the humans to forget everything. Get your soldiers to hunt the Cursed who attacked. No one finds out about this."

My boots crunched into the glass, and I looked down at Nyna, her eyes still lost in shock.

I needed to get her out of here...

Now.

My power flared to life, and I prayed it wouldn't hurt her, but I refused to let anyone else touch her.

The gap swallowed us whole, and we fell through the void's dark embrace.

CHAPTER SEVENTEEN

NYNA

My heart raced as I took in the darkness, the blues and purples lightly swirling past us.

We landed in my room at Elias' place, and my chest ached from how hard I was breathing.

"Are you okay?" Ezekiel shouted, his eyes glossed over with tears. "Damn it, Ruin. Are you okay?"

I took a moment, trying to focus on any pain coursing through me from the gap. Hell, even the stab wound to my heart. But it wasn't there. I felt fine.

"I'm okay..." I breathed out. "It didn't hurt me."

How?

"What the hell am I?" I asked, panic taking root as I stepped back until I bumped into the bed.

"Who was that? Did you know that vampire?" he demanded.

I nodded my head, my jaw still open in shock. Kali... She was alive. She was alive and tried to kill me. My eyes watered.

What was I?

That should have killed me.

"Nyna!" Ezekiel shouted as he grabbed my face, forcing me to focus on his silver pools. I took a deep breath, trying to settle the way my body was shaking.

"She was my friend...I buried her." It came out as a whisper, my stare becoming vacant for a long moment before I met his gaze again. "Who was she talking about?"

Now it was his turn to pull back, his eyes falling to the ground. "Persephone."

"Your betrothed..." I whispered, crossing my arms over my chest. "She wants me dead."

Kali turned her back on the Cursed, on me, for that woman. The woman he was to marry. I felt sick, my stomach turning.

Not only did I have a friend try to take my life, but a powerful fae witch was after me now. Because I was with...him.

"Nyna. I have never cared about her. I only wanted to use her for the spell she offered me."

"I know that..." I said, crossing my arms over my chest. I saw his true intent with her in the stone. He wanted to use her power to become more like a god...so that way he could undo his curse and go up against the one who made him. He wanted power. And I believed him, but it didn't make this hurt any less.

"She is nothing to me. She has never been, nor will be. I told her as much when you were sleeping last night. I don't want her," he protested, his chest rising and falling.

And the look he gave me screamed his true desire. Clearing my throat, I took a step forward.

"What does she want?" I asked.

"What all of us powerful fae want. More power..."

I nodded. "So...that's all you want? Right? Nothing has changed."

He moved in, grabbing my chin and stilling my rapid heartbeat. "How do you want me to show you? What words do I need to speak to convince you?" He fell to his knees slowly, dropping his head. "I would gladly give you my crown, Nyna. Or throw it in the ocean if that would make you happy. I would burn worlds down. Kill anyone and everyone to make sure you take your next breath." He gazed up, tears falling from his eyes. "I am cursed... by you... And it is one that I would never want to be broken unless you wished it. At that point, take the heart out of my chest."

Another tear fell, and I slowly lowered onto the bed, keeping my gaze on him.

"I never fully grasped why the fae in my realm would turn against all they were for the sake of another. But now, I do..." He brought his hands up to my thighs before piercing me with those silver eyes that were glowing brighter than ever before. "Fate. You are my fate. My redemption. My soul, if I even possess one anymore."

I wanted to tell him to stop, but everything he was saying rang out within. This was happening so fast, and yet, I didn't want anything to slow. I wanted to question every single detail of our time together, but I didn't want the answers. Because my very being urged me to hold on to this.

I never wanted him. I never saw this coming, and yet, here I was, falling into his inferno, basking in the warmth as if it was giving me new life.

He slowly smiled, his eyes longing for the next thing I would say. And I stalled, thinking back to the dreams of him. The ones that reminded me of nightmares...but they weren't. They were of what was coming.

I saw this before it happened.

What did all this mean? What type of power was this? I wasn't a fae seer. And they weren't part of the Cursed at all.

"What is this?" I placed my hand over one of his, and a spark flew off his skin. "What are we?"

"If you don't stop touching me, I'll be forced to show you," he growled, and I swallowed hard.

The heat between us grew, causing my stomach to tighten. And against the fighter inside me who wanted to demand an actual response, I fell in... I fell into how my power called to his, and how for the first time in my life, I realized, I only felt completely alive when he was near.

And I wanted more.

"Then show me..."

His silver pools darkened, his hands drifting until his fingers traced the top of the dress. He tore it open, causing me to hold my breath as he bared my body before him.

His hands moved back to my legs, pulling me down until I lay flat. I gasped as I felt his tongue on me again, but instead of slowly savoring, he devoured me. Devoured me as if I were the last meal he would ever have.

My body blazed, my skin tingling as my core tightened. I felt my climax building, and it was faster than ever before.

Sliding two fingers into me, he moved slowly, curling them, and I couldn't hold back the moans falling from my lips. I arched, a silent plea for more, but he stood there, teasing me with just enough to make me unravel further for him.

He stood up, placing one knee on the bed, and leaned down. Taking the peak of my breast into his mouth, he slowly flicked his tongue over my nipple and my eyes rolled back.

His fingers continued to plunge into me, moving faster. His tongue was quickly replaced with his teeth, giving me a mix of pain with the euphoric pleasure.

Fuck... Everything was on fire. And I noticed his scent and mine swirling.

"Do you feel that?" he asked me, thrusting his fingers deeper and pulling a gasp from my lips. "How our power calls to each other. Getting closer with each touch." He growled before moving closer to my face, our lips brushing. "Do you want more?"

"Yes... Gods. I want it all."

Pulling away, he took off his shirt and my eyes widened, my chest tightening from how fast I was breathing.

He was immaculate.

I sat up, pulling him closer, running my hands down each muscle made of stone, seeing the scars that decorated him.

Standing, I pulled him around and sat him on the edge of the bed, kneeling before him. I brought my lips to each scar on his chest, leaving kisses and bites in my wake. He groaned with each one, his fingers tangling through my hair.

Undoing his pants, I pulled them down as he lifted his hips. His cock sprang free and I let out a breath.

Holy fuck...

He made a soft noise, almost like a hum, and I glanced up, taking in the grin on his face.

Leaning in, I ran my tongue up his shaft and watched as his eyes rolled back before closing. Taking him into my mouth, I worked him in slowly.

"Fuck, Nyna..." His grip on my hair tightened before guiding me down his length.

My nails dug into his thighs as he fucked my mouth, and I basked in how it filled me.

With each second that passed, I was wholly aware of our scents intertwining like thread on a tapestry. And there was nothing in this world that would make me want to undo the last thread.

Pulling me off, he grabbed me by my throat. I moved closer until I was forced to straddle him on the bed.

"Take what you want from me...because I'm yours," he breathed out, before slamming his lips to mine.

My hips tilted, grinding against his cock, and my entire body vibrated. I continued to move over him, breaking our kiss to lift my hips. He lined his dick up with my entrance but stopped, and my eyes opened.

He grabbed my chin, pulling it down until our eyes locked. "Let me see your face as I fill you. I want to see the beauty of making you all mine."

My heart skipped a beat as his hands came to my hips, and he dragged me down. Each inch made me suck in a little more air, my jaw falling open.

"*Fuck...*" he growled, pulling me up slightly.

I let out a frustrated moan, trying to pull myself down again, but he denied me, only giving an inch at a time.

"Please...Ezekiel," I begged.

He gave me a breathy laugh. "As you wish, Ruin."

Pulling my hips down, I yelled as he filled me and wrapped my arms around his neck.

And there it was...that feeling within.

Fully awoken. Fully emerged.

He moved me over him and I met his pace, chasing the pleasure that was something beyond this world.

"I was made for you," he groaned, and I felt his words sink in.

Pulling back, I looked into his eyes, the pleasure still coursing through me.

"And I was made for you..." I whispered, and he flipped us over, pinning me below him.

He thrust harder, and my toes curled, my eyes closing.

My core tightened past the point of pain, and I let it take me.

The intensity of my orgasm was overwhelming, the darkness blazing bright red as if the heat within was too much to bear.

I basked in each wave, feeling him slow, letting me notice how each nerve seemed to light up.

Opening my eyes, I watched as sparks fell from him, hitting the bed and burning holes through the blanket.

He was beautiful. A perfect contrast to the hard man I knew, with a softness that made me feel safe, cherished. And I couldn't pull my eyes away from him, watching as he came undone, pouring himself inside me.

And then I felt something shift. Like two worlds colliding, with a whisper in the wind that this would never end. That we were... something, yet I didn't have the word to name it.

My heartbeat doubled, and anticipation flooded me.

After a what felt like a few minutes, he pulled out of me, lying by my side, both of us trying to catch our breath.

"What are we?" I turned my head, taking in his profile.

He slowly smiled, and it was something to behold. Like the pain he'd held from all the years alive on this earth fell away, and he was just at peace.

He turned his head, meeting my gaze.

"Mates, Ruin... We are mates."

CHAPTER EIGHTEEN

EZEKIEL

One month later in the Mortal Realm
Or one day in Valyner

Blood dripped from my face, my breath growing wilder as I turned to look at Nyna with corpses of the Cursed scattered around us.

It had been like this almost daily for the last month.

"What did she promise you?" she yelled, pinning a male witch to a tree with her sword.

He laughed, looking at me as I took a step in before meeting her gaze. "Our cure...since our *Queen* sold herself to the enemy," he bit out, pushing forward. Crimson slowly trickled down his throat, and he smiled.

"I made a deal to save you all!" she roared. "And yet you spit on my oath and loyalty to our people?"

Her voice commanded power. Yet it wasn't just that. Her compassion for others was something that shook me to my core.

She was a leader. A true-born leader.

My mate.

I moved in slowly, evaluating the witch. Furrowing my brow, I paused, feeling his emotions shift.

"Yes... We do. Because you couldn't stay true to your word and kill the King. And let's face it, *Your Grace.* You were never one of us," he seethed. "Persephone also promised something else..."

"What?" she demanded, stepping in and pushing the blade tighter against his neck.

I started moving, the flames sparking in my hands.

He pulled a dagger from his pocket and slammed it into her side, causing her to cry out.

He began chanting a hex and Nyna growled, her anger growing unmatched and singing out to the beast inside me.

Flames shot out, but through the blaze, I watched her push the sword through his flesh, decapitating his head from his body.

As my fires died out, she stepped back, dropping the sword before his ashes. I moved in, placing my hand on her arm.

Her mouth was slightly open, her breath shallow, and her eyes... They held a pain that made my own body hurt.

"How can I save them...when I am the one killing them?" she whispered, and I could hear the brokenness in her voice.

This was hurting her...and in turn, hurting me.

I was to blame for this, and I couldn't figure out how to tell her. The gods' power aided me as I channeled the stone and it fueled my power. It had never been the same since. I wasn't sure I could break the curse after all these years...and it needed to be me since it was done by my hand.

Glancing down at the blade, I studied the hilt and slowly brought one hand to it.

She hissed as I touched it and anger flooded me, causing me to drown in the sea of fire within.

"This is a Crystal blade," I said. "Hold still, please." Pulling it out fast, it caused her to lean forward. She placed her hand over the wound, blood quickly coating her hand.

"What?" she asked, turning to look at me.

I held up the dagger, showing the crushed sapphires in the leather with an amethyst blade.

After a moment, I looked down at her side, and pulled her hand away, watching the wound close. And it felt as if the stars above finally permitted me to breathe. Not that I had even realized I wasn't.

"Why hasn't she come to kill me herself?" Nyna asked, her golden eyes shining brighter.

"She doesn't get her hands dirty. She uses pawns." I gritted my teeth. "I'll call for Osiris. He will get the Embers to go raid the Court."

"She won't stop, Ezekiel. We need to figure out how to get you the power you need to stop her. And that means I need to figure out what I contain."

Her hand reached out, taking the blade from me, and I watched as her blood dripped to the ground before hearing a branch break behind us.

Someone was out there.

"We have to go." I pulled her into my arms and fell through the gap, landing outside Elias' home.

I instantly began chanting protection and cloaking spells, erasing our traces.

"Who was it?" she asked, looking around, readying herself for another battle.

That was the thing... I didn't know.

If I had to guess, it was someone working for Persephone. But it could've also been Persephone herself. Either way, the only thing I cared about right now was keeping Nyna safe.

Elias came around the house and met my gaze.

My eyes went to Nyna and then back to him, a silent plea to get her inside, and he nodded. I watched out of the corner of my eye as he got her into the house.

I stood outside for what felt like hours, placing every spell I could over the property, my heart beating faster with each one, because this fear would not go away. And it was something crueler than anything else in this world...

Losing someone you loved.

Osiris met me around midnight, and I gave him free rein to rain hell on that Court. To kill whomever he pleased, along with my soldiers. I wanted the Crystals to feel my wrath all the way from here. I wanted their homes burned down, their fear so potent that you could taste it in the air. And the pain of loss shrouding them for the next hundred years, so that they knew what happened when they followed a cunt like their lady.

Whether they knew her dealings, it didn't matter.

Anything associated with her would die for trying to hurt my mate.

I made my way down the hall, my hands shaking as I slowly grabbed the doorknob to the room we had been sharing since our first night together.

I could feel her emotions running rampant and took the deepest breath I could before I walked in.

"At the ball...my hands flickered with white. Do you remember?" she asked, keeping her gaze locked out the window on the trees beyond.

"Until the day I die." I moved forward, sitting next to her at the end of the bed.

"That power...it was..." She closed her eyes. "It felt like something I felt from my father the last time I saw him."

She stood quietly for a few minutes before turning to face me. "What if we get her here, and I use it on her?"

"Do you even know how to use that type of power again?" I asked, my trepidation growing. "And what if it hurts you?"

"I will. And it's my power. How could it hurt me when I am the vessel in which it stays alive?" She grabbed my hand, her gaze falling down. "If she comes near you...I will use whatever power I possess to make sure her eyes never meet yours again." She slowly looked back at me, tears staining her cheeks. "I may not fully understand a fae mating bond, but I understand this, Ezekiel. I would die protecting you."

"And do you not think I feel the same way?" I pulled her in, her warmth bringing me peace like no other. "She isn't after me. Not in the same way. And I will not let her hurt you. I will not."

Pulling back, I placed both hands on her face.

We had talked a little about the mating bond since I told her. I could sense she was confused by it, but she didn't resist it. And with each touch, it only grew wilder, begging us to fuse our souls in the bonding ceremony. I worried that would make her turn away from me, that it would be too much right now with everything going on. She was already fighting my battles that she hadn't asked for. She was killing her people, *our* people, and that was taking a toll on her.

And I needed to do at least one thing for her. She had fought so long for her people. And they deserved this...because of her.

Standing up, I pulled my stone from Elias' office, still under my spells, and pulled the dark obsidian dagger from my sheath. As I sliced my palm deep, Nyna jumped off the bed.

"What are you doing?"

"What I should have tried doing months ago..." I whispered before placing the Ember stone in my bleeding palm.

I called out to our gods in my mind. Waiting for an image, a sound, but nothing lay within the ruby walls but the memories of the past.

"Ezekiel?" Nyna's voice was distant, like it was underwater.

I needed to do this for her. I needed to make this right...

Pain gripped my chest, and the power in my veins faltered, causing me to suck in a sharp breath.

What was happening? Why did it feel like I was getting weaker?

"Ezekiel!" Nyna placed her hand over mine, and light shot out, turning the ruby walls into pure white, stunning me.

I felt the urge to bow, to look away from it, and fear worked its way through every nerve until it all went black.

Coughing, my eyes fluttered open, and I looked at Nyna across the room, on the ground.

"Are you okay?" she asked, pushing herself up, carefully avoiding the broken glass from the windows surrounding us.

I shook my head and looked over her ears, which were still rounded.

"You were trying to break the curse," she breathed out.

"They won't help...the gods won't help."

She slumped back, her eyes widening. "You channeled more than the stone for that spell, didn't you? You can't break it alone?"

I nodded, my eyes blurring with tears.

A minute passed as I felt every emotion roll off of her. Ones of shock, anger, and worry...and then one that gave peace to the broken man within me.

Placing her hands on my face, she forced my head up to meet her eyes. "We will figure it out. Together."

"I did nothing to deserve your loyalty, Nyna... Why did the stars above give me you?"

Her lip quivered before she leaned in, tucking my hair behind my ear.

"Because they know everyone deserves to be loved..."

"I don't deserve it." My voice broke, and the tears fell.

"And yet, you have mine... You have my love."

She moved in, kissing me softly. And I slowly fell into the comfort of what this was. What we truly were.

A mate was someone you would do anything for and protect at any cost. Who you couldn't bear to be without because that would be like living without a soul. Who you needed in every way, like they were air itself in your lungs.

But it was so much more.

It was comfort. It was seeing the pain in one another and accepting it as your own. To sit in the darkness of failure or pain and hold one another until the last tear fell. It was so much more than I could have dreamed of. And it made me feel whole.

I felt whole for the first time in almost 1,500 years.

The pain of the past was a mere glimpse now, like I hadn't truly lived through it. My life began the day I saw her in those woods. And I wanted lifetimes with her. I wanted all the years I missed loving her to be filled with memories we could cherish until we were no more. Because it would always be us.

Just us.

I pulled her onto my lap, dropping the stone to the floor. Wrapping my hands around her waist, I sat up until our bodies were flush, and even then, I needed to be closer.

Her hands went between us, undoing my leather jacket and pushing it off my shoulders before I used the spell to remove our clothes.

Standing up, I placed a barrier over the room and walked over to the window seat. Sitting down, the breeze from outside slammed into us, causing her nipples to harden even more.

She lifted her hips, guided my cock to her entrance, and slowly lowered onto me. I groaned, burying my face in her shoulder as she rocked her hips over me.

She arched back, riding me, and I just became mesmerized by her. Memorizing each curve. How her body shuddered with pleasure. How she looked at me.

I think that was my favorite part.

Those eyes on me...filled with love.

She loved me.

Wrapping my hand around the back of her neck, I pulled her in, our lips brushing.

"I love you too," I whispered.

Her lips pulled up, her moans becoming louder as she chased her pleasure.

A few minutes passed, both of our heavy breathing being swallowed up by the wind rushing into the room. But all I felt was her warmth. Not my fire, but the fire she started within me. And I was wholly entranced by it, by her.

Her muscles tightened around my cock, the sensation making everything more sensitive. And I knew she was close.

"Come with me."

Her body tensed as she fell over the edge, and I moved my hips up. My balls tightened and my release poured out into her.

Our moans filtered through the room, slowly dying down with each breath as peace washed over us both.

Yet, I wanted her again. I wanted to be inside her until I took my last breath.

Standing, I held her to my chest and moved over to the bed.

After placing her down, she looked up at me.

"I think I have an idea... Someone who could help us."

"Tell me about it tomorrow." I got on top of her, her hands trailing down my chest. "Because tonight, we are the only ones in this world."

CHAPTER NINETEEN

PERSEPHONE

My hand tightly gripped the Crystal stone, waiting for the gods, but my eyes were locked on the blood.

Her Blood.

I collected it a month ago in mortal time, but it had only been a day for us. A month for *her* since the Cursed tried and failed to kill her. I saw her stabbed with the blade, but the witch's hex was cut short by his death. I was hoping it would weaken her at least, but it didn't.

And with each passing attempt to get to this...creature, to eliminate her, it proved that I needed something more to seal her fate.

It would be so much easier to do it myself, but it was a risk.

My spell to kill was different.

All witches had a signature in how they killed with a hex. Mine were strongest with hexed blades, But I had to stab the person for it to work. And with Ezekiel there...I didn't want him to get in the way. I didn't want him dead.

Just her.

I figured, with her being one of the Cursed, this would be easier to accomplish. Keres and Verena failed with the witches I sent because of Ezekiel showing up. I could understand that. But the stake didn't work. A hex by her own kind didn't work. A spelled fae dagger didn't work.

What would it take to kill her?

Could... No. Unless...

I moved over to the spelled blood floating midair in a black salt circle and studied it. I could feel the power from her––great power––and I wanted to know how she got it.

I would bet my life on Akari knowing something. It was why I'd tried to get her stone––to see what she'd hidden inside it. But that wasn't going to happen now with Ezekiel's Embers guarding her.

I ran my hand around the barrier of blood, my skin tingling.

So what was this? What made Nyna this powerful?

Did Ezekiel give it to her? And if so, how?

Or was she born that way?

Ultimately, what mattered was how I was going to take it from her. Because he was only with her for the power she held. It had to be that.

A deep voice sounded in my mind, and I straightened.

"What is it?" Obsidian asked.

"Does our deal still stand?" I swallowed hard.

Obsidian chuckled, and I closed my eyes, allowing the power of the stone to pull me in and see the black mist within the purple walls.

"Ezekiel will lose the power of the throne the more he uses his magic since he is neglecting Valyner. If he wants it back, he will have to bond himself to you," he said, his tone tainted with humor like he knew that would never happen.

My lip twitched, but I quickly controlled the anger rising within. It wasn't wise to show that in the gods' presence. I would know since I had been working with them both for some time.

"And the girl?" I questioned.

"Can you not kill one of his little Cursed? That is a problem for you."

"Yes, my Lord," I said, casting my eyes down. "What if I brought you more power?"

The black mist stopped before me, the smell of brimstone pungent.

"I'm listening."

"I will get the stones for you. I will siphon magic from whoever you ask, but what if I brought you someone more powerful... Would you honor me with that?"

"In what way do you want to be honored?" he asked.

I took a deep breath and slowly exhaled. "Ezekiel wanted to merge power, to become untouchable. Like you and Tanith. I ask that you give me that instead."

"You want to be a god?" He laughed. "I admire your courage to even ask...and also loathe it. Why would I give you more power?"

"Because it's all that I'll ever have." The pain in my heart branched out, touching every nerve, and I buried it down. "I will serve you faithfully."

The mist of onyx moved around me, and I stood still, waiting.

"If you can find something stronger than a fae or some Cursed beings, sure. I'll honor that. But beware of those creatures, Persephone. They will kill you and send your soul to a place where no peace will ever be found."

"Then it's a good thing I know how to get what I want. And play a game no one else can win."

"Very well. Don't make me have to come down there and do all this myself. Because the second I see you faltering, I will allow you to fall. So, prove yourself worthy to the gods who gave you life."

I pulled out of the stone, and my breathing was ragged.

Was I really going to do this? Was I really going to betray Ezekiel? Yet I knew the answer to that...

I already had.

He was my everything from the moment I saw him at the gathering for that first Lunavas that made us fae. How he stood up against our king: his father. Speaking up for the weak and the unjust. That vengeance was ours.

He gave me hope that night and I had longed to be with him.

And just when I was about to have him as mine, she came in...and took him.

I had waited lifetimes for his love. I played the loyal subject with my bleeding heart, all while dreaming for the day he would just look at me. Look at me with eyes that said I was the one. But he never did. He never saw me...

He was my King. My world.

Every deep seeded wound caused in my mortal life bloomed.

Neglect. The unworthiness. Never being enough...for anyone.

When you search your whole life for a love that makes you feel whole, yet it never comes, should anyone be surprised when the organ in your chest that used to bleed now only resembles stone?

I played the part... I hid my own child, found comfort with Keres when needed, but it was never what I really wanted. He was a pawn. It was always Ezekiel.

We were equals as untouched fae. In our love of magic. And still...nothing.

Moving over to my table, I placed the stone down, and a red glow beamed from behind me. Turning, I looked over Nyna's blood and watched as it shimmered.

My brows furrowed as I moved closer, looking it over.

Magic from within her blood shifted, and I didn't need a spell to tell me what that meant.

No... No.

He couldn't.

He couldn't have gotten her...

No!

My power shot out, breaking the salt circle, and her blood fell to the ground.

Tears threatened to spill over, and just for a second, I almost allowed them to fall. Until a wrath I didn't know I possessed bubbled up and swallowed it whole. I could feel my heart hardening, turning dark with a fury that I grasped onto, that I let devour all senses.

I loved him...I did. But if all I'd ever have was power...

Summoning Keres and Marta, I waited until the door swung open. Turning around, I knew they saw the anger in my face, and I didn't care. I would show everyone the monster life created––that he created––if it meant I got what I wanted.

I had a feeling I was about to become something far worse than he had ever been, and I welcomed it.

"I want her dead. And both of you are going to help me do it."

CHAPTER TWENTY

NYNA

A month later in the Mortal Realm
Or one day in Valyner

Over the last month, Ezekiel called for more of his Ember soldiers to hunt down the Cursed plotting against...me.

Because of Persephone.

Ezekiel had seen how killing them was affecting me. He ordered the fae that day to only capture, and help subdue them.

Not kill.

Ezekiel had also commanded more of the Embers to the Mortal Realm, with the order to kill on sight if any fae were here without orders from him. And since then, the attacks had stopped; not even the Cursed had tried anything again. And we had time to search for my father, following every lead we could, while still trying to practice diving deeper into my power.

But both were a challenge. My father had become a ghost, his presence nearby, but we were never able to catch sight of him. And my power felt as if it was chained, weighing me down and requiring more each time.

The only thing that felt right in this chaotic world was being with Ezekiel. The comfort he brought was like a spell, entrancing me into a peace I didn't know I craved.

And it amplified when he was inside me, begging for more that I still didn't understand. The Cursed formed relationships like the mortals. The term "mates" wasn't used among us. And no one was connected to a fae.

Ezekiel told me he was just as stunned as I was because of his curse. He had believed he was made to be alone, never furthering his bloodline. And for him to be connected to me—someone who had Valyner's power but was something unknown—it made little sense.

Yet, us together, made everything else insignificant.

I moaned, being brought back to the present where the ocean breeze caressed my face, my body quaking as he thrust deep inside me.

Slamming into me without pause, I couldn't hold back the cries of pleasure.

I came gripping the helm of the ship, and he followed me. Our moans danced across the sea, and it was almost like the waves themselves stalled, the whitecaps disappearing to allow us the utter stillness of our bond.

Yet just as fast as they disappeared, they returned, and our breathing was masked by the crashing water around us. Glancing back, I took in his smile as he redid his slacks.

We were anchored so far out at sea for this meeting, making sure no one would cross us or overhear our conversations. And while Ezekiel could glamour a room—hell, even the location we were at— he didn't want to take any chances. And since we got out here earlier, we had time to... Well...

"Pull your pants up or I will fuck you again," he demanded. "Do you want Orla to show up to see that?"

I shook my head and straightened myself. But before I could pull my pants up, he stepped in behind me, and grabbed my hips.

"*Gods...* I will never get enough of you," he whispered, before smacking my ass.

Pulling up my leather slacks, I turned, facing him with a smile on my face. Yet, he was looking over at the water, his expression quickly changing from light to dark.

I had learned over the last two months what that meant.

He was strategizing, angry, or worried. And the way his heart was beating right now told me it was probably a mixture of all three.

"How much time do we have to stop Persephone?" I asked.

"For her, three days...for us, three months," he explained.

"The time difference between our realms is strange... Why's it like that?" I moved over to him, resting my elbows on the railing of the wooden ship.

"No idea. We were once on the same plane. Same time. But after the lands separated, it was like we were still on this earth, but not. A question for the gods, if they would even entertain such a thing."

I heard the disdain in his tone, and my face fell.

"You hate them, don't you?" I said, waiting for him to look at me.

"Gods are cruel and selfish beings. And we were made in their image."

"Anyone can be cruel and selfish. It's a choice. And I've learned that even the cruelest of them all can still surprise you."

He smirked, his eyes softening.

I touched his face before smelling the overpowering salt in the air.

Turning, I took in Orla and dropped my hand. "Nice to see you again." I moved in, hugging her.

"Again?" Ezekiel questioned.

Pulling back, I took in her fearful expression.

"She helped me with the sirens. And gave me dark obsidian." I smiled.

He went to speak, but was completely silent.

"Don't do it," I spoke within his mind.

Ezekiel had taught me how to communicate recently through the bond we shared. And in that moment, it almost looked like he regretted it.

I smirked.

"Fine, then I'll punish you later for it." A small grin lifted his lips to one side.

"Osiris says you have a message for me?" Ezekiel asked, coming closer.

Orla's expression held concern as she studied the man before her. She knew him. Knew what her King was capable of.

Slowly, her focus worked its way over to me, standing beside him. Her eyes lingered on me, maybe a beat too long, as if trying to recognize the girl she'd quietly helped—the one burdened by the weight of the Cursed.

Her features softened as she looked between us. It was quick, but something about it almost spoke of change. The change we both always wanted, but never thought Ezekiel would be a part of it.

"Yes, we were all summoned to the Crystal Court. The Lords and Ladies, excluding Osiris. Persephone said you have a weapon that could destroy our realm... Is it true?"

He patted down his leather jacket before sucking in a breath. "You know, I left that in my other set of leathers," he said sarcastically.

"Did she say what it was?" I asked.

"No...but the Courts believe her," she added.

"The Embers?" the King questioned, his eyes beaming brighter.

"No...but there are some fallen soldiers who are in on this. I don't have names. Osiris is working on it." She took a step forward. "Your sister told me of her visions a while back. She said change is coming. And the Salt Court will be ready, Your Grace. Persephone can't get what she wants. But if she doesn't get you, she will take what she can get...and I fear for Valyner."

"What do you mean?" I asked.

Orla's eyes shifted down my body, narrowing for a moment before they widened.

She met my gaze, swallowing hard. "The throne. And you, Nyna. The power you hold. She will come for your—"

I hissed, feeling the sting of metal pass my left arm.

Orla stumbled back, her eyes going wide. And I looked down, seeing a black blade sticking out of her chest...right where her heart was.

No!

I dropped to the ground, holding her in my arms, shaking her. "Orla! No...Please!"

Where did that come from?

There was no one here but us, but slowly I felt it. Fae presence was all around us.

"Nyna, we have to go!" Ezekiel pulled me off of her, my eyes blurry with tears. He went to pull us into the gap, and my heart stalled in my chest. My power grew, sensing something, and panic took over.

Something was coming for him.

I moved over a few inches and closed my eyes, waiting.

And then I felt it.

A sharp yell left my lips as the dagger buried into my shoulder. Right next to my heart. I stumbled back, unable to breathe from the pain. My eyes widened as I looked into Ezekiel's, seeing the horror that consumed every feature.

My vision was spotted with black as I stumbled away from him, my body hitting the rail of the ship.

And then I felt it.

The sensation of falling.

I watched Ezekiel dive through the air, following me. The image of him above me was distorted as my body slammed into the water.

My eyelids became heavier as the darkness of the ocean swallowed me up. And I thought that maybe this wasn't such a bad way to die...*protecting the one you love.*

I'd do it, over and over again.

My heartbeat slowed, my power became mute, and then I heard something.

Soft, growing in speed.

I opened my eyes, but there was nothing but darkness.

And one heartbeat racing as mine slowed.

It was a beautiful sound as the world faded, taking me away to the unknown.

And I prayed as I took in a shallow breath that he would find me again.

PART 4

THE TRUTH WE FACE

CHAPTER TWENTY-ONE

EZEKIEL

"ELIAS!" I screamed, carrying Nyna across the lawn, my entire body violently shaking.

She wasn't waking up...but I heard her heart.

I heard... No.

It wasn't just her heart, but one that was beating fast.

It was mine. It was just mine. Right?

Elias ran out, meeting me on the front lawn.

"What happened?"

"Fae in the gap, they were trying to kill her..."

He looked her over, his eyes filling with panic.

"She stepped in front of me... Why would she step in front of me?" I cried out, realizing tears were coating my lips.

"I'm going to pull the blade out, okay? Her heart is beating... It's going to be okay."

His hand slowly wrapped around the handle of the dagger and pulled, and I turned away, not wanting to see her blood. I couldn't bear a single drop falling from her body.

I gritted my teeth as he stepped back, holding the dark obsidian in his hand.

"Why would they use this on her?" he asked, and I slowly met his gaze.

"Because they know the stake didn't work," I growled, dropping to my knees and cradling her to my body.

"Please...wake up... Wake up..."

Nyna began coughing, water passing between her lips and onto my already drenched shirt.

She looked around with wide eyes, trying to back away from any other threat, but I held her tighter.

"They..." She coughed. "They were trying to kill you," she got out. I loosened my grip on her, allowing her to look up at me.

And what if that's what they were counting on? Her protecting me...

Nyna winced, and pain washed over me.

"It's not healing, Ezekiel..." Elias said, looking at her back before meeting my gaze.

Dark obsidian could kill her.

"I will kill them. I will make them suffer in ways they never thought possible!"

"Ezekiel...listen!" Elias stopped me.

My anger faded as I listened to the wind and the birds chirping in the distance. I tried to focus on the power of any fae nearby. It could be my own soldiers right now, and I'd rip their hearts out.

My heartbeat filled my ears before Elias' joined, followed by Nyna's...but there was another.

It was fast...faster than all of ours.

No... It wasn't possible.

It wasn't possible!

Getting up, I took Nyna with me and made my way into Elias' house. Her own eyes were stunned as she listened to the pace of the heartbeat within. After placing her down on the small couch, I went to his cabinets in the dining room and started rummaging through them.

He was right behind me, opening the drawer and pulling out salve and alcohol.

"Ezekiel...how?" he whispered.

I couldn't speak, my gaze vacant as I tried to process what was happening.

After a few moments, he made his way over to her. I slowly turned, watching her in the other room as she pushed herself up into a sitting position.

I could feel her shock radiating off of her and it was merging with mine.

"Here, let me help," he said before sitting behind her and opening the bottle.

She hissed as he dumped out a good amount onto her shoulder.

"Who have you been with?" I asked her as I moved back into the parlor.

Her eyes opened wide before a spark of anger flashed over them. "Are you serious!?" she spat out.

"That's not mine... It can't be!" I yelled, taking another step in.

Elias applied the salve, and she strained to stand up, stumbling slightly. Part of me wanted to reach out to catch her, but I resisted.

"Fuck you!" she seethed.

"I can't have children, Nyna! I can't be a father!" I shouted.

Elias moved past her, placing his hand on my chest.

"Brother...put your hand on her stomach."

I shook my head, tears stinging my eyes as if I had shards of glass in them.

"Ezekiel..." he said again, softer.

When I met her gaze again, the pain in her eyes revealed what my reaction was doing to her.

And shame burned through my fury.

I moved in slowly, holding my breath.

Did I want the truth?

I was cursed. I'd made peace with that long ago.

She lifted her shaking hand and grabbed my wrist, placing it on her stomach.

I looked away, holding my breath as I focused on the heartbeat. It was fragile. Small. But there was no mistaking the power it gave off.

Like a mark etched in fate itself, it matched me, and my power. Although it was something else. Something stronger...just like its mother.

Glancing back at Nyna, tears fell from my eyes, and hers followed.

I didn't know what to do.

I was just frozen in place.

After a minute passed, I pulled my hand away and turned towards the door. "I'm sorry, but I can't do this. I can't be a father."

I walked out, not looking back, hyperventilating as I made it outside.

"Ezekiel," Elias said a few moments or minutes later. I didn't know. He was standing at the top of the stairs of the porch, and I glanced up, wondering when I walked down the stairs.

"Akari said she was the key to me... I thought at first it meant she was the key for me to have more power... To become untouchable by everyone, including the gods." I sucked in a half breath, the air getting caught in my throat. "And then maybe it meant she was the person I needed in this life...that maybe I could have a mate...not that she was the key to breaking my curse."

He walked down the steps, sitting on the bottom one, and waited for me to join him.

I slowly did, staring out at the trees beyond.

"Do you really not want the child? Or are you afraid of being a father?" he asked, and I shook my head.

"I can't be a good father. Look at Ezra... Look at how I turned out. I can't do that to a child."

"No...you don't get to use Ezra as an excuse anymore." He raised his voice, pulling on my arm until I met his gaze. "You have had fifteen hundred years to deal with it. And now you have to because she needs you. *Your* child will need you."

"You said it was a blessing the gods didn't let me carry on my line," I retorted, still feeling hollow. Numb.

"The man you were a hundred years ago... Yes. The man you have grown into... No." His emotions matched his words, pulling my gaze to meet his blue eyes. "She is your mate. That is your child. And I know you... You will protect them to your final breath."

"Like I protected you and Akari." Guilt washed over me, another tear sliding down my cheek.

"We are all still here, aren't we?" He smiled. "Now get your fucking ass in there and talk to her."

I stood still, the insidious tendrils of fear slowly taking root within me.

"Look at me, brother." I did as Elias asked. "You are enough. You always have been. And they need you."

He offered me his hand, and I took it as I stood, but held him from taking another step. "I'm afraid."

"So am I...but we will be better for our children."

I swallowed hard, my eyes locked on the front door, feeling her emotions of anger and shock, with a hint of amazement and joy.

And it was intoxicating, making my own form.

I was going to be a father.

He tapped me on the shoulder. "Smile, brother, it could be worse. You could marry someone you barely know to raise a child together."

I shook my head, and he chuckled.

He had a point. I was getting everything I never deserved. And now that it was within arm's reach, I couldn't let anything take it away.

We both made our way up the stairs and he went inside first. I took a cleansing breath, my hands shaking.

Taking the step over the threshold, I paused as I was met with a man with blue eyes and long blonde hair standing next to Nyna. And her hardened eyes said it all before I even felt her disdain.

It was her father.

"Sorry, but it's time for my daughter and me to have a chat."

He looped his arm around her waist, and I sent my fires out, my rage returning like it had never left me. He vanished before our eyes, taking my mate with him.

Taking *my* child with him.

I let out a scream, my blood boiling.

Elias looked at his furniture on fire, and I quickly pulled the flames back.

"How did he use the gap?" he asked me, and my nostrils flared.

I felt his power in the air, similar to his daughters, and yet, it was so much more.

"I'm pretty sure she is about to find out."

"He isn't Cursed… He wasn't from Valyner," Elias said.

Nyna had told me everything about him. And I didn't trust him, which was no surprise. Fathers had a way of scarring you beyond your wildest nightmares. Mine was more physical, hers was emotional. And I couldn't shake that whatever he had planned with her was going to cross a line…

And she would be the one to suffer.

"Can you feel her? Can we follow?" Elias grabbed my arm, turning me to face him.

I tried to feel for her, but she was just gone, like she never existed to begin with.

But I refused to believe that, and I refused to sit here while she was out there with him.

"No. But I'll tear the realm apart until I find them."

CHAPTER TWENTY-TWO

NYNA

My father released me, and I stumbled back, placing my hand out against the stone wall. My vision spotted black as I breathed through the pain in my shoulder.

Glancing over, I slowly took in the ruby-red walls of a...cave.

"Where are we?" I asked, pushing myself up to stand straight.

My father walked around to the opposite wall, running his hand over the symbols etched into the rock. They were strange, like nothing I had ever seen before, and yet, I felt like somewhere deep down, they made sense.

"Somewhere no one can find us. No one can get in unless we allow them to. I spelled it that way."

I pushed off the wall, moving over to him. "You're a witch..." I said, causing him to turn and face me.

"I will tell you the truth. I'll tell you everything if you do one thing first."

He pulled a blade from a sheath at his hip, and my hand went to my stomach, fear taking over.

He glanced down. "I wouldn't harm your daughter, Nyna..."

"Daughter?" The air ripped from my lungs, my entire body freezing in place.

I was going to be a mother... I was going to have a daughter?

How was this all possible?

"I knew this day would come…I was waiting for it." My father broke the silence, and I slowly looked at him.

"What?" I breathed out, shaking my head. "You're a seer too?"

"As are you. You have experienced it with your dreams. Your mate's blood opened that power within you to see into the past, the present, and the future. Your child will have that too. But her power will be focused on what's coming."

"What are you?" I asked, stumbling back. "What am I?"

He looked down at the blade, causing me to follow his gaze. One side was completely black, like the obsidian dagger that Elias had just pulled out of me. And the other side was completely white.

"This is called shadowquartz. And if you want to know everything, you will swear to me you will not speak of what I am about to tell you."

I swallowed hard, meeting his gaze, and thought of only one person.

Clearing my throat, I met his blue eyes. "If it's anything concerning my child, her father has a right to know," I demanded.

I was angry with Ezekiel right now, but this concerned him, too. And what if it also helped the Cursed and his realm?

My father's eyes fogged over, turning completely white for a moment, and I leaned back.

"Very well… I see no problem with that. But you'll have to complete the bond first to share what you know with the King."

Complete the bond?

"Come here," he commanded.

I moved forward, gritting my teeth. Each step built this war inside me, mixing with anticipation and anger. I was finally going to learn what I was, and yet, why did he have to wait until now?

Stopping before him, he waited for me to offer him my hand, and I hesitated. My reservations slowly fell, like walls that no longer had their foundation, because I needed to know everything.

Lifting my hand, he sliced into my palm, causing me to hiss. My fingers curled, protecting the wound as he cut his the same way.

Crimson covered the dagger's blade, and he brought it up to his mouth, letting one drop fall in before offering it to me.

"Vas aluh matrium lavousa. El nah sol vasmatrais," he said, closing his eyes.

"What does that mean?" I asked, swallowing hard. And somewhere, in the depths of my soul, a part of me understood, trying to explain, but it was too far away, leaving me with panic and wonder.

"Do you want to know who you truly are?"

My nostrils flared as he repeated the phrase, and I opened my mouth, allowing the drop of blood to fall to my tongue.

And something within shifted.

I stepped back, placing my hand over my heart. Moving through my body, it invaded my head, and it was all-consuming. It wasn't painful, but something so intense that it made me fear this was a mistake.

"A blood oath. Meaning you swear to hide the truth until your soul passes on. And it will include Ezekiel too."

It took me a minute to meet his gaze again, and I waited.

"I am from a realm called Adonys. The home of the gods. I am the heir of King Cyro, your grandfather."

I backed away, the world feeling like it was swaying. Sitting on a large rock, I stared at the ground.

What the fuck?

"You...you're a god?"

"Yes." He placed his hands behind his back and looked over the cave. "I was exiled for siding with my brother, Arcadyus, after they accused him of crimes against our realm... I believed they were wrong. So, I fought for him, and my father taught me a lesson. That sometimes you need to let someone go or they will take everything you hold dear." He paused, his eyes closing as he took a deep breath before continuing. "And so, we were both sentenced to this world."

His eyes scanned the markings on the walls again.

"Little did I know that the crimes he was convicted of were true. He stole the stones from the gods, relics, shadowquartz chains, and two of these daggers." He held it up, examining it.

"What's so special about those daggers?" I asked.

"They can kill gods like us. Like dark obsidian, slate, or onyx can kill the fae...and you."

"What do you mean? If I'm like you, then..." I leaned forward.

"But you aren't exactly like me...I will explain that, but there is more to this story..." He let out a breath, rolling his shoulders back. "I believed my brother when he said he took it for us. That when the time passed, we could use it all to go home and beg our father for his forgiveness. But then he wanted to test the power of the stones since he had studied them his whole life. He was a stone keeper—an honor our mother, Elowen, gave him. Well, *my* mother."

"He's your half brother?"

He nodded. "I didn't know until everything took place and they were about to exile him. But he was still my brother. Half blood or not." His eyes closed, and his throat bobbed.

"So, what made you change your mind about your brother?" I asked, trying to understand, because the way he talked about him seemed like he still held so much love. Something I'd never seen from this man.

"When we got here, after a few centuries, my brother's true power manifested. He wanted to do a spell using the stones so we wouldn't be alone with the humans. And we ended up creating a realm, naming it Oasis." He dropped his head, and his expression turned hollow. "That's where we made the six gods using the stones as well. The ones who made the fae and fae Realms. But none of them got his power. Only mine. And for the first time, I saw what he really wanted...more gods like him."

"Like him? Wouldn't your power be the same?" I asked, a chill running down my spine as I stood up and moved closer.

"No... It's why his power was suppressed. It was to protect him from people who would have wanted him dead. Arc's from a cursed bloodline. In fact, he had no magic at all while we were growing up. But I... I carry all of it."

He continued. "My bloodline was blessed by the stars before my birth as a gift granted to my father for his bravery during the war against Arc's mother—his former mistress. She shattered the stars' blessing over her realm, her people, all to harness dark soul magic— magic that let her control life and death itself, and it made her line unstoppable. They could do horrid things with their power. And that imbalance threatened everything."

His fingers curled into fists, forcing his skin to turn white.

He met my gaze.

"So, the stars gave my father's line the one thing strong enough to stop her. The stones were used to harness the power of each type of god and goddess. And it was bestowed upon our bloodline alone to hold that power and responsibility to fix what she did. And so, we became her weakness. Her downfall."

I shook my head. "Our bloodline is the only thing that can go up against your brother? What did you do to him? What am I missing?"

"I did a spell...to lock him away and protect the balance of power. And he cursed me. Well, cursed my line. Your daughter will be affected by this. She will hold his toxic power."

I could feel the blood drain from my face, my throat closing.

He stood and moved over to the symbols again. "I spent a lot of time with the humans, appreciating the simplicity of their lives. I lost track of the years, but then I noticed the relics were missing. The chains...even one dagger. I brought a relic here when I saw some pieces missing from it and hid it behind spells. And then I noticed...he was getting closer to some of the gods, and keeping secrets between them." My father's nostrils flared as he took a breath.

"I knew I needed to stop whatever he had planned. And when he asked me to help him join the six stones into one, I said yes..."

His voice shook, his fist slamming down on the stone and causing me to jump slightly.

"The six stones?"

Valyner had six for the untouched fae...it was a gift to them when they were made.

"They were never Valyner's. They were my father's," he growled.

After a long moment, I asked, "What did you do?"

"Once I finished the spell, I placed the stone in the handle and stabbed him in the heart with this very blade," he said, gripping the handle, eyes downcast, before looking at me. "I sent him to a realm I made for him... The Abyss. He was dead...in a way. There is only one way to kill his kind..."

"How—"

"It's not important. Not to you," he continued. "But...he was ready for the betrayal. Like he knew it would come. The spell we did combined our blood...which meant it was in me."

I stood, moving over to him.

"I've been losing my power ever since... The gods created the fae, and I blocked them from entering the Mortal Realm. And drained a lot of my power by doing so. Obsidian was determined to find and kill me, along with the humans, to punish me for what I did to his King. And he had the other dagger, so..."

The god that created Valyner with... Tanith, was it?

"Is that it? Are you telling me we are cursed to lose our power if we use it?"

He didn't answer me, standing perfectly still.

"No. That's just me... Maybe you should sit back down."

"No, tell me the rest!" I yelled, and trepidation set every nerve on fire.

His gaze turned hollow again, distant. And it wasn't the first time I had seen him that way. That had been his state of mind for most of my life. Yet, right now, it shook me to my core.

"I cared for your mother...but it wasn't until she became pregnant that I started seeing visions of how I could break the curse on me." Turning to face me, I watched as a tear fell down his cheek. "When you were born, you had a twin sister. The power of two goddesses being born created a tear in my spell that was locking Obsidian out. And I knew I needed to keep you alive..."

"What did you do?" I asked, my voice shaking.

"I let him take her... I let Obsidian take Aesyra and turn her into the new goddess that would rule Valyner. And I promised your mother she would have a full life, but she won't...she will die by his hand one day..."

Dragging my fingers through my hair, I couldn't believe what I was hearing. My heart ached for my mother.

The sister I never got to meet was out there, somewhere, and would die at the hands of her captor.

"That's why Mom said she lived half a life...with half her heart." My voice shook as a tear trailed down my face. "You let him take her daughter."

He avoided my gaze, and my anger grew wilder.

"What happened to my power?" I asked.

"I locked it away. Because I needed you. I only needed *you*."

"Needed me for what?" A scream escaped my lips.

"Your revenge always drove you. Whether it was against me or another. And your power responded to it," he said, shaking his head.

"What did you need me for?"

"I needed your power to stay locked away. For you to listen to me until it was time for you to meet Ezekiel. I needed you two not to kill each other until the bond became obvious and led to this." He pointed at my stomach. "Your child's birth is necessary, as is both of your deaths."

Every muscle froze as I stopped. I was going to be sick...

We were going to die?

"Your mother knew what you were. She didn't want me to lock away your goddess side, but it needed to be done. And I directed you the best I could so that way you controlled that door from opening." He took a breath. "She was going to tell you. She couldn't live with guilt of lying anymore...and I couldn't let her."

His voice got louder, his tone frantic.

"Our blood oath wasn't like the one I just created between us and your mate. She was going to tell you everything... How you were a goddess of the most powerful bloodline to exist. That I denied you the right to your true power. And with that, you needed to be careful with dark obsidian because it made you more like the fae and would kill you. She couldn't lose another child. She didn't want your life to be lived in hiding." The anger physically rolled off him, his eyes filled with the reason behind his motives.

"Oh my gods..." I stepped back, placing my hand over my mouth.

"I didn't have a choice."

"You killed her..." My breathing came in rapidly, the nausea twisting my stomach into knots.

"I used my fading power to keep her around longer. For you," my father shouted. "She would have been dead within five years of us meeting. Every minute after that was a blessing from me...to *you*."

I moved in and slapped him, slamming my fists into his chest, but he didn't fight back. He didn't move an inch.

I thought it was the fae this whole time. That the King passed the order. It had fueled my rage towards him, what he had done to the Cursed, but it was my father's hand that had pulled the blade across her throat.

His power shot out, holding me immobile, and he backed away. I tried to break through its iridescent white vapor, but it tightened, forcing me to cry out.

"You can't understand what this curse feels like. I will become human and die unless I undo what I did. I need your daughter. She holds his blood; his magic. She holds the key to raising my brother. But she can't hold all the power she has. Not yet."

"I would never deny MY CHILD the right to her power!" I bit out, seething at the man I called father for just about 150 years.

"Nyna, I have seen it. All of it!" he shouted, moving in. "If you don't, she won't make it past ten!" he yelled again. "When the flames sit upon the throne...light and darkness will rage war until one stands between, able to control both. *That is your daughter.* She is the balance between light and darkness. But loss will be her friend, betrayal will be her follower, and love will be her fight. The walls will fall, forging something new. She will *fix* what I did to my brother. Fix *me*."

"I don't give a fuck what happens to you anymore!"

"But you care about what happens to *her*, don't you?" he bit out, pointing down at my stomach through the white mist. "If you don't control the power in your veins and keep it from fully emerging, I will have no choice but to kill you myself after you birth the child. And then I will raise her." He held the dagger up, and my throat went dry.

"Persephone will kill you. She already knows that dark obsidian works on you. But she cannot take your power or your child's if you die like a fae. Even now she turns his kingdom against him, anger fueled by rejection and pain because he didn't love her," my father explained. "She is communicating with Obsidian. And she believes if she gets your power, then Obsidian will turn her."

"Turn her into what?"

"A god."

I shook my head. "Why would you do this to me? To your granddaughter?"

He placed his hand on my face, and I tried to move, but he brought his other hand up, holding me still, and he showed me what was to come.

Different lines of alternative futures played out for her, my beautiful daughter with silver eyes, like her father. Her long, dark brown hair. How she fought, how she moved. She was something to behold. To cherish in each vision.

Yet my body shuddered at each one. Because in most visions, she died young. Too young. And in only one did I see her live. She grew to find love and friendship. She grew into her power, her strength. And she was good. She was everything a parent could want.

So many paths flickered in and out of my mind, but that one stood at the center. I tried to see how it ended for her, but it wouldn't show me.

I saw moments with Persephone dead before her. A copper throne on fire. Collecting the stones. And a war, fighting a dark mist before her. And then it was nothing. I didn't see whether she lived or died.

Or maybe...he didn't want me to see it. Because if I truly knew what would happen to her after that, what would I do?

But something that remained constant in all futures for her was the fact that Ezekiel and I were not with her. And that thought ripped my heart to shreds within my chest.

My father pulled back. "I want to go home... Please try to understand that. I was never meant to be here."

I couldn't believe what I was hearing.

The gods were selfish and cruel.

Or at least this one was.

"I will not let you use her."

"You won't have a choice," he said calmly, no emotion in his tone.

"I will never forgive you for this..." I said through gritted teeth.

"I believe you. But after today, I am going to a place the sun cannot touch, where I can be free of the weight this world has put on me until it is time. And you won't be here, nor will your mate."

"Fuck you!"

"You have seen it, daughter... It's coming for you either way. But it doesn't have to be the end of our line." His gaze fell, and he began walking to the opening of the cave. Placing the dagger down, he turned back and looked at me. "Hiding something you love is the only choice." He took a few steps towards me, looking around at the cave one last time. "Go through what I have left behind for you...it will help you prepare."

He began walking again. And the power fell from me.

"Dad..." I shouted, and he turned his head over his shoulder. "I will do everything in my power to make sure she never does what you want. And I will smile wherever I am the day you die, knowing you failed."

He hummed, nodding his head. "My daughter, the goddess of revenge. Time will tell... But I like my odds."

He vanished before my eyes, and I ran out of the tunnel, looking around, my fury growing hotter by the second.

Falling to my knees, I screamed, my power shooting out and snapping trees all around me.

Minutes passed, my breathing became ragged, and I looked out at the surrounding destruction. Fury took root, and my vision turned red.

If he wanted a goddess of revenge...he just got one.

CHAPTER TWENTY-THREE

EZEKIEL

Hours had passed, and I rode by my brother's side, my eyes scanning, my ears listening...

And nothing.

We were getting close to Eldros, where many of the Cursed lived within some towns still occupied by the humans. Yet, as we passed the town, it seemed quieter.

"The humans have been moving up north... Too many attacks," Elias stated.

I pushed the horse to ride harder. Where was she? Where was my mate?

I should've known that I couldn't find happiness in this life without setting it ablaze.

The problem was always me; it always would be.

Or maybe...I could finally step up and just admit that I was wrong. Because I was. I was wrong about everything.

Slowing to a stop in a clearing between the mountains, my heart raced.

"Ezekiel... What is it? Is it Nyna?" Elias asked, pulling on the reins of his horse.

Unmounting my horse, I walked a few steps before glancing up at the sky. It was painted in shades of orange and red, creating its own inferno. It dawned on me that I didn't even feel an ember of my power. It was just cold. Freezing.

"What if she never comes back?" I whispered, hearing Elias move up behind me.

Turning around, he placed his hand around the back of my neck and pulled me in until our foreheads touched. "She will... She will."

His emotions were drenched in hope, and I pulled back, looking into his blue pools.

"I don't know how to be a good father..."

Tears filled our eyes, both of our worries mixing.

"We will figure it out. Whatever it takes. They will be the best of us," he reassured me.

"There was only ever good in you, brother." The tears fell, and my throat tightened.

He paused at that, blinking away the tears. "Listen to me. There is good in you. There is... I was wrong when I said there was no redemption for you. I see it right now. I see the man who raised me. Who cared for me. Protected me. And loved me. You will only do more for the child. Your child. I am sure of it."

Heat flowed over my body and I stepped back, looking through the trees to my right. And then I felt it.

I felt *her*.

A scream echoed through the woods, and Elias and I both froze.

"Go! I'll follow with the horses!" he shouted, running back to them.

I fell into the gap and found myself in the woods, the trees broken over and Nyna on her knees in the middle of it all.

I rushed over, dropped to the ground, and held her close. Panic took over as I listened to her heartbeat, and then...my child's.

They were okay...

The fear that had settled into my bones over not knowing where they were was over, showing me how much I loved her. How breathing was at its hardest when she wasn't near. And now a newfound strength had formed, building wilder by the second to protect what she held in her womb...

The thing I was never supposed to have.

The thing that drove me resentful over the years because I was denied a family. My *own* family.

And now I couldn't lose them. It would kill me.

"I am so sorry. I am so sorry, Nyna..." I said, pulling her gaze up to meet mine. "Are you okay? What did your father say?"

"No...I-I'm not o-okay..." she cried. "My father told me... He... he said..." She stumbled over her words, anger growing as she tried to force them out.

Iron filled my senses, and I looked down, picking up her hand to see the slice through her palm. "What did he do to you?"

She went to speak again, but nothing came out.

"You don't need to tell me until you are ready. But give me the order and I will hunt him down and do whatever you ask," I declared, watching another tear stream down her face.

Wiping it away, her lip trembled. Her eyes were so heavy, so haunted as if she was caught inside a nightmare.

Elias rode up behind us, and I looked over my shoulder, his eyes wide and scanning over her. I picked her up, holding her to my chest.

"Meet us back at your place. And if we are all lucky, the spell on the Cursed will fall before you arrive."

I didn't even stop to take in his shock before I fell into the gap, landing in Elias' office.

"Ezekiel...what are you doing? You already tried once... It didn't work." Nyna asked as I placed her softly in the window seat.

Turning, I pulled the Ember stone from my jacket and wrapped my fingers around it until they throbbed.

"I need to try harder. I promised you I would undo what I did. So let me... For you, for Elias, for every fae I cursed...and for our child. I will not have any of you afflicted by my anger for another minute."

"Ezekiel...I..." She tried to speak, but again stopped, her brows furrowing.

I walked over to her and kneeled, my other hand softly touching her face.

"You will be by my side in Valyner. You will be my Queen. And our child will be raised with the Embers and the rest of the Courts. It is their home. Your home, Nyna. Let me do this for you both."

I stood up and backed away, recalling the curse, and adjusted my grip on the stone. I could feel the curse working through my veins like it did all those years ago, and I felt the fury all over again.

The betrayal of my brother wasn't the root of my anger, nor the fae who followed him. It all stemmed from the man who raised me. The man I called father.

Elias' intentions were pure, but it gave Ezra an edge in the fight when he found out what could kill us...and that's what drove me. I needed to prove to that pathetic excuse of a father that I could stand up for myself. That I wasn't weak.

But I never was... I survived him.

I began to try to reverse it without the gods' help, feeling the floor rumble below me. And I gave it more. Because now I had something far greater than anger: It was love and fear, merging to become one.

Nyna rose, grabbing onto my arm, her voice distant, but I couldn't stop.

I couldn't.

As I was towards the end, seeing the light bloom before me, I took a deep breath, letting it come for me.

"Ezekiel!"

Her voice rang out in the darkness that was turning into pure light, and before me sat the throne.

And then everything vanished.

Coughing, I sat up in my brother's study, seeing broken glass, books on the ground, and his desk turned over. I looked over at Nyna, hiding behind a barrier.

Fuck...did it work?

"Are you okay?" I asked.

She nodded, and I slowly stood.

"Do you feel any different?"

"No..."

Fuck.

What was the problem? Was it too rooted in place to break? Did I need more power?

"It's not enough..." I said, turning my head to look at her. "My power isn't enough to undo it."

She moved in, dropping the barrier, and ignoring the mess of the study.

"Then channel me," she said, placing her hand out.

I looked at her, stunned, and shook my head.

"No...what if it hurts you both?" I glanced down at her stomach.

Closing my eyes, I turned away, seeing the throne behind my eyelids.

It was made by the gods...

I had been away for some time, and maybe my connection to the power it gave me was weakening. And I knew what I needed to do.

I turned and pulled her close, capturing her lips with mine. Pulling back slightly, I breathed out, "Do you trust me?"

"What are you—"

"Do you trust *me*?" I asked again, needing the answer.

She pulled back, her hand running down my face. "I do."

"Then I will be right back."

Landing in my throne room, I turned to face the throne and saw Persephone standing near it with a crystal crown adorning her head, and stopped.

"Good, you are back. I knew you would choose wisely."

Flames poured from my hand, roaring like untamed beasts as

they lashed out at her. She blocked them, her barrier rippling as the inferno bounced off and turned to embers.

I tried to pull it down, but it was no use.

Gritting my teeth, my fires built, ready for another blow when purple mist slammed into me. Stumbling back, my eyes narrowed as I steadied myself, readying my power to devour everything in this room.

And then I felt it...my power fading away.

Dropping my hands, I heard the metal cling together. My eyes drifted to them, seeing the dark obsidian chains.

She used a spell to place them on me.

My gaze met hers again, and gone was the mask she wore in front of me. No charm, soft demeanor, or smile that promised warmth. Now it was just hard, cold anger.

Throwing her hand out, she pulled me to my knees and began walking towards me. I tried to stand, but I couldn't. Her spell held me to her will.

The doors behind me slammed into the stone walls, and I looked back, seeing my Ember soldiers rush in, their hands burning bright.

Yet each one was stopped in their tracks, their eyes bulging from their skulls right before their hearts were ripped from their chests. My eyes closed, a chill running down my spine.

"Now... Where were we, my love?" she asked, her voice smooth, but as sharp as broken glass. Her heels clicked on the stone as she grew near. Something scraped against the floor before me, and I slowly turned my head back to look.

A dark obsidian dagger.

"Cut your palm."

My lip lifted into a snarl, and I shook my head.

"No..." I growled, looking up at her.

"Cut. Your. Palm," she repeated slower, her tone unwavering.

"I will not bind myself to you."

"We were supposed to be bonded. It was supposed to be us, Ezekiel!" she shouted, and I met her gaze. Tears lined her eyes, shining through her wrath. "I will *raise hell* like your precious Fallen Court...but my fury won't end with them. Some appreciate a leader who will give them what they ask for, not that I will ever give it." She huffed. "Unlike this Court who is loyal to you... I will kill every last Ember if you do not cut your hand right now and say the words."

My stomach twisted, bile rising into my throat.

"No," I growled again, refusing to look away from her.

"I'll go to the gods..."

I laughed. "Something tells me you already have. Have they answered you yet?" I taunted, and she gave me a vile grin.

Fuck, had they talked with her?

Was that why they were ignoring me when I was trying to use more power to undo the curse?

It had to be...

Kneeling before me, she picked up the blade, bringing the tip to my cheek. "There is no way out of this for you, don't you get it? You can save yourself, or I can hunt down your family..." The tears in her eyes fell slowly. "I'll start with your sister, then I'll find your brother over in the Mortal Realm. That won't be hard. And then, I'll take her...and the child inside her womb."

I pulled back, the sting of the blade cutting my cheek. My breathing was erratic, and I had never felt this before, this feeling...

I thought I had been enraged before. But nothing like this.

How did she even know?

"I have spies everywhere, Ezekiel." She wiped her cheek with her other hand before standing up and walking around me. "Did you think I wasn't keeping track of you? Of her. And now I know why you like her so much. Her power is a strange thing... But soon, that will be mine. Well, ours, if you do what I say."

She made her way back in front of me and pointed the dagger at my hand.

"Bond to me...and we can forget it all. We can live the life we both were destined to have. By each other's side..."

I leaned in, my body shaking from the rage, trying to push through her spell to wrap these chains around her throat.

My jaw locked, my vision blurring at the edges.

"You will never be Queen."

Another tear fell, her lip quivering for a moment before her face hardened all over again.

"Yes, I will... I will take your kingdom. I will take your throne, and everything you hold dear before I kill you."

"Why not just skip to the last chapter, and do it now!" I yelled. "Do it!" I laughed, and she stepped back.

Osiris landed behind her, his shadows wrapping around her throat, and her magic on me faltered. Pushing myself up, I ran in, sending out a war cry.

Her hands went out wide, the purple in her palms growing brighter before she broke through his hold and sent him flying back.

Osiris stopped himself, his black wings appearing and pushing him up into the air.

Persephone sent her power out towards me, and it slammed into my chest, throwing me back to the ground. And I watched as my stone rolled across the floor.

Fuck...

Her eyes locked on it, and she began moving towards it.

Pushing myself up, I paused as Crystals appeared, their power focused on me.

Their magic coursed through my veins, stealing the air from my lungs. I cried out, but one by one their power fell, and I looked back, seeing Ember and Fallen Soldiers filling the throne room.

Osiris must have called them.

He joined the fight, and I moved through the chaos, making my way towards Persephone. She held my stone in her hands and was wholly entranced by it, and I reached out.

Her wide eyes were all I saw as I wrapped the chains around her throat and pulled her back. I slammed into the wall, and she pawed at my arms, her long nails cutting into me.

"Axel!" I yelled to Kadeyan's friend, the closest person to me.

He snapped the necks of two Crystals and moved in, taking the stone from Persephone.

"Get out of here! Now!" I ordered him, and he fell into the gap.

A bolt of pain sliced through me as Persephone pulled the dagger from my side, causing me to scream and loosen my hold on her. Warm blood flowed down inside my leathers, and I met her gaze as she turned.

Pain filled her features, tainted with a fury that matched my own. And I knew she wouldn't stop. She wasn't going to take no for an answer.

Yet I would not bend for her. I would not give her any part of me.

She must have seen it in my eyes because it only made her wrath grow as she let out a cry that could only be described as a broken heart.

Her hand went up high, the dagger gripped so tightly that her knuckles were white.

I went to move, but her power filtered out, slamming my head against the wall, and causing my vision to spot. Her hand sliced through the air, the blade so close.

And within the blink of an eye, the world fell away, the darkness taking me somewhere unknown. And it hurt knowing that if Nyna was there, our child wouldn't be.

I could have sworn I heard her screaming for me.

And that hurt most of all.

CHAPTER TWENTY-FOUR

NYNA

Three weeks later in the Mortal Realm
Or seventeen hours in Valyner

"Nyna!" Elias yelled after me as I walked out of his cabin, a few miles back into the woods behind his house.

I had been a wreck with each passing minute since Ezekiel left. He should have been back by now. If all he was doing was the spell, he would have tried and come back to me.

No. Something was wrong. And I needed to find him.

"It's been over three weeks, Elias!" I said as I kept walking, not looking back. "I can't sit here and wait."

Elias' hand wrapped around my arm, stopping me from taking another step.

"What you are trying to do will kill you. I have seen fae take the Cursed to Valyner over the years, and they never came back. And even if you—by some miracle—make it there, what if it affects your child?"

I glanced down between us, my stomach taking on a small oval shape below my leather jacket. I was already showing.

She was growing fast...faster than she should since the Cursed who could have children endured a mortal pregnancy length.

"I can do this," I bit out, burying the fear that was coursing through my veins.

Not only for the baby, but for him.

The Cursed couldn't muster the amount of power needed to open the gap between our planes.

But I could. I was something more than them. More than the fae. I had contained a power in my veins since the day I was born that was beyond this world entirely. Even if it was locked away.

I could do this.

I had no other option.

"You can't stop me," I finally said, pulling my arm free and pulling for the magic within.

I remembered what it felt like when I studied the power that Ezekiel fell into. Or the years I summoned that power with the Cursed. I could do this. I knew this magic.

Elias' eyes were filled with worry as the essence of power opened around me and I tried to make sense of what I was seeing.

It was dull white, just like when I used it at the mortal ball. Similar to my father's, but not as strong.

I could feel that place inside of me, where it was locked away behind a door. It was rattling, begging to be set free, but I held my ground, only giving it as much as I allowed because, if I was being honest, it scared me.

As I sucked in a breath, it swallowed me whole, and I felt myself falling through the darkness. Panic coursed through me, my heart racing as I tried to steady my thoughts on Valyner.

Yet that was the thing. I'd never been there.

I didn't know what it looked like.

Taking shallow breaths, I closed my eyes, picturing Ezekiel, my heart slowing a bit.

I could see his eyes, smell his scent, and hear his voice. And peace washed over me. A focus that was wholly consumed by him.

A shift in the gap pulled me down faster, and pain slowly invaded my hands and feet, forcing me to open my eyes.

I gritted my teeth, and the pain grew as the darkness faded around me.

My feet slammed into stone, and I fell, rolling across the ground.

Did I do it?

As I pushed myself up, I cried out, every bone feeling as if it was grinding together. Every nerve was on fire, searing from both ends, and it was only growing stronger.

"How thoughtful of you…" A female voice sounded from behind me, causing me to turn. "To come to me for your death rather than forcing me to hunt you down."

A woman sat on a step in the large room we were in, with a large copper throne behind her. In her hand was an obsidian dagger, dripping with blood onto the floor in front of her dark purple gown.

And I knew that smell… It was his blood.

My eyes widened.

Persephone.

"Good, it seems like you already know who I am." Standing, she approached slowly. Long black strands swayed slightly, shining from the light spilling in from the surrounding windows. She moved as if she were royalty. Looked the part too. She was beautiful…and yet, it made her all the viler.

Pushing myself up, my entire body protested the movement. "Where is he?" I choked out.

Her purple eyes beamed brighter, narrowing as though she were amused.

"That is none of your concern now, is it? He isn't yours." She gestured to me with her long nails, painted the same color as those eyes.

"Where. Is. He?"

She paused, looking me over, her face void of all emotion. "He is mine. He has agreed to bond himself to me and is preparing as we speak."

I laughed through the pain growing within, holding back the tears that wanted to fall. "He will never be yours..."

"Not while you live. Or that little abomination in your womb."

Her power shot out, a ball of purple mist slamming into my chest. Falling to the ground, my head slammed into the grey stone, my vision blurry as I tried to sit back up.

"You seemed to have more fight in the Mortal Realm when I watched you. Why are you holding back now?" she asked, throwing her power out at me again and tossing me further across the room. "Is your life or your child's not worth fighting for?"

Coughing, I felt the warmth of my blood pour from my mouth.

Something wasn't right. Everything felt off.

It felt as if I was dying slowly...

"The Cursed can't be here. And while I know there is something different about you, you are still one of them, aren't you?"

My lip trembled.

I could get here unlike the Cursed, but I was still one of them. I was still bound to the same fate as them. Even though it was different.

Elias was right. *Fuck, what do I do?*

The visions of the last few weeks filtered in from my dreams. Seeing our daughter fight Persephone. Although, if I killed her right now, then my child wouldn't have to do it alone. I could stop Persephone from taking the throne, killing me, Ezekiel, and all the Embers.

And we could raise our child. She would know exactly who she was. What she contained. She could grow up with her people. We could fix all this together as a family. The Cursed. Stop the gods and their games. And my father would never get to use her to raise his brother.

This fate had to exist for us, even though I hadn't seen it, right? It had to. I could change it right here. Right now.

Couldn't I?

Get up.

GET UP!

"Tell me, Nyna... What is it about you that calls to him?"

I laughed through the pain, pushing myself up. I held back the tears as every fiber of my being was shredding to pieces.

"You really want to know, Persephone?" I took a shaky step forward. "I'm not you."

Her face turned hard, her anger showering over her entire body. I tried to pull for my power, but it was fading with each breath. And panic set in.

Purple mist flowed out of her hands, slithering through the air and wrapping around my arms, legs, and throat. I choked as it tightened, my body unable to move an inch.

"Ezekiel..." I called out through our bond.

"I am going to enjoy this." She flipped the blade in her hand, moving in.

Pausing in front of me, she pressed the dagger against my cheek. I hissed as it sliced my flesh open, and the smell of iron grew. Pulling it back, I watched as she took in the crimson, before glancing down at my stomach.

"Let's start with that first."

Everything within me was screaming. The curse in my veins. The fear of not feeling Ezekiel. For the life we created. And I couldn't do a damn thing to stop it.

Unless...

If I pushed into that power...the power my father locked away.

I focused on it, banging on the door it was locked behind and begging it to come out. And then I heard his voice—my father's voice—from deep within.

"If you don't control the power in your veins and keep it from fully emerging, I will have no choice but to kill you myself after you birth the child."

"But she cannot take your power or your child's if you die like a fae."

His words haunted me, stopping me from pushing forward.

My gaze focused on her hand pulling back, and I closed my eyes, finally letting the tears fall.

What if that was true? When you were born for no other purpose but to die, what other choice was there?

Persephone let out a cry, and my eyes shot open, seeing Ezekiel behind her.

His skin was pale, sweat beading against his brow, but it did little to stop the fury radiating off him.

Blood pooled from Persephone's mouth, and her stare became blank, lost in shock.

Her power fell from me, and I dropped to the ground, my whole body sinking deeper into the agony of the curse.

More blood poured from Persephone onto the ground, her screams of anger and pain echoing around us. Ezekiel stood over her, an obsidian dagger in his hand, and I knew he wanted to finish her.

I wanted that too.

As he moved in towards her, I closed my eyes and let out a shuddered breath.

It was almost done.

This was all going to be done. And we would make it all right.

My heartbeat slowed, and then I noticed it.

Our child's heart was also slowing down.

No.

Panic took over, and my breathing became shallower. My vision tunneled, the edges turning dark. But I couldn't mistake the warmth of the thick liquid trailing down my face.

Did I cough?

Was I dying? Was she?

"Nyna!"

It was his voice...right?

I didn't know as everything vanished and I fell into a dream that was just as horrific as reality.

Where I had to accept that my father was right. I wouldn't raise my daughter because fate had already written the ending to my story.

CHAPTER TWENTY-FIVE

NYNA

A month later in the Mortal Realm
Or one day in Valyner

I could see her so clearly.

How her wide silver eyes took in the darkness shattering before her, letting in white light that illuminated every feature.

She was beautiful. I wanted to walk up to her, and at the same time, I wanted to just watch. To just take in every detail of who she was.

Everything blurred before I saw her with an obsidian dagger in her hand, containing her father's stone in the hilt.

"Goodbye, Persephone," *she said, plunging it into her heart.*

I turned, looking over the Cursed in the woods. They were all stuck in place, their eyes hard until something shifted. The air lightened, and I felt it.

The curse lifted.

My daughter was going to break it.

Not Ezekiel.

But her.

She hugged a girl with red hair, and I laughed... was that Elias' *daughter? She looked so much like him, their eyes and hair almost identical.*

I watched my daughter...Davyna. I couldn't take my eyes off her and the man watching her.

He looked like Osiris, and I could feel what they had. Matching what I had with Ezekiel.

She had a mate.

Tears sprang to my eyes, and the vision shifted, pulling me further into the future, seeing the throne burning, her fighting with the power in her veins.

The power of the gods and the curse from my uncle.

It was real.

She was surrounded by people who loved her, but she was so alone in her battle.

Angry.

Turning, my daughter faced me, and I froze, my breath vanishing. That look was crushing me because I knew how it felt to look at a parent that way...

Unable to forgive what they did.

And she said...

"This isn't living...and a mother would see that."

Jumping up, I tried to catch my breath, but it refused me.

I looked around the cabin I grew up in, in Eldros. It was worn down now, dust coating everything, and I'd left it that way when we got here a few nights ago.

It had been a little over a month since I had gone to Valyner. Ezekiel had gotten us out and back to Elias' cabin. We were both weak, in and out for days, and in bed for almost two weeks. I didn't know the extent of his injury, but it had missed his heart by a few inches, only adding to my anger that she almost took him from me.

He wasn't able to break the curse again, but after all the visions I had, it made sense.

The effects of Valyner simply took time to fade for me. It made me question why I was affected like that, with what I was.

My only explanation was that I was cursed. Cursed to not be who I was. Cursed that if I let it out, my father would come and kill me without a second thought. Like he did to my mother.

I was my own type of *Cursed*, connected to another by blood and a fate so cruel that if a devil existed, it would make even him shudder.

Osiris had been back and forth a lot lately, reporting on Persephone's movements.

She was cloaked, and no one could find her.

Hera, the woman Elias had married a few weeks ago, had moved in, and we in turn moved away from the area to protect his child and his new role in society as a lord of the mortal king's court.

Two months into this pregnancy, and I still didn't know what to do. We were moving from place to place and using our power to put protection spells over us. Yet it had been utterly quiet. Eerie. Like all the problems we faced had just vanished from existence. And I knew that couldn't be true.

They were just beginning.

The worst part was...I still hadn't told Ezekiel what I knew, or what I was. He had asked me multiple times, and each ended with me unable to speak, my throat burning at the attempt.

My father said I could tell him. That we needed to complete our bond, and when I asked Ezekiel what it meant to be bonded, he said we were and that was that.

I knew there was more, but he was hesitant to tell me the rest. I could sense it.

Both secrets were creating this storm between us. And I couldn't take much more of it.

Nausea rose at the thought of the dreams. I hadn't gone a night without them now, seeing the future play repeatedly. So many paths, so many with her dying...except one. And regardless of the path, I couldn't be with her.

Tears flooded my eyes and streamed down my cheeks. Taking a

few minutes to collect myself, I then moved through the dusty cabin, making my way outside. It was early morning, the sun just cresting the horizon in the distance.

"Hey, are you hungry?" Ezekiel asked as he walked towards me, holding up a few items from the market in town.

I nodded, forcing a smile as he made his way over to me. Bending down, he kissed my stomach before rising to capture my lips. We stood like that for a long moment, a grin gracing his face as he pulled away. Although I saw it in his eyes, he wanted to push for answers. He could feel my emotions, and there was no hiding what I was feeling lately. But he resisted.

"Osiris will be here soon with more information. I'll go get this made for you."

He walked into the cabin, and I ran my hand over my neck, still slick with sweat from the dream.

This past vision made me feel nothing but sorrow.

I couldn't put her through this... I couldn't put my child through this.

Bile rose into my throat, the thought taking on a life of its own. That maybe we were all better off if we didn't make it out of this.

If she didn't take her first breath, none of this would happen to her. And I wouldn't have to do what my father did to me. Lie and take away what made her...*her*.

I didn't want him to win. He couldn't win.

Returning to the cabin, I made my way down the hall. I glanced back at Ezekiel in the kitchen, using his fire to heat the hearth before grabbing the food. I un-spelled the door that was hidden from him and walked in.

My eyes landed on the books I'd found in my father's cave, filled with spells and what they did. Some for protection, binding, joining, and more.

Numbness washed over me as I looked over at the shadowquartz dagger.

Could I do it? Could I truly do it?

I didn't care about my life, but hers...

I strolled over to it, picked it up, and inspected the blade.

My lip quivered, and I swallowed hard.

She kicked my stomach, and it broke me from my trance, my breathing growing heavy. Looking down, I cried, throwing the knife down and backing away.

And in that moment, I knew...

It wasn't an option.

Not even something I could bear in death. So how could I help her, encourage her not to aid my father in his freedom? To guide her towards the truth of what and who she was, and break free of this cursed family?

Remember who the true enemy is.

Akari's words that Orla brought to me... They were about my father. About a god.

I wanted revenge more than anything right now. For the life I lived. For the sister I never met. For the mother he killed. For using my child to free himself. But maybe there was a different way to get it. One that he wouldn't see coming.

What if I could help her...in death?

"Nyna!" Ezekiel yelled for me, and I left the room, making my way back down the hall.

Osiris was standing in the living room, his hands behind his back, but he was bleeding from his arm.

"Are you okay?"

"I'll be fine. It was just a good fight." He smirked.

"What happened?"

Ezekiel walked over, his eyes hard.

"Persephone happened. Again. She had Crystals attack my Court." Osiris walked over to the couch and sat down, looking up at his king. "I went to talk with Katarina. She overheard Persephone talking to Keres in the Crescent Estate library. And she gave Keres a journal to hide. She found it when he was out of the house and read it. She wrote a lot about the two of you. The gods. And a prophecy. But you never know with Persephone; she could have made it up herself. She could have been saying those things to further her own agenda."

"Do you think it was a lie?" I asked.

Osiris took a deep breath, his eyes cast down for a moment before meeting my gaze again. "As much as I want to say it's a lie... Something tells me we shouldn't ignore it."

And that was good enough for me. He was Ezekiel's general and had known Persephone for just as long as his King.

"What was the prophecy?" I asked, thinking about the one my father told me about my daughter.

"The child born to light and darkness will fail them. It will fall on the lost child to restore the rightful power to whom it belongs to. For if not, the one who holds light and darkness will rain fire and turn the Realms to ash."

I had seen a man in my vision with red hair, and heard him speak of this prophecy to our daughter. I then learned that he was Persephone's son. Did she fabricate this? Did the gods give her that to talk about her own son? This man was close to Davyna for a time, but then distant, angry. He had wanted her dead from the start, but he didn't succeed. I watched him die. So it couldn't be about him...

And then it hit me.

Did that mean she was going to burn Valyner down? Or was someone else going to?

I couldn't see that far into the one vision she lived through. It was like I got to where she was about to fight Obsidian and then... nothing.

"You are showing," Osiris said.

I cleared my throat. "Yeah..."

"We think it's because of me being fae. She is growing like one," Ezekiel added, but I heard him enter my mind.

"What's wrong?"

I shook my head.

It was more than that...but I couldn't speak it even if I wanted to.

"What else did Katarina say?" Ezekiel asked, breaking the silence.

"She believes that the Ember Court is going to fall. And she heard some soldiers in the Crescent Lands talk about hunting down Elias. Which means she is going to go after Akari, too."

Ezekiel ran his hands through his hair. "Fuck... She is going to kill us all, isn't she? Why haven't our men been able to get to her?"

"She had the Crystal Court put up so many barriers, there is no way to get through them," Osiris growled, and I could tell he was angry at himself that he couldn't do this for his King.

With each word falling from their mouths, I remembered things from the dreams. Osiris wasn't there...like us. My heart became heavy, the pain of loss for his son and Ezekiel settling in my bones.

Shaking my head, I tried to focus. Most times, Persephone killed us all, but there was one option...one where Akari, Elias, and our daughters lived. Even Osiris' son.

And the Embers... That was until Obsidian came.

I needed to think about what I could control right now.

Ezekiel had his soldiers out here protecting the Cursed, defending me, and our daughter. They didn't deserve to die. And she would need them. She would need a connection to her father's Court.

"I can help the Embers," I said, making them both look at me.

Leaving the room, I heard them both follow behind. Before they entered, I swung the door open, sheathing my shadowquartz dagger and waving my hand over my father's grimoires. I called out to the spell like the one he made with the cave.

"Nyna!" Ezekiel called out, but I ignored him.

"Osiris, is there a place in Valyner that is hidden, a place that could house a Court if needed?"

He looked at his King, keeping his mouth shut until Ezekiel nodded.

"It's a tunnel system underground that only me, Ezekiel, and my son use. It's between the Ember and Fallen Courts."

I flicked my wrist, watching the book flip open, the pages turning on their own until it showed me the spell I wanted.

"You need to close the entries. Seal them off completely. We don't have much time."

"Nyna...I don't want you using that much power...what if..." Ezekiel grabbed my arm, turning me to face him.

"She'll need them, Ezekiel. Our daughter will need her Court."

He stopped, his eyes widening.

And I realized I could tell him it was a girl.

Osiris stepped in and looked right at me, breaking my gaze with Ezekiel.

"What do you need from me?" he asked.

"I need both of your blood. The spell will be linked to Ezekiel's life, but if he falls, then it will fall on you and your bloodline. As... extra protection." I cleared my throat, averting my gaze down. "The spell will only stand for as long as your bloodline lives."

Osiris pulled the dagger back out and cut his palm, his eyes turning a deep red, and I grabbed a bowl, collecting it. I turned to Ezekiel, and his eyes narrowed on me.

He knew I knew something more.

After a minute passed, he took the blade from Osiris, cut his palm, and moved closer to him, letting it fall into the bowl.

"What is going on, Ruin?" he whispered. "What are you not telling me?"

I went to speak and again, was denied by the fucking blood oath. Rage grew, and I placed the bowl down, trying to breathe in and out.

"Osiris, I need you to go straight there. I am going to start the spell in a few minutes."

He nodded and began walking to the door. Ezekiel grabbed my arm, pulling me in.

"What is going on?"

Our bond circled us, and relief washed over me, but as I went to speak, the blood oath worked through my veins. And a chill ran down my spine.

You'll have to complete the bond first.

My father's words surfaced.

"I am trying to save your people. Like I promised. Let me." Pulling myself free, I ran to the door and called out to Osiris before he fell into the gap.

"What is it?" he asked.

"Can you do that privacy thing for a minute..." I asked, and he furrowed his brow before waving his hand over us.

"What's wrong?" he asked.

"How do fae bond?"

He was taken aback and glanced at the house. "It's a ceremony we call the mating bond ceremony. Both cut their palms and say the old words... It joins you as one."

I stepped back, my jaw falling open.

That's what we needed to do—become one.

"But doing it with anyone other than a fae... It's never been done. And since you are Cursed..."

"Thank you." I walked away, but I stalled, biting my lip. "Osiris..."

I turned, and he stood at attention.

"What is your son's name?" I asked.

He smirked. "Kadeyan."

I thought back to the dreams and seeing her with him. "They are going to be...*close*...."

He stepped in, tilting his head, and I could tell he was reading between the lines. "Are you saying... How do you know?"

"I'm not one of the Cursed. I never was."

And it was the truth. No blood oath could even deny me saying so.

His jaw fell open slightly, as if he wanted to ask for more.

He moved in, his eyes narrowed. "What are you, Nyna?"

I swallowed hard, and he just looked at me, waiting, trying to decipher the silence I was giving him.

My throat tightened, my veins burning.

Osiris went still, his expression shifting. "You were never one of the Cursed..." he repeated, realization dawning on him. He gave me a soft smile and reached out, taking my hand.

"Then you shouldn't worry. She will always be protected."

He stepped back, and my heart felt lighter.

She would have someone.

Like I had her father.

Making my way inside, I waited a few minutes before starting the spell. I stood over the table with the bowl of blood, giving it all I had.

Ezekiel paced the entire time, watching intently, waiting for any sign of harm to stop me. Yet, I was fine, more than fine. The power in my veins answered my call and cracked the door within where my goddess power lie. It felt right. Utterly beautiful and strong, although I could feel it wanting to open more and had to steady myself within my mind to push back on it.

I couldn't let it out. Not if I wanted to help her... I needed to wait.

Heat filled my veins, but it wasn't my magic. It was like a small ember, growing into its own blaze, that aided me. Keeping me in control and allowing me to complete the spell.

Was my daughter helping me? Was that her power?

After I finished, I looked down at my hands, glowing a dull white, and stepped back.

Turning to Ezekiel, I took a deep breath as he felt it wash over him: the link to where the tunnels were.

"It will be hell for them... Trapped and hiding to survive," he said.

"Then that should be its name. Hell." I moved closer to him and cleared my throat. "I want to tell you everything, but we need to do something first..."

It was the only way.

He arched a brow. "What?"

"We need to do the bonding ceremony. Now."

CHAPTER TWENTY-SIX

EZEKIEL

"Are you out of your mind?" I shouted, stepping back from her.

Pain passed across her face.

"Fuck, I didn't mean it like that. But fae only bond to fae...we don't even know what would happen to you."

"Ezekiel. We need to do this. It's the only way I can tell you about..." She trailed off, running her fingers through her hair.

"What did your father do to you?" I asked, and she didn't answer.

I've wanted these answers since I was strong enough to sit up in bed after Persephone stabbed me. Since she was healed and our child was okay. But I was done waiting. I needed to know.

"I will kill him," I growled.

"Get in line. But he is long gone," she bit out, her eyes hard.

"I can't put you at risk..." I said.

She moved in, grabbing my hand and pulling me towards the door.

"Where are you taking me?"

"I am going to show you some"—We fell into darkness for a moment, and I deepened my hold on her hand as we dropped outside a cave—"thing," she finished, just as stunned as me.

That wasn't my power.

"How did you do that?"

"It wasn't me..." She glanced down at her stomach, her mouth open in shock.

Did our child just... Was her power mixing with Nyna?

She shook her head and walked through the opening of the cave. "Come on... My father said this place is spelled, and only our bloodline can allow people in."

As we made it to the large circular room inside, she dropped my hand. I took in the ruby cave, the symbols etched all over.

"What are those?" I asked.

"He didn't tell me, but I think they are..." Her mouth was open, the words refusing to fall out. Running her fingers through her hair, she turned.

"Fuck!" she yelled. "This is why we need to do this. He said I could tell you if we finished the bond."

"But what if..."

"Do you trust me?" she asked, her eyes glassed over.

That used to be a loaded question for me, but looking into those golden pools, I knew the answer.

"I do..."

"Do you love me?" she asked, stepping in, and my heart pounded.

She touched my face, and my eyes closed. My hand wrapped around her waist, pulling her closer.

"Is that even a question at this point? My heart bleeds for you, and only you."

I took a deep breath and swallowed hard before using my power to pull a blade into my hand. Slowly, I cut into my palm and met her gaze again.

"But answer this: Is this what you want? Do you want me?" I asked.

She smiled, standing on her tiptoes and kissing me softly. "Is that even a question?"

I smirked, taking her hand, and slowly dragging the blade across her palm.

"Then repeat after me, Ruin..." I joined our hands together, our blood mixing. "Until the seas dry up. Until the earth withers away."

She repeated, and I smiled. "I will be yours, and you mine."

The lines between us celebrated, swirling faster as they merged.

"Until the sun burns out and the stars die... until death and Beyond," she began to say along with me, and we both got lost in each other's eyes, the bond fully guiding us through the binding of our souls.

And maybe I was wrong all along. It didn't affect us on a level that was damaging to who we were or would become.

It completed us. It made us who we were always meant to be.

Our souls were made for another, to hold that part of us, to be our safe haven. And that's what she was. And I'd gladly give her all of me.

"You are mine...now and forevermore."

Power bloomed between us, taking both of our breaths away, and I reveled in how it felt. How it felt to have her be mine. And only mine.

Our lines of power weaved together, interlocking, and I noticed something deep within me became whole. It was magical, beyond this world. It was soul-altering, and maybe that's what a mating bond was always meant to do: alter one's soul to become something far greater than it ever could have been alone.

Pulling her in, she let out a cleansing breath, her smile still in place.

"Is that it?" she asked.

"Well, yes...but usually..." And I knew she felt it, how my body called to hers.

I took a step in.

"Hold on..." She pushed back, her cheeks hot.

I could sense her arousal, but she was fighting it.

As her eyes met mine, I saw the change in her face, her eyes holding a weight that shook me to my core. And against every fiber in my being, I stood completely still.

Waiting for something that I knew would change everything.

"I'm a goddess..."

I froze, my eyes staring through her for a moment before I focused.

"And I need to tell you what's going to happen to us...and what we need to do to save our daughter. To save Davyna."

Hours passed, and I made her run through it all multiple times. Every dream she had, everything her father said. And each time she said it, more anger flooded out, filling the cave we were in.

I was drowning in it.

"She is going to undo the curse?" I finally turned to face her.

"Yes..."

"And she will kill Persephone?" I asked, and she nodded.

"But that won't happen for some time. It was never something we could fix," she whispered, sniffling.

"And what of your father? Where is he? If we use that dagger and kill him—"

"Ezekiel..." She looked at me, her eyes red and puffy.

I shook my head. "Fucking gods... What if we stayed in this cave? What if we never left? Then we could raise her."

She shook her head. "Are you willing to let your brother, your sister, and everyone else die? To have our child live a life of hiding? Plus, you are just as bound as I am to this oath now. How are we to share this with her?"

After a few minutes, I ran my fingers through my hair, gripping the strands.

"You said she dies...she dies when Persephone stabs her. How does she come back?"

"It wouldn't show me. I've been trying to figure that out."

"Fuck, Nyna!" I shouted.

She got up and vanished into the gap, and I followed her, landing in the cabin.

"Nyna! Don't you dare walk away from me again!"

"Why, Ezekiel? You clearly can't handle the truth."

"No, I can... I just won't accept it! The truth and what will happen are two different things," I shouted, my heart racing in my chest.

We were not going to die. I wouldn't allow it.

"No, they are one... Everything I told you will come to fruition."

Heat flooded my body and I could feel it behind my eyes as I burrowed my gaze into her. After a moment I turned away, feeling the tears begging to fall.

I shook my head.

This couldn't be happening... This couldn't happen.

"I don't want this for Davyna, but it will happen. My father told me everything, Ezekiel."

"How the fuck is any of this possible?" I yelled, throwing a crystal vase across the room as I turned, taking in Nyna's gaze falling to the floor. "Why didn't you tell me sooner? Why didn't you tell me what you were?"

"I didn't know until recently... He told me the day I found out I was pregnant."

"So, you kept this from me for the last two months?" I bit my tongue, realizing she didn't have a choice, but it still hurt.

Hurt that she made the blood oath with her father. Hurt that for two months she carried this alone when I was asking over and over what was going on. And I thought she was just pulling away. But it wasn't that. She was bound by blood to a cruel god who she called Father.

I steadied my breathing and looked back at her, my heart cracking open for my mate.

"If what you are saying is true, then we have...."

We were quiet for a long moment before her eyes softened. "You have one more month with me...and maybe two more months with her."

It took me a minute to collect my thoughts, and the tears fell. Looking back at her, I saw her face stained with her own, and I felt any remaining anger fall away.

I just made her mine. She was mine. Every part of her. And I was hers...

But this was about our legacy. Our daughter.

Davyna.

What was I going to choose? Myself, my mate, or my daughter? And as much as it broke my heart beyond repair. I knew the answer. Because I finally knew what it took to be a good father.

A good father would do anything for their child. They would move the stars in the sky to see them happy. Burn worlds to the ground if they were hurt... And they would give up everything, *everything,* to make sure they continued breathing.

And if it was the only thing I could give her in this life.

The only way I could be a *good* father.

Then I would...because I loved her.

I rushed over to Nyna, grabbing her face and pulling her close. "I love you so much, Nyna. I love you more than the air I breathe, more than life itself, and that will never cease to captivate my world... Even in death." My breathing was heavy, matching hers, and our gazes locked on one another. "So...what do we do next? How do we protect our baby girl?"

"I need time to study my father's books. She is going to need help. Protection. I don't want her to be used, Ezekiel. I don't want her to feel like she was abandoned in all this."

"She won't. She will have people in Valyner. Here in the Mortal Realm. And Kadeyan. He is a good man... I know he will help her."

She nodded, and I pulled her in, kissing her softly. A tear ran down her face, coating my lips, and I deepened the kiss.

"You don't have to do this alone. You are not alone," I whispered into her mind, and realized I needed to hear that too.

Pulling her jacket off her shoulders, I ran my hands down her bare arms, sparks flickering off my fingertips. She moaned, and I swallowed it down, causing everything in me to vibrate.

Pulling us into the gap, we landed on the bed, and I used the Crystal spell to remove both our clothes.

The desire and want pouring out of us matched each other's, the bond taking over and pushing every worry and fear out.

I leaned her over the bed, her back arching, and I growled in response. Lining my cock up with her entrance, I slowly thrust in, her moan echoing out into the small room.

I wanted to savor every noise, every touch, because we wouldn't have forever. We wouldn't have lifetimes. And it broke my heart. It shattered me beyond repair.

Yet, it also grounded me in a way. That this was the way life was. You never truly knew your time was coming, and in that, we could miss out on these moments because we were so focused on ourselves. When the truth of the matter was that we were always fleeting. We just knew when, now.

And I wouldn't take it for granted. Not for another second.

I let her find her pleasure, using me how she saw fit as I met her pace. Pushing her hips back onto me, she came undone, her face turned to the side to let me see.

I couldn't take my eyes off her.

Everything about her was perfect. The way her eyes closed, how her mouth parted slightly.

We both fell deeper into each other, our breaths growing heavier with each passing second as the pleasure built beyond our control. And we both fell over the edge, heat engulfing us. The warmth filled the room, extending through the cabin and beyond.

And I believed I'd finally found it. Found what my soul had craved for 1,500 years.

Home. I was finally home.

It was everything I needed; *we* needed. Piecing back parts of our hearts, knowing that we were not alone. And for the first time in my life, I didn't feel weak, because strength was found in this.

In us.

Pulling out of her, I slowly picked her up, laying her on the bed before crawling in with her. I waited for her heavy eyelids to open, our gazes locking, and I couldn't help but smile.

"You brought me back to life, Nyna...to die a man worthy of love."

CHAPTER TWENTY-SEVEN

EZEKIEL

Almost two weeks had passed since I learned everything, and the world felt as if it had stopped turning. Like we were waiting for something to erupt into chaos.

And I guess we were.

There were moments when I wondered if there was a way around all this. A way to make sure Nyna lived and that we could be a family.

It was a natural want, wasn't it?

I looked over at her, sleeping on her side, with a pillow under her stomach. The night was still blanketing us, the muted blues slowly shifting. A sign that, once again, the sun would come and obliterate the night.

Darkness could not live in the light.

And maybe fate deemed we were the darkness for Davyna. And the light she held needed to outshine it all.

Or fate was just one cruel bitch.

Maybe it was both.

Nyna's breathing picked up, her brows furrowing. Fuck, it was another dream. She had been having them a lot lately. Her mind was captivated by the paths before us, and I hated seeing her struggle with it.

I had used some spells to ease the effects of her stress lately, but with each spell, or using any line of power...it felt off.

Turning my stone within my hands, I looked down at it, taking in the ruby red. Osiris brought it back to me after I gave it to Axel during the fight. And I had been taking memories from my mind and storing them within, just in case. To protect not only Nyna... but our child as well.

She jumped up, her heartbeat matching our little one's within her womb.

I moved over, placing the stone back in my pocket, and dropped to my knees by the bed. "It's okay. You are okay..." I said, taking her hand.

I could feel her fear, and it was suffocating. Yet it wasn't for herself.

"The vision changed." She pushed herself up and walked out of the room, forcing me to follow.

She was frantic, grabbing the books her father left behind.

"What is it?" I asked, following close behind her.

"She died...she died when Persephone stabbed her." She dropped the books onto the table and grabbed the closest one.

"It's just one vision," I said, trying to ease her anxiety, but my heart was racing along with hers.

"Persephone doesn't get to win. Our daughter will not meet her end by her hand, too."

She paused, her head falling. "I won't be here to help her...and neither will you."

Her words slammed into my chest, and my heart stopped beating.

Anger slowly bloomed within, and I looked over the books as she flipped through them, searching for anything to change what was to come.

Picking one up, I moved into the small kitchen and flipped through it, the only sounds being our breaths and paper scratching together.

I felt like I was living in a trance, my world upside down. And I wanted to fight this. I wanted to fight all of this.

Turning to the next page, I stopped, looking over the spell to create a void. Taking in the words, I then studied the symbols curving and connecting to one another. And a chill ran down my spine. Something about it promised torture...darkness.

"I don't know what to do." She threw the book down, her lip quivering.

"What about this?" Her eyes met mine, and I slowly walked over, placing the book before her.

She read it over, her brows pulled down.

"That won't work."

"What if you use my power and my stone?"

She met my gaze.

"This would have to be tied to your death."

I spread my hands out wide before dropping them. "I'm dead either way."

"Yes, but there is still the problem of her power, if she is detected in any way...especially as a goddess."

"I know a spell for her fae side..." My throat closed.

The binding curse was one I had used freely on fae when I wanted them to die as humans. And the thought of having to use it on her... It sickened me.

"Are we really going to take away all her power? Make her human?" Nyna asked, her stare blank.

Neither of us wanted this for her.

"Is that how she survives?" My voice broke.

The silence was the answer.

"Do the spell on me. Make sure she can come back from death," I said, clearing my throat.

"What if there is another way?" she questioned, looking over the other books.

"Maybe this is the only way."

"Your soul won't pass on if I put it in this place. You will be alone. And if by some slim chance, she lives her whole life without opening her power, you will be in there until she dies as a human," she explained, and I slowly nodded.

"Which means I won't be able to find you in the next life." I filled in the blanks of what she was saying.

Moving over to her, I pulled her in, our lips crashing together. After a minute, I pulled back, my lips brushing hers once more. "Then I will find you when the day comes."

I picked up the shadowquartz dagger from the table and placed it in her hand before pulling my stone out of my pocket and placing it on top. "Do it."

"What if I do this wrong? This is a spell for gods...and if I use too much of that power..."

"Look at me." I gripped her jaw, forcing her gaze on me, and only me. "You can do this."

I stepped back, waiting as she weighed the options, faced with her fears. And then I saw it––her determination that had been captivating me since I met her. She used her power to move the gold on the hilt, my stone spinning through the air. It fell in, the metal hugging close.

She looked down at her stomach. "Help me with this one, little one." Rolling her shoulders back, she directed me over to the chair.

"I need you to take off your shirt," she said, her voice shaking. And I slowly did as I was asked.

I leaned over the back of the chair, gripping the wood hard enough to snap it.

She looked over the book again, her body tense as she tried to figure out how to adjust the spell.

"My blood is mixed with hers...so as I carve the symbols into your back, she will be connected to you through the stone. And her power as a goddess that's flowing through her veins right now will block the dark obsidian on that day. And when you..." She couldn't say it, and my eyes shut. "The void will hold your soul and enough of our power. From your line and mine to send her back."

"What type of magic is this?" I asked. And she turned, looking at me, shaking her head.

"It feels dark. Something that is used to torture a soul. I do not know what you'll feel there."

"Well, I've had some experience with being a tortured soul. How bad could it be?" I joked, but it did little to lighten the tension.

She moved behind me, and her hand slowly ran down my back as she chanted. I looked over my shoulder, watching her cut her palm before feeling the warm crimson paint my flesh.

The tip of the blade touched my skin, and I could feel her shaking. I reached back, stopping her, and met her gaze.

Pulling her to me, I kissed her deeply, savoring the taste of her like it was the first time.

Leaning down, I placed my hand on her stomach.

My lip quivered, and I thought about her...and only her.

"This world will see you fall, Dy...but you will rise above them all. You will lead, not because it is in your blood, but because you will fight for what is right. You will be just like your mother. And I can only hope you get the best parts of me... You will be a Queen who shakes this world. That molds it into something beautiful. And I will be with you...we both will, wherever we are. You will not be alone." I met Nyna's eyes before wiping a lone tear away.

Turning back around, I let out a harsh breath and rolled my shoulders back.

"Do it."

She carved into me, and I gritted my teeth, a cry working its way up my throat.

I held it down, letting her go through each marking, each slice. And I focused on one thing.

My child.

My heir.

After a few minutes passed, she stepped back, her cries mixing with the spell. And then everything burned, and I couldn't hold back the yells. It was blinding pain, making my vision go black, and I realized I was seeing it.

The void.

The utter darkness that beckoned me, taunted me with where I was going.

As fast as it was there, it was gone, and the cabin came back into view, my breathing rapid as I noticed I'd snapped the wood on the back of the chair.

Turning to Nyna, she threw the blade onto the table, her sobs heavy. I pulled her in, holding her, letting her face the reality of the choices we were making.

Pulling back, she looked into my eyes. "I'm sorry... I'm so sorry..."

"I'm not," I said, tucking her black hair behind her rounded ear. "I have lived many lives, and this one will forever outweigh them all. Because I had you. I had you both."

CHAPTER TWENTY-EIGHT

NYNA

I rolled over, and Ezekiel let his arm fall open, inviting me to come closer. I did, and he pulled my leg over his.

It was early morning. And we had only gotten a few hours of sleep, spending the night lost in each other. Most nights for the last week were like this. And I wouldn't change anything about it.

"What if I leave her something––a journal?" I asked, looking up at him.

Slowly, he met my gaze. "Can you even say any of this to her?"

My head buried itself in his bare chest as I exhaled.

"I can't just leave her with nothing...so I'll try. I'll try to say as much as I can."

Looking up, I met his silver gaze.

Soft. Warm.

"Then do what you can."

"You know you won't be able to tell her about me... You are going to have to tell her this was your power...not mine." Sorrow tainted my voice.

"I know..." He slowly sat up, his eyes hardening. "I am going to kill your father all over again when he dies."

That pulled a chuckle from me because I was thinking the same thing.

I'd tried to use my power to locate him a few days ago, but it was gone...like he never existed once again. And I thought about what he'd said: Being where the sun doesn't touch him, where the world was lighter.

I had an idea of where it could be, but it wasn't worth chasing... Not when we had maybe a couple weeks left.

Getting up, I moved through the cabin and picked up a journal. It was empty, so I sent out a spell engraving the leather with my name. Looking up through the window, I saw a few soldiers standing on the lawn, looking at me.

"Ezekiel?" I asked as I turned, watching him walk out of the room, buttoning his slacks. He moved over to me and looked out the window, his eyes hardening.

He walked past me, and I took in the symbols on his back, seared into his flesh from the spell. I moved after him and stopped at the door.

"What are you doing here?" he asked them.

There were about fifteen of them, all dressed in deep crimson leathers with swords strapped to their backs.

They were Embers.

"We heard you were seen walking this way from town. We wanted to know if orders had changed. Are we to return to Valyner?"

"Why are you asking me that?" Ezekiel commanded.

"Because of this," the soldier with cherry-black hair said, handing him a letter.

Ezekiel opened it, reading it over, his face shifting into the cruel man I met a hundred years ago.

"Oh my gods..." one soldier said, looking up at me. Well, not me, my stomach. The rest followed, and I swallowed hard.

Another whispered, "Is that the weapon they are talking about?"

They weren't talking about me... They were talking about Davyna.

Could they feel her power from here? Of course they could.

They were fae.

Ezekiel tilted his head towards me before turning and grabbing the dark obsidian sword from the closest soldier. He cut the head off one before running it into the next.

One by one, they fell, with only a few trying to fight back. I set my power out, stepping onto the porch and holding them in place so they could not strike my mate until he took their lives.

Ezekiel moved back in, blood dripping from his face and chest. He burned the paper in his hand and walked into the cabin.

"We need to leave. Grab your things."

"Ezekiel, what did the note say?" I rushed in behind him.

"That I ordered them back to use the weapon I had on Valyner."

"Did it say anything about Davyna?" I asked, my stomach turning and causing her to kick.

"No... Persephone wants them to think I have something that will destroy our realm."

That was the thing though, Davyna could...

I had seen her power. It was something to behold, yes. But it was also something to be feared.

"All power is to be feared, Nyna," Ezekiel snapped, turning to face me, and I realized he'd heard my thoughts. "One of the Cursed. A fae. A god. We are all monstrous beings doing unspeakable acts. The only question is why we are doing them?"

I swallowed, looking at the blood on his chest again, and knew he was right. Because he just showed me the reason he slaughtered his men.

Why I helped.

"What do we need to do next?" he asked me, wiping his chest clean with a wet rag.

"I need a fae who is from another realm than Valyner to give me a ward to protect the stone and what we left inside it for her to see. Since her power as a goddess is from a royal bloodline, she will get inside. But no one else in Valyner will."

He nodded and walked over to the paper that was laid out on

the table. He grabbed the feather, dipped it into the onyx ink, and scribbled his note. His power made it break down, sending it to the only person I knew he trusted over there in Valyner.

He looked pained for a moment, like using his power was hurting him. He'd explained to me he felt like he was getting weaker...and I hadn't been able to figure out why.

Yet something told me Persephone had her hand in this.

I walked up behind him, placing my hands on his back.

"I'm sorry you had to do that," I whispered.

His pain was clear, but through the bond now, I could feel it.

He didn't want to kill his soldiers. Ones that had been loyal. And it was all to protect her.

Our secret to the fae of Valyner.

And I feared he would have to do it more before this was over.

We were the monsters, making monstrous choices in the hope of a better future.

"What if you are wrong?" he whispered, slowly turning to meet my gaze. "What if Persephone dies? And we live...with her?"

There were no visions of that happening, but did that mean that it couldn't happen? That somehow fate could be altered and turn in our favor?

And a glimmer of hope seeped in, begging me to let it stay.

And I wondered if it was possible. Could you change the course of fate to something they did not write?

We waited in the cabin, the silence deafening between us.

Faelynn and Osiris finally appeared in the room, and I let go of the breath that I was unknowingly holding.

"Faelynn, this is Nyna," Osiris said before she put her hand up.

She moved in, her black eyes taking me aback. It was such a contrast to her white hair and skin, which were almost the same shade.

"The Cursed Queen." She offered her hand, and I slowly laid mine in hers. "Your aura...is something to behold for sure."

"She is just *the Queen*, Faelynn," Ezekiel corrected her.

I looked over at Ezekiel, and then back to Faelynn. She nodded before facing me again.

"My apologies, Your Grace. How can I help you?"

I pulled my hand back and removed the stone from my jacket. Placing it in her hand, I cleared my throat. "Is there a ward from your realm that can protect this? And that would only allow our bloodline to access it?"

She tilted her head, running her fingers over it.

"Yes. There is something you could use from my home realm–– Anawyn... But we will need the blood of you both to coat the stone in."

We moved through the cabin, getting everything prepared for Faelynn to help us. She told me that channeling her would make it easier since it was from another fae realm, and I took the help because I was a little worried that if I did it alone, it could pull more of my own power out.

And I still needed to do one more thing with it...one thing that I had blocked in my mind from Ezekiel because I didn't have it in me to explain my plan for what was to come. It was going to hurt...but I needed to stay focused, in control.

Osiris stood guard by the door, his eyes scanning the woods beyond for anyone coming near. Ezekiel had given him orders to kill on sight, no matter who they were.

Our blood was in the bowl, and Faelynn dropped the stone inside, using her fingers to mix the crimson liquid. Picking it up, she smeared the blood over our foreheads before joining mine and Ezekiel's hands. And my heart only drummed harder by the second.

I couldn't stop thinking back to what Ezekiel had said about a different path. But even with that, I was bound to my father's oath. And so was he. How were we going to raise her––if that was even possible––or share who she truly was, unless she figured it out on her own?

I was setting her up for pain...and either way, I would end up with the same look she gave me in the vision: betrayal.

Faelynn placed her hand on my shoulder, and I went through the spell, lost in a trance as each word poured out. This would work...it had to. After reciting it a few more times, the magic in the air faded.

The spell was completed. And another secret slid into place.

No one stayed long after that, and we said our goodbyes. Ezekiel went onto the front porch to speak with Osiris, and I looked down at the journal on the small table and stalled. Picking it up, my anger grew towards the one being who deserved it.

If my soul had to pass on for her to have answers, then that's what I would do.

But just in case I couldn't pull off the spell when the time came, I'd give her everything in this godsdamn journal to help her kill the fuckers.

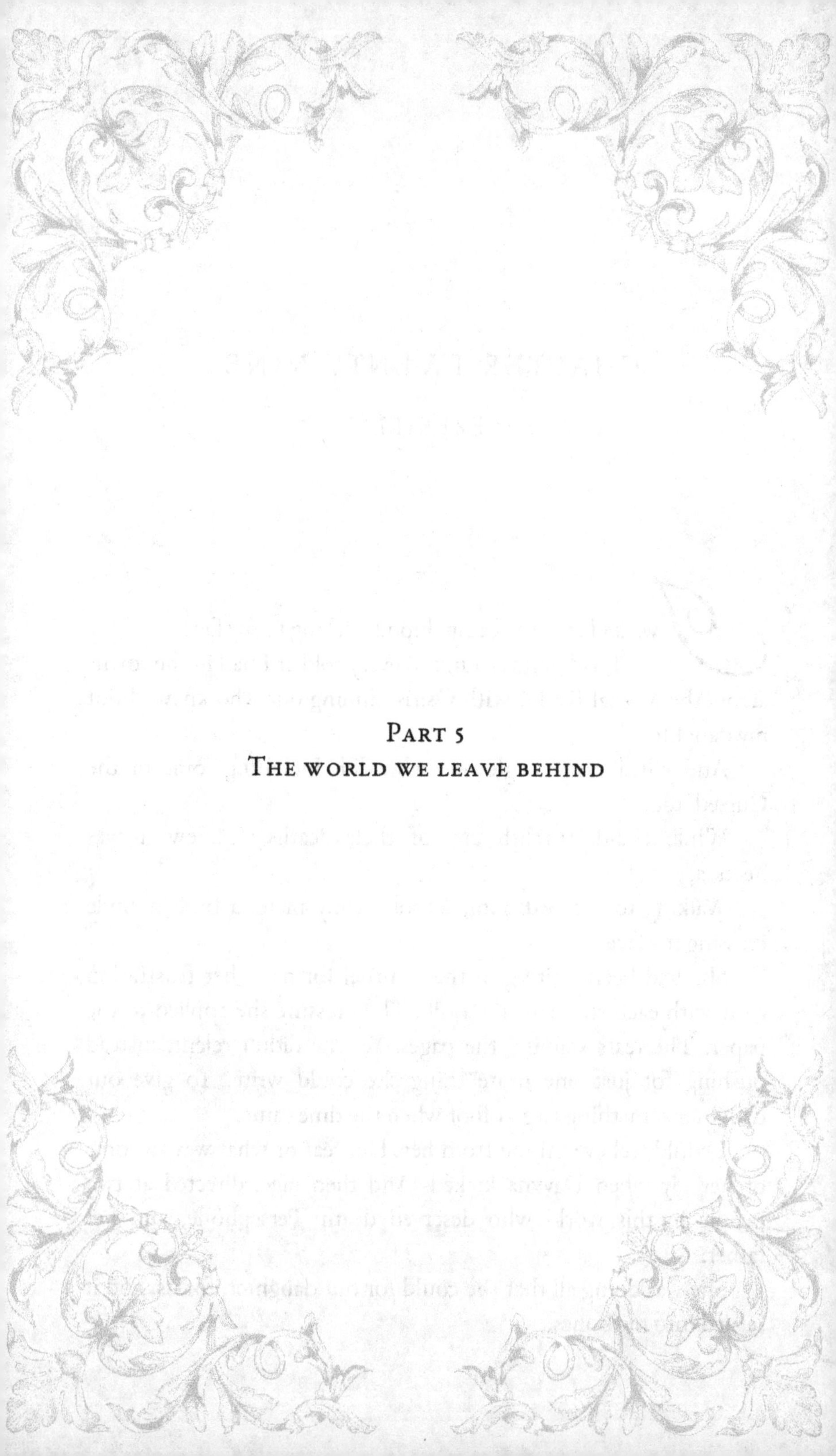

Part 5
The world we leave behind

CHAPTER TWENTY-NINE

EZEKIEL

I walked into the cabin, blood sticking to my face.

I had gone around to every soldier I had in the towns across the Mortal Realm with Osiris, finding out who knew about my daughter.

And killed every single one who did. Including some of the Cursed, too.

While I didn't relish any of their deaths, I knew it was necessary.

Walking to the bedroom, I took in my mate, a broken smile crossing my face.

She had been writing in that journal for days, her frustration clear with each stroke of the quill. The pressure she applied to the paper. The tears staining the pages. Yet she didn't relent, instead pushing for just one more thing she could write. To give our daughter something to go off of when the time came.

I could feel everything from her. Her fear of what was to come or her joy when Davyna kicked. And then rage, directed at two people in this world who deserved death: Persephone, and her father.

She was doing all that she could for our daughter, for us, and it settled into my bones.

It was always okay to care, to love...and now I felt those emotions more than I could even express.

And she had done that to me. They both had.

She folded a loose page in the journal, and I took in her expression, noticing something was different today. She was writing something else.

Wiping her eyes, she looked up. "Hey, I didn't hear you come in."

"Don't let me interrupt you." I smirked, feeling the love pour out of her.

She folded it up and placed it in the journal, her magic forcing it to vanish within the pages.

"Now, all we have to do is put it in the cave. She will be able to enter it."

"How will she know it's there? Or what if your father comes and takes it?" I asked her, and her eyes fell.

"He won't. I spelled it so that only she could find it, and she will..."

Then I felt it, her pushing something down.

"Come on, let's go." She got up slowly, and I moved over to help her.

"How much time do we..." I trailed off, waiting for her to meet my gaze.

"We will have forever. Hold on to that."

After a minute passed, I pulled us into the gap, and we appeared in the cave. She looked around before walking towards the back, where a solid stone wall lay. She placed her hand on it, and I watched as her power filtered out. It shifted the outer layers, exposing the inside. And slowly, the stone moved within, creating a shelf.

She brought her hand to her stomach, dropping her head. "I'm so sorry...you don't deserve this," she said to our daughter.

I placed my hand on her lower back before placing my other one over hers.

"She will be strong...just like you."

Slowly she placed the journal within, and whispered under her breath, closing the hole in the stone.

Turning, she faced me. "And like her father. But we both know that being called strong when you hold the weight of so much can make you feel more alone. I worry she will feel the need to stay strong for everyone and neglect herself...and the pain that will cause her..."

I paused. "I know... She doesn't deserve any of this."

Pulling her in, I kissed her forehead and slowly guided her out of the cave.

"Wouldn't it be better to keep the dagger in there with the journal?" I asked as we made it outside.

"I mean, yes...but I didn't see it there with the recent dreams. I think I am supposed to put it somewhere else. Or maybe someone else needs to find it first." She looked around.

"Well, let's figure that out tomorrow before—"

My fires flooded my veins, and I turned, watching wolves pounce towards us. My heart stalled in my chest, and I sent out the flames, devouring one of them before the other fell into the gap.

Adrenaline took over, and I turned to grab Nyna and get away from this area as fast as possible, but tendrils of black vapor wrapped around my arms, ripping me back.

Fallen fae.

I screamed, my fire pouring out of me as more fae appeared around us.

Crystals, more Fallen, and Crescents.

And they were all moving in towards her.

Pulling for the all the power in my veins, I wrapped my own shadows around the ones holding me and pulled the fae in. The power felt forced, weaker, but I demanded it come to me. My hand sank into the chest of one before my flames poured out in a wave, taking out the other three.

And the cruel beast I lived with for over 1,500 years came out, waging war.

War on anyone who dared to touch them.

My heart refused to beat as I ran towards her. Her eyes met mine as magic spiraled through the air towards her from the Crystals and Fallens. And all I felt was fear as the Crescent's growls pierced the dying day.

This couldn't happen. I couldn't lose her.

Her eyes hardened, and I felt it. The shift in her power, her hands rising with a furious glow...

A glow that could only be described as one thing.

A pillar of flames shot out, devouring all the fae coming towards her. The blaze whipped past me, forcing me to turn and see it taking out the fae who dropped in from the gap. It stole my breath away as I felt the power matching mine in ability, but more powerful.

That wasn't her power....

It was Davyna's. She was helping her mother.

I pushed through the blaze, grabbing onto her as the flames ceased from her fingertips.

Her breathing was heavy, and I looked her over. She was okay... they were both okay.

"Let's go."

I turned to leave and was met with the glinting point of a dagger. Pushing Nyna behind me, I sucked in a sharp breath as the metal slid into me.

"Hello, *Your Grace*," Marta said, twisting the blade in my stomach. Her power shot out, knocking us both back. My head bounced off the ground, my vision spotting black.

I needed to get up. I needed to get us out of here.

Rolling to my side, I pulled the blade out and slowly rose, seeing Nyna bleeding from her head.

Rage grew as I met Marta's gaze again. "I am going to rip you limb from limb!" I yelled.

She sent her power out, and obsidian chains locked around my wrists. My power faded, but I refused to stop. To stay down.

"The new Queen has a message for you," Marta explained, moving over to Nyna as her eyes fluttered open. She mumbled a spell... One I knew.

No.

I pushed myself up, shouting from the pain, and forced myself into a run.

"She said...how does it feel to lose?"

The light purple mist of Marta's spell slammed into her chest, and Nyna screamed out.

The death spell.

Just as I was about to reach her, Marta's power wrapped around my throat, holding me completely still.

No...

NO!

"Let's see if you can get to her in time to say goodbye," Marta teased before the gap took her and Nyna away.

CHAPTER THIRTY

NYNA

*P*ure agony worked its way through my veins, consuming every fiber of my being. And with it, my stomach began to cramp.

I was in the gap, and I knew I needed to get out.

Looking at the fae with iridescent white hair beside me, she kept her expression cold. "Sorry for my part. But it needed to be done," she said. "Don't worry, it will be over soon. Persephone is waiting."

No, she would kill Davyna.

And I still had the shadowquartz dagger. Persephone couldn't get her hands on it.

She couldn't get her hands on either.

I pulled for everything within, and flames shot out again, filling the darkness with their hues of destruction. The fae screamed, letting me go, and I fell away from her.

I sucked in a breath, focusing through the pain, and on the Mortal Realm.

My knees slammed into the dirt, my breathing rapid. The cool air caressed my face before another yell ripped from my lips.

Everything hurt...

Everything.

And it was mixing with the pain tightening my stomach.

I looked around at the mountains surrounding me and held back the tears.

This was it, wasn't it?

Pulling the dagger from my back, I began digging a hole, gritting my teeth with each inch into the soil. I had to stop multiple times, placing my hand on my stomach, the torture stealing my breath away before I forced myself to continue.

Once the hole was deep enough, I threw it in and pushed the dirt over the black and white metal, my fingers becoming coated.

Falling back on my ass, I let out a low hum, trying to bear the pain of the Crystal's power. I could feel its purpose, how it wanted to decay my insides, to freeze the power in my veins.

And my power was fighting it, shaking the door inside to open and remove the stain of her spell.

I could do it...I could save myself right now...

Another wave of pain ran over me, my stomach tightening with it, and I gripped at my blouse.

Shaking my head, I pushed myself up and began walking, screaming out for Ezekiel.

How far away was he? Was he okay?

I gripped every tree I passed, crying out as I tried to breathe through the next wave.

"Look what we have here, boys..." someone said, and I looked up through half-lidded eyes. "The whore of the King and her abomination."

My teeth ground together, my gaze darkened as I looked over the three Cursed.

"I don't want to kill you...but I will," I breathed out, causing them to laugh.

One moved closer, and I pushed myself up straight, every muscle shaking.

"Well, you see... The Queen of the fae has promised us freedom. Something you couldn't do." He rushed in the rest of the way, his fangs out.

He stopped before me, blood running out of his mouth as he

tried to cough. I kept my gaze on him as I took an unsteady step forward before flicking my hand.

His heart flew past me, the dead organ slamming against the ground, and I let out another cry of pain before doubling over.

The other two moved in, their voices growing as they began their spell. And I tried to straighten myself.

Even my power begged for me to let it free, to stop all of this.

Yet I couldn't...not if it meant she didn't live past five, ten... No, I needed her to live more than me.

Straightening, my vision spotted black, and I stumbled back as I looked at Osiris.

His shadows filtered into their bodies and turned them grey.

How did he know I was here?

And then I saw him...

Ezekiel stumbled forward, and my heart skipped a beat. A broken smile graced my face until I saw the blood staining his shirt.

He forced himself to move, and my lip quivered, the fear setting in. And I knew I wasn't ready for this.

Another wave of pain washed over me, causing my stomach to tighten again.

"The spell started my labor. She is coming." I gripped my stomach as he lifted me into his arms, ignoring his own pain. "I need to finish the spell... I need to."

Osiris moved in, using his power to pull us back to the cabin, and Ezekiel placed me down on the couch.

Another wave of pain came over me, and my screams grew.

"Grab the book," I yelled, my voice breaking.

Osiris moved over to the table. "Which book?"

"The red one..." I winced, curling over and groaning low.

"Please, Nyna... Tell me there is a way to stop this. Tell me there is a way to save you," Ezekiel begged. "I need more time with you."

Our eyes met, tears blurring my vision.

Osiris slowly stepped in, his head cast down. He placed the book on the small table before me, and I reached out, my power calling out to what I needed.

The book flew open, and I took a few deep breaths.

"Ezekiel..." Osiris called out, looking at the windows.

I could feel them––the Cursed. The fae...

They were here.

Ezekiel stood, muscles tense as the fire spun down his hand, creating a sword of flaming death.

"No one will harm our Queen, Your Grace," Osiris growled, his black shadows twisting around his body.

Sitting up, I pulled the book forward, located the spell, and began chanting, crying out as each word fell from my mouth.

"Go!" I yelled. "I need more time!"

Osiris took his order, walked through the front door, and I peered out, seeing at least a hundred men and women ready to fight.

Ezekiel was frozen in place, and I nodded to him, resuming the spell.

I pushed through each stabbing pain, feeling the door deep within where my power was locked behind open more. And anger took over.

I didn't want to do this to her...

Placing my hand on my stomach through the next contraction, I let out a guttural yell, shattering the surrounding windows. Glass rained down, pricking my skin, but I felt nothing compared to the battle of life and death within.

War cries filtered into the house, and I knew who they were from. The fire illuminated the night, his wrath traveling into the cabin and merging with my own.

Focusing on the last bit of the spell, tears fell from my eyes as I spoke the words, my hand gripping my stomach.

My daughter's power roared within, almost as if it was begging me not to do this. To not lock it away. Her power and the force of the spell brought me to my knees, and I gripped onto the small table in front of me, pushing it as I cried out.

I'm sorry... I'm so sorry, Davyna.

The goddess power within her vanished, falling away with each passing heartbeat, and I tried to catch my breath.

I took away her choice...like my father did to me.

Was I any better?

And I had to believe in this moment that I made the right choice. I did it not to deny her who she truly was, but to protect her in what was to come. My actions were not intended to deny her true self, but to shield her from the future long enough for her to have one.

I did it because I loved her. Not because I wanted to use her for something...I just *loved* her.

And loving someone that much meant you would do anything to make sure they lived.

I needed our daughter to live.

I went to push myself up but fell back down, the Crystal hex taking root and making me completely paralyzed.

"Ezekiel!" I choked out, my voice fading.

My eyes closed, the sounds of the raging battle still echoing around me.

He ran in, dropping to the ground, his face and jacket covered in blood.

"Get her out. Cut her out now..." I spoke through our bond, and my eyes slowly looked over the cabin, remembering this in all the visions.

This was the night I died... This was the end.

"No! You don't stop fighting! You can't leave me, Nyna!" he cried out, pulling my head into his lap.

But it was time.

The look on his face reminded me of when we first met. One that was angry and cruel. Yet it was now filled with layers that he probably never saw coming.

I could see his fight to protect. His fear of losing someone that he cared about. But most of all, love. Love that was untamed and unwavering.

And I loved the way he looked at me. It made me feel whole. Alive.

"Stop. Please..."

He was listening. Good. I wanted him to.

"Save our daughter, Ezekiel. She needs you now."

He leaned down, tears falling to my face, mixing with my own.

His lips touched mine, and I tried to kiss him back, but I was becoming numb, lost to the spell.

"Now..." I spoke into his mind, and he sobbed, forcing himself up to move over to the table to grab a dagger.

My eyes followed him, and only him, memorizing everything at that moment.

Tears filled my eyes, and I closed them for the briefest moment, before...

Pain erupted, causing me to suck in a sharp breath. It felt exactly like it did the last time I was stabbed. And I knew it was dark obsidian.

My eyes opened and looked up, seeing Keres standing over me before my eyes slowly shifted down to see the hilt of a blade sticking out of my chest.

And that dagger held a stone that was dark purple.

"Goodbye, Nyna," he whispered before ripping it back out.

Flames rushed out, passing over my body, but he was already gone.

Ezekiel hurried over, falling to the ground as I gasped for air.

It grazed my heart, working slowly through my system.

He dropped to his knees, and the world fell quiet, like nothing else mattered. Ezekiel looked over at me, unsure what to do, but he knew... It was just a matter of if he would.

My eyes closed, and my heart slowed from the toxic metal mixed with the spell.

I didn't feel the pain as he cut across my stomach, or when he pulled at my flesh.

No, it was all far away...fading fast.

Forcing my eyes open, I watched his lips move, screaming for someone, and I smiled.

If loving him always brought me to this moment... I'd never change a thing.

He slumped beside me, his arms cradling her.

Our baby...

I wanted to reach up, to touch her, but my body denied me.

"Nyna, please...please don't leave me!" he cried out in my mind.

My heartbeat slowed further, and I stopped trying to find air...

"I love you both so much..."

I focused on my heart, waiting for the final beat, and pulled for the spell I had memorized over the last few weeks.

I would be with her...even if it was only in this way.

I'll see you in your dreams, Dy...

As the final beat washed over me, I pulled for the last bit of power, shattering the door within and letting death take me to the unknown.

CHAPTER THIRTY-ONE

EZEKIEL

I couldn't move, couldn't breathe, because part of my heart was dead and gone.

And I didn't want to say goodbye to my better half...to her.

"Ezekiel," Osiris said from behind me, his steps slowing. "Oh my gods," he whispered, and my eyes pinched shut.

A small noise came from my arms, and I sucked in a breath, my eyes shooting open.

Dark brown hair adorned her head, a perfect balance between my light brown and her mother's black strands. She slowly opened her eyes, as if she were peeking at me, and it stole my breath away.

She had my eyes.

Her lip trembled, and I shook my head. "Osiris, get a blanket."

He ran into the other room, his boots crunching over the glass.

"Is everyone dead?" I asked.

He reemerged, handing me the blanket. I slowly wrapped it around her, holding her closer to my chest.

"Yes."

"Good..." My eyes landed on Nyna, her eyes shut, and if I didn't know better, I would have thought she was sleeping.

The numbness was pleading to take over, the severed bond screaming with such agony, and I just wanted to collapse into it all. Yet, I couldn't do that right now. I needed to get Davyna to safety.

Keres believed he had killed them both. And I needed to keep it that way.

I needed to keep her hidden.

Sniffling, I rose from the floor and called my stone to me, catching it as it appeared. I looked around and took in the books from her father, her body.

"What do you want to do?" Osiris asked softly, and it caused my stomach to turn.

The fire ignited in my hand, shooting out and devouring the books. Books that held great power. Power I would have killed for once. Power that my child could use one day, but at what cost? What was power, really? Just a false safety that could never protect you from what truly broke you...

And that was losing a part of your soul.

It was losing the person you loved.

"Ezekiel." Osiris moved in, grabbing my arm. "You don't want to do this."

"No, but it needs to look like I lost it over their death." My lip trembled. "And I am trying really hard right now not to lose it."

He offered his hands out, and I hesitated.

"I can take her outside while you do this. You are allowed to break right now..."

I shook my head.

"Ezekiel. Nyna told me she and Kadeyan were going to be close one day... I don't know how she knew. And I think I know what our Queen may have been." I closed my eyes as he continued. "But I don't need to know. Your daughter is part of my family, and I would die before I let anyone touch her."

Tears fell from my cheeks as I turned, slowly putting her in his arms.

He walked out, and it wasn't hard to find the rage, the pain... It consumed me the second Davyna was far enough away, bleeding out into an inferno that erupted from me.

Falling to my knees, I cried out, shaking the ground below me as the fire quickly devoured the cabin. Devoured *her*. I watched her skin blacken, her bones turning to ash from the heat.

I let it out. I let it all out.

Yet it did little to take the pain away. And I knew... I knew deep down this pain would last until I found her again.

My anger towards my father or the fae who betrayed me against the mortals was surpassed by it. It was deeper than my own insecurities and shortcomings. I had experienced nothing like it before her.

After a few minutes passed, I slowly brought my gaze up, looking at the forest beyond, taking in the destruction I'd created. And yet, it wasn't enough...

I wanted to burn every city, every realm, every fucking god out there who gave me this fate.

I wanted to find whoever deemed me worthy of her, only to rip her away...

I wanted them to feel what I was feeling right now.

Pushing down the grief, I picked myself up and moved outside.

Osiris placed Davyna in my arms, and I watched as she sucked on her hand before I met his gaze.

"I will tell you what I can, what Nyna told me to tell you. But you cannot tell Kadeyan until it's time...and you will know when that is. She made sure you would have another chance."

His brows furrowed, but nodded.

My stomach turned because both of our time was almost up, and Nyna had told me a few weeks back to tell him this because Kadeyan would need it.

My daughter's mate...would need it.

"My daughter is the future of Valyner. She will be the Queen one day, and she will struggle with her power. With a darkness that rivals all others around her. I cannot tell you the depths of her power, but Kadeyan will learn of it. They will need all the stones... Two endings lie before our children, and your son needs to help her pick the light. It isn't his place to stop what's coming. But he will need to protect her at all costs. Do you understand?"

He looked stunned, but quickly nodded, not questioning me. "Yes. You have my word."

I shook my head, glancing back, the pain blooming over me once again.

She did all this for Davyna...for me to step up and be the protector she needed, and I wouldn't fail her. Which meant we needed to see someone.

"I need to see my brother. Now."

We were at the cabin beyond the river, and I stood in a trance, staring at my daughter. I was afraid to move, to wake her, or scare her.

Did she sense my sins? Did she know how I'd failed to give her a future beyond this fate? Failed to keep her mother here with her?

Osiris walked in, with Elias right behind him. I slowly met his gaze, and I knew my eyes were bloodshot and puffy.

"Where is Nyna?" Elias asked, his shoulders falling an inch.

My eyes closed, my chest tightening.

He came closer, his emotions shifting, and understood what my silence meant. Sitting down by my side, he stared out at the fire before us.

"I would have been there to help... I would have done anything for you to not..." Elias said, his voice breaking.

"You were where you needed to be," I said, my voice hoarse.

Magic swirled before us, and my body tensed. Osiris and Elias stood, readying for a fight.

A letter appeared, floating down in front of us.

I refused to move, holding my daughter closer to my chest.

Elias leaned down, picked it up, and showed me the seal.

The Sky Court.

He opened it up, took a seat next to me, and read.

"Hello, brother,

"I was sitting here for the last hour, mourning the loss of someone I never met. But I could see her in my visions. She felt like a sister from the moment I saw her. She was the light in your life, Ezekiel. And now, you have a new one. One who needs you. Her father.

"I told you long ago that she would free them. That she would reign. And I know you finally see that to be true now. You have learned a great deal you can't speak of. Don't worry about her. I see more than I ever imagined now, and I will make sure she gets what she needs when it's time.

"But for now, you need to cover your tracks. And protect her in the way only you know how to. By fighting for your family.

"You will find peace in what's coming, I promise you, brother. And I'll wait for the day we meet again. And please tell Elias I'll see him soon.

"All my love,
"Akari."

Elias got up, throwing the letter into the fire. "Persephone doesn't know your daughter lived?"

"No. And we are going to make sure it stays that way."

I stood, channeling the throne's power, its line weak but still there, and poured everything I had into a cloaking spell over her.

"Osiris. I need you to get into Valyner. I need you to get as much dark obsidian here without a word getting out about it."

"Ezekiel... what are you planning?" Elias asked me.

"You once wanted to protect the humans of this realm, and I

cursed you for it. Now I am asking you to teach the humans about the Cursed and tell them the ways to kill them. They are going to decline rapidly without her help. You need the humans to fight them, or the fae will keep finding reasons to come." And that was the last thing I needed. I needed them to stay away from my daughter until she could protect herself.

"And make sure there is enough dark obsidian to burn all over this realm," I added.

"Dark obsidian doesn't affect us with the curse," he said.

"I know…but it will affect the fae. Fae that will come to hurt my child. And I won't have it."

I wanted to add that it would also dull hers as she grew here, until it was time for her to go home. But the blood oath from Zaryk refused me.

Elias moved in and nodded his head. "I will do whatever you ask." He looked down at Davyna, a grin raising his lips to the side. "May I hold my niece?"

And it brought a smile to my face, my eyes watering.

I slowly handed her over and watched him as he looked at her. A small tinge of jealousy hit me because he would have more time with her. And yet, I knew she would be in good hands.

Maybe better ones, even if I could change what was to come…

All I had to do was kill Persephone. And I could be there with her. Save the Embers from what Nyna saw coming.

Persephone was her threat until the gods came. I could help her…couldn't I?

Looking over at Osiris, I could see his eyes narrow, realization falling over him as he focused on the power in the room.

"Osiris, could we talk for a moment?" I walked outside, moving to the firepit Elias had put in.

"How is it even possible?" he asked. "How can a child hold that much power… It's from every Court."

I shushed him. "And that's why she needs protection."

"Are you sure about doing this?"

I knew he was talking about the dark obsidian because it would also affect my power if I was near it. But it was the only option.

Someone cleared their throat from behind us, and I turned, ready to send my fires out, when I realized who it was.

"Kadeyan..."

He stepped in, looking at the cabin, but quickly turned back to see us. And I was grateful his emotions didn't turn, which meant he couldn't sense her in there.

The spell worked.

"What is it?" Osiris stepped in.

"Persephone is taking the throne in two days. And is ordering the Lords and Ladies to be present. Along with the King. She wants you back in Valyner." He turned, saying the last bit to me.

I gritted my teeth.

"I heard she is gathering fae to come here to find you and bring you back..."

"Thanks for the heads up," I said, looking into his amber eyes.

"Is there something you want me to do? Maybe stir up something to delay the fae?" he asked.

Looking to Osiris, I nodded.

And then it hit me...

He took my mate...and I was going to take his.

Katarina would be okay, of course, with her daughter, Alta, but since Keres was close with the cunt, it would give us a distraction.

"Go raid the Crescent Court. Take Keres' mate and daughter. Do not harm them...but make it look like you are there to kill them. And then, Osiris, take them to Hell."

"Hell?" Kadeyan asked.

"Your father will explain, but go... Get it done. And then bring me what I asked for," I said to Osiris, and he nodded.

They both vanished, and I let out a shaky breath, my heart slamming against my ribs.

I promised I'd get her out, her daughter out, and I would keep my word.

Now all I hoped for was that this worked in delaying the fae.

I looked through the window, and saw Elias still holding Davyna.

It had to.

CHAPTER THIRTY-TWO

NYNA

One month later in the in-between and Mortal Realm
Or one day in Valyner

I couldn't say this was peace...but it was a version.

Watching Ezekiel with Davyna this past month had brought tears to my eyes.

She was growing so fast, like a true fae. Her little body created flames when she got frustrated. And she would use shadows to cover herself when the early morning sun was in her eyes.

I got to see her smile, laugh, along with Ezekiel. He was broken...yet she was holding him together.

I successfully completed the spell, and now my soul was trapped between the living and the dead. Which meant I could help her when the time came.

Ezekiel was currently kneeling, his arms outstretched to her. And she stumbled a little, falling to her butt before pushing herself back up, taking her first step. And the smile on his face was everything.

So much pride. And joy in the simple things.

He was so afraid to be a father, but seeing him with her... He was a good one.

I wondered if he could feel me next to him right now, touching his face.

I missed him...

My lip trembled, and my eyes fell.

He was still determined to change fate...to not lose her, too. And it broke me to see his pain.

If anyone had asked me in the beginning if I would cry over his pain, I would have laughed. Yet now, it was as easy as breathing. If that's what I was even doing in this place.

Leaning in, I kissed his cheek as his arms wrapped around Dy. Pulling back, he looked over, his eyes meeting mine before looking through to the trees beyond.

He had been working with Elias and Osiris for the last month. Dark obsidian was being ground down and distributed in all lamp oils, in fireplaces all over so that if the fae came, their powers would be weakened. The humans were learning about the Cursed, but they remained ignorant of the fae.

Fae had come looking for Ezekiel, but not as many. I had a feeling he set something in motion, and it brought a smile to my face.

Pulling back into the in-between, I looked over the darkness, the quiet stabbing into my ears.

Until I heard a laugh.

Turning, I looked around, knowing that sound.

"Hello, daughter? Did you think this would work?"

"How are you here?" I asked my father.

"I'm not. I'm still alive where I said I would be."

And I knew exactly where he was.

"I figured I could waste some of my power to talk to you one last time."

"Fuck you!" I yelled.

"Everything is coming to pass. You will not stop what's coming. She will do it."

My lip rose into a snarl.

"Maybe...but I will make sure she knows everything. And then she can decide for herself."

He laughed.

"Did you think dying was enough to release you from this oath with me?" He chuckled, and the sound sent glass into my nerves. "Until your soul passes on. And you didn't really do that... You opened your goddess power to hold your soul from true death," he sighed. "I figured you would try to find a way around your oath."

"And what if she figures it out? Learns about the gods and who you are?"

He went silent.

"She won't," he retorted after a minute.

"Are you sure about that? Because if she figures all of this out on her own, then I am bound by nothing to you," I seethed.

"You and your plots and schemes... I am not afraid of you, daughter. You have no power in this," he growled.

"It's because I had you as a father! And *my* daughter is not a pawn for you to use!"

"No... She isn't. She is just the key to freedom," he countered.

I swallowed hard, a lump forming in my throat as a tear rolled down my cheek.

"I am sorry... It was the only way for me. You know what it means to make that choice now."

"You son of a bitch!" Shaking, my anger grew. "I'm not you! I didn't use my family to get something for myself. I only did it to save her!"

"Well, if that was completely true, then you wouldn't care so much if I live or die."

I shut my mouth.

"Face it, you are your *father's* daughter."

His voice vanished, and I yelled out into the void, falling to my knees.

I didn't know how much time passed, or how long I cried, but eventually, I got up, pulling my soul back to the land of the living, and watched Davyna.

Regret washed over me...because he was right. I wanted him dead. But what I wanted more was to make sure Davyna didn't play into his game. And there, in truth, lay the answer he failed to realize.

When you truly love someone and would do anything for them...you hold an untouchable power.

I possessed it. So did Ezekiel. And I saw it in her in all those visions fate gave me.

That same untainted love that would destroy worlds. That would forge a new path. That would bring down anyone who dared take it away.

He was right... I was not the one he should fear.

It was her.

CHAPTER THIRTY-THREE

EZEKIEL

*One month later in the Mortal Realm
Or one day in Valyner*

"Daddy... Why are you sad?" Davyna asked, walking over to me, her silver eyes soft.

The light in her small face dimmed, mirroring my fear as the end neared. Could she feel that?

"Come here, Dy," I asked her, sniffling and forcing a smile.

She crawled into my lap, and I wrapped my hands around her, holding her against my chest. She pushed back her messy dark brown hair and met my gaze.

"Do you know how much I love you?" I asked her.

She shook her head, and I lifted her and walked over to the fireplace. Placing her down, I kneeled as she waited patiently.

I lifted her hands, turning them up so her palms faced the ceiling.

"More than the flames that sit upon the sun..."

Slowly, I pulled my hand back, bringing my flames to my fingertips, and she studied it. A smile grew as she focused on her own. Slowly, sparks filtered off her skin, embers floating up between us.

A small blaze ignited, and I could instantly see and feel her joy.

"More than every shadow that covers the night..."

She focused on her hands, and I watched the power change, and it took my breath away. Light grey shadows filtered up, the tendrils dancing as one.

"More than the deepest depths of the ocean..." I continued, and she met my gaze.

Water rose between us, creating a sphere.

"More than the most powerful spell ever cast..." Purple flared from her small fingers, and I held back the tears.

"More than every moon cycle, and the rest to come..." I grabbed her hands, and looked into her eyes, watching the silver shift into a red.

"And more than all the prophecies ever foretold about who you will become. My love for you has no limits...and it will live on forever."

"Is this how much you loved Mommy?" she asked, and I chuckled, nodding my head. "I love you too, Daddy. Just as much." She threw herself forward, wrapping her little arms around me, and I slowly wrapped my own around her.

"Hey! Look! It's snowing!" she called out. Her little voice was drenched in excitement, and she pulled back. "Can we go play in it?"

And how was I to say no?

I nodded my head and rose to my feet, noticing she was already pulling on her deep red jacket. Her little giggles filled the small cabin and it was infectious: her joy, forcing me to smile.

Walking to the door, I opened it, and she ran out to look up, lost in the beauty of something as simple as a snowflake.

I moved out, keeping my eyes on her, when I felt a chill run down my spine.

Turning, I took in the woods, my heart slowing.

"Daddy?" Dy said, her voice shaking.

As I turned, I took in the two fae standing in front of her.

Fuck...the fae were here. Which meant...

They were stunned, looking from her to me, before a vile smile rose on their faces.

No...if they left...Persephone would find out.

Rushing in, I stepped in front of my daughter. I summoned a sword into my hand, using all the power I had to bring the fae to the ground.

Yells filtered into the sky, and I turned.

"Dy, run!" I yelled, and she began moving back towards the cabin.

My wrath flooded every nerve, every bone, as I swung my sword, removing their heads, blood splattering back and coating my face and chest.

Crystals appeared, pushing through my power, and I sent out my flames, devouring them, my breathing uneven.

My link to the throne was growing weaker by the second... It had been for a while now, but it was worse, fading away like it was never mine to possess. And I needed it. I needed all the power for one last spell.

A powerful scream sounded off behind me, and I didn't think. I just ran.

Davyna was on the ground, pushing back through the light dusting of snow, her heartbeat wild with fear.

"Who's the kid?" the fae before her asked, smiling at me. "I'm sure the Queen would like to know you've been hiding something from her."

I guarded my daughter as the Fallen female sized me up. Raising her hands, her shadows poured out, slithering through the air with determination. And every flame within became charged with a ferocity that could only be described as catastrophic for anyone who dared touch my daughter.

Just as I was about to send the flames out, the female sucked in a breath, her eyes going wide. She glanced over her shoulder, seeing her Lord standing behind her.

He pushed harder, and the tip of a dark obsidian dagger pierced through the front of her chest. Her eyes quickly went flat, and Osiris pushed her body forward, letting it fall to the ground.

He moved in, his chest heaving.

"More are coming. The meeting is taking place now... What do you want to do?"

I turned around, picking up Dy, feeling her little body shake against mine, and realized I was shaking too.

"Ezekiel," Osiris called out.

"I know." Hesitantly, I turned to face him. "I know..." I said softer, my lip trembling.

Osiris moved closer, his chest rising and falling fast. I pulled him in, hugging him the best I could. He pulled back, and I took in my friend. His soft expression, his own fear.

"You have been my closest confidante. A loyal general. A friend I didn't know I needed. You became my family when I denied even the thought of one. It's been an honor to fight by your side, and to have you in my life, Osiris. And I can never thank you enough for it all."

He wrapped his hand around the back of my neck, bringing his forehead to mine. "The honor was all mine, my King. My friend. My brother..." He pulled back. "But this isn't the end of our story. We are going to make her pay."

I nodded, my heart shattering again, and I didn't think it could break any further. But it was.

"Go back... I need to make sure she is safe. Tell the cunt I will be there in a few minutes."

I watched him vanish before my eyes, and the air was ripped from my lungs.

Would that be the last time I saw life in his eyes?

I couldn't take any more grief, yet...I was destined for it all.

"Daddy?" Dy asked, pulling me back to meet her gaze.

"We are going to go see your uncle, and then how about we play a game of hide and seek? Does that sound like fun?" I asked her, and she hesitantly nodded.

Making my way into the cabin, I grabbed the small white chest.

One I had spelled shut a few days ago with the stone. I had crafted it into a necklace and put in inside, along with the letter I wrote her.

She would be the only one who could open it one day.

This was it...

I was doing this for Nyna.

I was doing this for our daughter.

The gap swallowed us up, and with it, the end of our time together.

Falling near my brother's estate, I paced back and forth near the tree line, staying in the shadows of night, waiting for him to sense me.

I knew he could...

After a few minutes, I saw him come to the window of his study and look out.

I walked across the lawn, making my way to the woods on the east side of the estate. The same place I tested Nyna's power.

Looking back, I could hear him running to catch up and noticed the bloody footprints I was leaving in the snow.

Dy waved her hand, and they vanished, looking as if no one had been there. My lip quivered as I finally made it to the spot and stopped.

Elias' heavy breathing filled the quiet woods as he met up with us, and I slowly turned.

"What is going on?" he asked.

I rocked back and forth, feeling Dy's body becoming limp in my arms, and took a deep breath.

"I need you..." I finally said.

"Anything." He took a step in, his eyes filling with worry.

"No... I need you to take her. Protect her. Raise her," I choked out, and his heartbeat quickened as the silence fell between us, the words of my plea sinking in.

"Ezekiel, what is going on?"

I shook my head. "Will you do it?" I asked, my voice breaking.

And without hesitation, he said, "Of course."

"They will come for her..." I finally said, the blood oath denying me to say anything more.

"I know," Elias said, touching my shoulder, his eyes holding sorrow that probably matched my own. "What about you?"

"I'm going to kill them all if it means she is safe."

It was partly the truth. I was going to kill as many as I could... but her being safe meant I was the one who was dead.

"Her magic will lead them here." He reached out, touching Dy's back softly, before meeting my gaze. "They could track me, too."

I nodded, leaning in and kissing my daughter on the forehead before doing the hardest thing in this life.

Hand her over to my brother.

A circle of fire rose around us, and I felt for the throne power, a sliver still there, and I knew this was it. I was going to use it all, and after it was gone, I would only be an Ember. And I knew this was the only way...

All paths lead to ruin...except one. And I would walk it a thousand times for her.

I chanted the binding curse, locking down his power, which in turn would protect his child, who was going to be born any day now. It would make them human...along with Davyna.

Their power faded fast, and I gritted my teeth, feeling the line to my extended power snapping apart, and pushed through.

As I chanted the last bit, I sucked in a breath, feeling my connection to the throne vanish, and with it, Davyna's and Elias' powers.

I focused on my brother's magic, my daughter's, and sensed the embers of them, sleeping deep within.

I did it.

"One day, when you see fit, tell her the story of the Cursed Queen and the fae King...and how they did everything to protect her."

His eyes were wide, still taking in the weight lifted from him, his freedom from the curse.

"I'm sorry, brother. You were my rock, and in my anger, I sent you here. You deserved more from me... Your own blood, and I failed you." I gripped Elias' shoulder as his eyes filled with tears. "But you are the only one I trust with my daughter. No one can ever know she still lives. They must believe she died within her mother."

Elias nodded. "I will protect her with my life, but please, come back when this war is over... She will need you, and she needs to be in Valyner. It's her home."

"She deserves someone like you to raise her. Someone who can show her kindness, joy, and love. Not me."

I turned and walked away, the fire falling and embers being left in its wake.

The ache grew stronger with the distance between me and them.

I pulled for the man I once was, letting it seep back into each fiber of my being. Because I needed to be with him one more time.

I needed to be the monster they all feared.

"Ezekiel! That man you speak of...is you. Never forget that," Elias called out to me, forcing me to turn back and meet his gaze. A tear fell as I took in my daughter's face one last time as she slept in his arms.

I swallowed hard, turning back and pushing my emotions down.

Red mist swirled around me, ashes spinning within as it blurred the world I had come to know as home.

This was it...

The day I proved to myself that my weakness was my greatest strength.

It was for her.

I closed my eyes and let the darkness take me to my fate.

CHAPTER THIRTY-FOUR

EZEKIEL

*L*anding in the throne room, I didn't wait to unleash my power. Flames surrounded me, covering every inch, and I unleashed them on anyone close. I walked through the fire, taking in their faces as I sent more out.

Screams rang out, filling the throne room. Ones of pain and others of fear.

Good.

I let every hurt fuel the flames until they became as hot as the sun. I wanted them to melt everything in their path. Every soul who sided with this bitch.

They deserved it.

Power filtered out, slamming into my chest, and my fires slithered back in, my skin slowly returning to its normal tone as the glow faded away.

And I knew this power all too well. I'd had it for 1,500 years. Yet now another did.

I took in the fae reappearing in the throne room, along with others who let their barriers fall. All their eyes were locked on me in fear, and I forced a smile onto my face, showing them I reveled in it.

Their cruel King.

That was before I spotted Osiris, and the air pulled from my lungs.

He was on the ground, with a dark obsidian dagger in his chest. Dead...

Kadeyan's eyes were hard, and I felt his pain within as he drifted his gaze to meet mine.

"I'm shocked you showed, Ezekiel. I thought you were going to keep running like the *cowardly* King you are...or should I say, were."

My eyes narrowed, looking at Persephone sitting on the throne, her vile smile forcing the fire to rise within.

I looked at the Lords and Ladies of the Courts, their eyes on me, their anger slowly filling the throne room.

"What is this?" I laughed. "Your attempt to scare me with a bunch of pawns in your pursuit to feel wanted?"

Persephone stood, her eyes glowing a brighter purple.

"Watch your tongue, Ezekiel. You are speaking to the new Queen of Valyner," she seethed.

"I see no Queen here," I huffed, smiling. "Just a hollow throne with a desperate woman playing dress-up in the hope that everyone will believe she is powerful. You will never truly be a Queen. Not now. Not ever." I stepped closer.

Her eyes shot daggers at me and I could see every muscle stiffen.

"Keres," she called out, and he came forward. "Chain him."

I smiled, my fury growing past the point of pain. I stood still, letting him get closer, keeping my eyes on Persephone the entire time.

Keres stopped next to me, leaning in. "Fuck you."

"Payback is a bitch, isn't it?" I smirked.

I was talking about his mate and child, and he knew it. Little did he know, they were safe.

Just as he was about to place the chains on me, I grabbed him by his throat, my eyes never leaving Persephone.

I threw him back, causing him to drop the toxic metal in front of me. He growled, and the throne room energy shifted, everyone pulling their power to the surface.

"Please...take your best shot! I will burn every. Single. One. Of. You!" I shouted, putting them on edge.

Keres shifted before me, running at me, and a wicked grin graced my face. I sent out my fires just as he was about to bring me to the ground. His anger blinded him, his wrath willing to take him to death's doors.

And I welcomed him in.

His cries rang out as the inferno devoured him whole. And it felt good to watch him shift back, clawing at his body. Yet, what made it better was how he looked to Persephone. Like she would stop it and save him...because she *cared*.

She didn't.

Burn, motherfucker. Burn.

Fae rushed in, and I let my power go, taking them out one by one. I relished the heat that took over my body. In being the villain one last time, who had a good reason to be one.

"Come on, give me a challenge!" I shouted through the flames at Persephone.

Her face distorted with anger, and she summoned the leaders of the Courts to her. I glimpsed at Kadeyan, in pain, moving against his will, his anger still overpowering the assembly.

I killed a few more fae as they all stood still. Marta handed over the Crystal stone to Persephone, and she chanted.

Every line of power shot out towards me, forcing me to cry out as it worked through my body, forcing me to my knees.

My nails dug into the stone ground, my vision blurring and spotting black.

"Chains, now!" she shouted, her tone uneven.

Some fae rushed in, clasping them on. And as they fell into place, my power faded away, along with the fae using their power on me.

Persephone slowly moved in. Her heels clicked against the floor, and I brought my gaze up. With a wave of her hand, the surrounding fae moved back, her eyes never leaving mine.

"Look, you are already on your knees. How perfect." She

chuckled before pulling a dark obsidian dagger from her thigh. She grabbed her purple gown and tossed part of the fabric back before kneeling in front of me.

"Where is the stone, Ezekiel?" she asked, and I laughed.

"Sorry, I must have misplaced it."

Bringing the blade to my jaw, she pressed the tip into my flesh, making me tilt my head back more.

"This is your last chance..." she whispered. "Be with me...and together, we can make this world what it always should have been. Loyal to power, and power alone."

"I found something better than power, Persephone. Something you will never have."

"And what's that?" she asked, digging the tip of the dagger into my skin further.

Warm blood flowed down my neck, disappearing below my jacket.

I forced a smile, showing her the only version of me she wanted. Yet inside, I was scared...because what did death feel like?

What would it be like in that void...without her?

I lifted my hands and gripped her wrist, causing her to hold her breath. I moved the dagger down to my chest, right over my heart.

"Love. No one will ever love you. So go on, get what you want, but be careful..." I whispered, leaning in and feeling the sting of the dagger pass my jacket and sink into my skin. "I know what's coming for you."

"What?" she said with so much disdain. But I could hear what was behind it.

Fear.

"Death." I smiled, and every feature on her face hardened. "It's coming for you. And there is no stopping it. You will never get what you want. Not me...not power...not anything. You will forever be alone. And I think that is the best part in all of this...you will *forever* be alone."

Her hand shook for a moment before she let out a yell, plunging the dagger into my heart.

I sucked in a breath, the world around me fading quickly.

She leaned in, whispering in my ear, "I will find the Ember stone, Ezekiel. And anything else you hid from me. Mark my words."

She pulled the dagger out, and I fell back, unable to breathe.

My last thought was of *them* before the world I knew vanished.

———

Sucking in a sharp breath, I sat up, my hand going to my chest.

Did I dream it all?

Was I alive?

My eyes scanned the surrounding darkness, and it settled in. I knew where I was.

The void Nyna had created.

Standing up, I looked around, slowly walking in one direction. There was no light, no sign of where it ended. And it was cold...

So fucking cold.

"Ezekiel?"

I stopped, my jaw falling open.

"Nyna?" I turned, looking for her, and began running.

Was this really happening?

I looked everywhere, my heart aching to see her face again, to hold her, kiss her...but she wasn't there.

She wasn't here.

Pain fell over me, and tears filled my eyes.

Maybe this was hell after all...tormenting me.

"Ezekiel," she said again. The tears fell faster as I cried out into the abyss.

No, I couldn't endure this. I couldn't...

"Listen to me," her voice sounded, and I stopped, my breathing shallow.

"When I did the spell on you, I wanted to make sure you had this when you woke in the void."

I slowly sank to the floor, if that's what was holding me in place, and waited.

She left me a message.

"I fought for so long...and I know you did, too. We both wanted certain things in our lives. Never expecting that it would turn into what we got...

"You woke something in me. Even from the moment I met you. And over the years, you were the one who made me whole. And I know I did the same for you. I will love you until the seas dry up. Until the earth withers away."

She paused, and my hand went to my chest, gripping at the heart that was no longer beating.

"I wouldn't change a thing because it brought us our daughter... And if all goes to plan during my death, I will not pass on. I'll open the gods power within me and hold my soul between the living and the dead."

My brow furrowed.

"I will be connected to Dy through her life source and my power. And I will do everything I can to help her after Persephone falls. But if I pull it off, that means I won't see you in the next life... until she has everything she needs."

My lip quivered as I looked up at the expanse of darkness above me. It hurt to hear her plan, but I understood why she was going to do it.

It was the reason I had her put me here.

"She is going to be okay, Ezekiel. Because of you... Because of us. And I have to believe this is what it means to be a good parent. I have to believe that one day, she will see why we had to do this. That she will break this dark curse that flows from both our veins into hers. She will be free. And that's all that matters now."

I nodded, the tears falling into the void.

"I love you...and I will see you again. Be strong, my King...this is only the beginning of the life we will have...I know it is."

Her voice faded away, and the sobs broke free.

"I'll see you soon, Ruin," I whispered. "I love you."

After minutes, or maybe hours, passed—I didn't know—I got up, wiped the tears away, and took a deep breath.

Fate was a cruel thing, but at least it got something right.

A broken smile lifted my cheeks.

Because I got to fall in love with the Cursed Queen. And together, we would live on through her.

Our daughter.

CHAPTER THIRTY-FIVE

AKARI

anding in the woods of the Mortal Land, I looked around, spotted Elias walking away, and ran towards him.

"Elias." He slowly turned, his eyes matching my own, filled with tears.

"Akari?" he whispered. "How are you—" he paused, his eyes widening. "If you are here...."

I moved in, my lip quivering.

"He's gone... Ezekiel is gone." The words broke through my sobs, and he dropped a small white chest to the ground and pulled me in.

Davyna was in his other arm, sleeping, and I slowly brought my hand up, touching her back.

Her power was deep inside, hidden behind walls, and it only made more tears fall.

It needed to be this way...for now. Yet it made my heart hurt for my niece.

A few minutes passed, and we slowly pulled apart, wiping our eyes.

"He knew...and he did it anyway, didn't he? To save us. To save her," Elias said, and I nodded.

"Listen, I have very little time. Things are about to change in the realm. Persephone is going to be looking for us."

"What do I need to do?"

How was I to tell him that eventually we would die protecting the heir to the throne? I wanted to tell him about his future, but what would it do other than make him look over his shoulder every day?

I forced a smile, taking his hand.

"You are going to live your life with your daughter and our precious niece." I touched her again, my hand slightly caressing her back. "You are going to protect the stones and her secret until it is time. And you will know when that day comes. You will find a joy that surpasses this world with them in your life. And you will be free."

"And what of you?" he asked.

I thought of my daughter––Maeve––back at the temple, still so young, just like Davyna. And my heart ached at the path I needed to take to protect her in the coming days.

"I will do the same until I fulfill the fate laid out before me. But we will never see each other after today."

"Akari...no. I can't lose you too..." His voice broke, and I kept my smile in place, another tear falling. "Stay here with me."

"I wish I could, but I need to protect my stone and my daughter. And to do that, I need to stay hidden."

"You have a daughter?" he asked.

I nodded.

His mouth opened again, probably to ask why it needed to be this way, but he stopped, reluctantly nodding.

"We were always going to be hidden beneath the embers of his fate, weren't we?" Elias asked.

I closed my eyes, seeing the future within my mind. I couldn't see it all clearly, or even the ending, but I knew deep in my bones that, with our children, they would do better than us.

And isn't that all we want for them in this life: To leave them better off than we were?

It pulled so many emotions to the surface, but one was the most powerful.

Pride.

Pride in knowing our family would live on.

"And one day, she will be seeking beyond the flames for the truths she needs. To find her fate written in the stars. And it will be found below the ashes of this curse upon us all. She will need to find him first... It will start this all. She will need to find her father."

His brows furrowed, not sure what I meant by it, but I just smiled.

Kissing him on the cheek, I lingered for a moment before stepping back. "Make sure she knows where to start... Goodbye, brother. Be happy."

Darkness swallowed me whole, and I took a deep breath, readying myself to return to the temple.

The one I hadn't been able to leave in 1,500 years. I'd made peace with knowing it would continue to be my home until I returned to those woods in the Mortal Realm. To face death willingly.

Just like my little brother.

CHAPTER THIRTY-SIX

ELIAS

ears threatened to spill over with each step through the forest.

My boots crunched into the icy snow, the air growing colder as the power in my veins vanished, as if I'd never had an ounce.

I was once again mortal.

My hands wrapped tighter around the small child, clinging to her little wool coat. It was deep crimson with apricot flames dancing up the sleeves, and it pulled a broken smile to my face.

My niece...

She alone brought warmth back into my bones. She was anchoring me as the grief took root. And it was she who held me up from falling to my knees and shattering.

Because...my brother wasn't coming back.

And I still had so much to say. Like how much it meant to me that he saved my life as a babe from our father. I appreciated him taking the time to train and raise me up into the man he knew I could be. And how sorry I was for standing against him all those years ago instead of helping him through his anger and rage. Because in my actions, I showed him that family wasn't worth trusting.

Even though it had been right at the time to stand against him.

For me and Akari. It hadn't been because we didn't love him. We just couldn't stand by with what he became.

Ezekiel lost his way for a long time. But seeing him change so much over the years, especially in these last few months... I saw my brother again.

Redeemed.

And it was all for her.

His daughter.

I hurried up the steps, sniffling from the cold. Or at least I told myself that was the reason before I realized tears had fallen onto my hand. I watched as the droplets rolled over my skin before they fell into the white powder dusting the wood.

Walking through the front door, I listened for Hera, but no floorboards creaked from the hallway upstairs or on the stairs themselves.

She was still asleep. She was due any day now with our child. They would be our only one.

I'd have to deal with her anger in the morning about Davyna. She would probably think I had been unfaithful, that she was my bastard child. But I didn't care. I would tell her only what she needed to know. She would never get the truth from me.

Relief struck me, causing me to stall and take a quick inhale. I wouldn't have to turn anymore. Nor would I have to break every bone in my body each night and hunt in my primal state. I wouldn't have to hide from the mortals anymore.

And neither would my child.

The Cursed were facing a war soon enough from the mortals... and I had only one choice now.

To protect my family. To protect my brother's legacy.

I didn't know if I felt relief for my niece, though. Knowing that one day, I'd have to tell her who she really was.

How would I do that?

I walked into my office, pushed the door open with my foot, and made my way over to the desk. Placing the small white chest down, I felt an energy coming from it and knew what it was.

The Ember stone.

I smiled, looking over at my bookshelf to the hollow book where I kept the crescent one.

They would go to our daughters.

Our daughters... I smiled, remembering the night Nyna told me she could sense what the baby was in Hera's womb. But as soon as the smile lifted my cheeks, it fell because I wouldn't see her again either. Nyna had been my friend. An ally. And hope that the Cursed needed.

Moving over to the window, Davyna's little hands squeezed my neck tighter as I lowered onto the bench, gazing out at the snowfall that was starting back up.

"I'm sorry that you won't remember your life before this night. But it was all to protect you," I whispered, changing her position so I could take in her features. She looked like Nyna. Her dark hair. And those eyes, which had been plagued with sleep before Ezekiel did the spell, were silver, just like his and Akari's.

I looked down at her little hand and slowly moved my own towards hers. Placing a finger in her palm, she gripped it, sighing as she cuddled into me.

"You are so loved, Davyna Ember..." I took a moment, looking back out the window, the tears building in my eyes. "I may not be your real father...but I promise you this right now." I swallowed, looked back down at her, and wrapped my other fingers around her small hand until it disappeared into my palm.

"You will have my name. My protection. And my life, if need be. I will be the best father I can be to you. And I'll honor your father in everything I do. It will be for him. For your mother. You have my word. Now and always."

I leaned my head back, gazing out at the dark sky speckled with bright stars that illuminated the snow as it fell to the ground. I don't know how long I sat there, silently crying with her in my arms, but eventually, I brought my eyes back to her. And forced a smile.

"I want to tell you a story..."

Davyna stirred in my arms for a moment before settling on her side, her head resting on my chest like she was waiting for me to continue.

"It's about a princess with magic like no other had seen. And how her parents—the King and Queen of two realms—fought...to protect her."

ABOUT THE AUTHOR

Fay Bec writes dark fantasy packed with cursed magic, broken crowns, and villains you probably shouldn't fall for—but will anyway. She didn't grow up with her nose in a book, but stories were always there, waiting. In 2022, she finally stopped waiting and started writing. Now, when she's not raising her four chaotic little humans, she's sketching, binging TV shows, or dreaming up new ways to burn fictional worlds to the ground. She swears villains do it better—and she's just getting started.

Follow her on Instagram and TikTok @faybecbooks,
or Goodreads

Want to stay in the know? Sign up for her newsletter.

ACKNOWLEDGMENTS

To start I need to give a huge thank you to my editor on this project, Callie: Thank you for being there through every random voice note on discord, or comments I brought to you in the document. It was so much fun writing this story, but also working on it with you. You are an amazing editor and I can't wait to on the next one with you. Love you!

To my alpha reader, Frankie. And beta readers, Ali, Annie, Sadie, Henriette, and Emma: I can't thank you all enough for taking the time to read the not so polished drafts. To give insight, feedback, reactions, and more. It meant the world and helped me more than you know. You are all amazing! Also, to my Arc readers: Thank you for the time in reading this book early, reviewing, and or sharing with friends and people you know online. It helps more than you know.

To my husband, Duane: This past year hasn't been easy. I think you know that better than anyone since you lived it too. But even in the chaos of everything, you encouraged me to keep writing. To keep doing what I loved even when I struggled to open my computer. Hell, somedays to even get out of bed... Your support, your comfort through it all is why I'm here today, publishing this books. I Love you.

To Ali, my best friend: What a year...and god where the hell would I be without you? Ali, you deserve everything you want in this life and whatever comes next. But beware we will be ghost besties, haunting people, and probably scaring the living shit out of people when we push our books off the shelf. (hehe) Your support these past few years, growing closer, and just well everything--I can't say just how much your friendship means to me. Love you girl... And always remember...My bullshit, is your bullshit, and your bullshit, is my bullshit!

To all of you, the readers: Thank you for your support. For being on this journey with me as I share characters that captivate my head first, only to give them to you to join in the craziness. And with this book specifically, it just means the world. It felt good to get back to what I love. And I hope you enjoyed it and are ready for the last book in the dark curse series coming in 2026.

Get ready, it's going to be...intense!

I'll get back to working on that and maybe another book idea... you'll hear about it soon.

With all my love,

XO, Fay

www.ingramcontent.com/pod-product-compliance
Lightning Source LLC
Chambersburg PA
CBHW011149310726
48973CB00010B/2841